D0955259

The Remarkable Life and Times of

Eliza Rose

Also by Mary Hooper

Amy

At the Sign of the Sugared Plum

Petals in the Ashes

Hooper, Mary, 1944–
The remarkable life and
times of Eliza Rose /
2006.
33305211920107
mh   01/24/07

WITHDRAWN

The Remarkable Life and Times of

Eliza Rose

MARY HOOPER

BLOOMSBURY

Copyright © 2006 by Mary Hooper
All rights reserved. No part of this book may be used or reproduced
in any manner whatsoever without written permission from the publisher,
except in the case of brief quotations embodied in critical articles or reviews.

Published by Bloomsbury U.S.A. Children's Books
175 Fifth Avenue, New York, NY 10010
Distributed to the trade by Holtzbrinck Publishers

Library of Congress Cataloging-in-Publication Data
Hooper, Mary.
The remarkable life and times of Eliza Rose / by Mary Hooper.— 1st U.S. ed.
p.   cm.
Summary: Thrown out of her home by her stepmother in 1670, fifteen-year-old
Eliza Rose becomes a companion to Nell Gwyn, a mistress of Charles II, and learns
a surprising truth about her parentage.
ISBN-10: 1-58234-854-5 • ISBN-13: 978-1-58234-854-4
[1. Identity—Fiction. 2. Gwyn, Nell, 1650–1687—Fiction. 3. London (England)—
History—17th century—Fiction. 4. Great Britain—History—Charles II,
1660–1685—Fiction.] I. Title.
PZ7.H7683Rem 2006   [Fic]—dc22   2006002153

First U.S. Edition 2006
Typeset by Dorchester Typesetting Group Ltd.
Printed in the U.S.A. by Quebecor World Fairfield
1 3 5 7 9 10 8 6 4 2

All papers used by Bloomsbury U.S.A. are natural, recyclable products
made from wood grown in well-managed forests. The manufacturing processes
conform to the environmental regulations of the country of origin.

Prologue

Somersetshire, 1655

The castle bedroom is large and richly furnished. Paintings and costly tapestries line the panelled walls and in the centre is a vast four-poster bed hung about with heavy drapes. Childbirth being a close and private matter, no outside light is allowed to penetrate the room, so the window shutters are secured tightly and heavy damask curtains hang across them. Light is provided by the fire burning in the grate and several silver candlesticks holding tall wax candles. A large white china bowl of lavender and rose petal pot-pourri standing on a table diffuses a faint fragrance.

There is a tap on the door and a woman within opens it. Notwithstanding her years, she is both handsome and elegant. A maid carrying a copper scuttle, full of coal, makes as if to enter. She is stopped by the woman, who takes the scuttle from her.

'Please, madam, it's very heavy,' the maid says. 'And you'll get all covered in smuts.'

'That's of no account,' the woman says. 'I don't want my daughter disturbed.'

The maid glances at a younger woman lying on the

bed. 'How does she?'

'She progresses well.' The older woman goes to shut the door.

'Are you sure that I can't get the midwife for you? Or the housekeeper or the doctor?'

'No one, thank you,' the woman says firmly, and, the maid not going away, has to shut the door in her face.

'Who was that?' the younger woman calls.

'Hush! No one – just the maid with some coals.'

'Did she –'

'Hush!' the older woman says again. 'She didn't see or say anything.' She puts some coal on to the fire and then wipes her hands and goes over to the bed where the woman lying on the linen oversheet is in the final stages of labour. She waits while another pain ebbs and flows through the woman's body and then, when there comes a moment of calm, helps her sit up on the bed and places pillows behind her. Then she holds a cup to her lips.

'What is it?'

'A herbal drink: tansy and juniper. I had it prepared by my own apothecary. 'Twill help and give you strength for the final ordeal.'

The other groans. She looks towards one of the tapestries on the far wall. 'Is the babe still there?' she whispers.

'You know he is. He's arrived and is quite safe.'

'Suppose he cries?'

'Then there's only you and I to hear him.' She dabs a cloth to the other woman's temple.

'Are Kathryn and Maria well?'

'Kathryn and Maria are very well and happy. They

are with their nurses. Now, concentrate on this coming child and –'

A mighty pain seizes the other woman and she throws herself back on to the pillows, turning to bury her face among them to stop herself from screaming.

'Soon, now. Soon,' murmurs the older woman when the pain passes. 'It can't be much longer.'

'You've been saying that for hours!'

There are heavy footsteps outside, then the door opens and a man calls from the doorway. 'Is he here, then? Is my son in the world?'

'Not yet,' the older woman says, and she and the woman in bed exchange anxious glances.

The man strides into the room. He has a large nose, puffy eyes and is weak of forehead and chin. He's been hunting and his hands are stained with the blood of small creatures.

'What, still not arrived?'

'Soon,' the woman on the bed says weakly. 'Very soon.'

'But where's the midwife? Where are the goodwives and neighbours to attend the birth?'

'My daughter wants complete quiet this time,' came the reply. 'She has asked – nay, insisted – that I should be the only one attending the birth.' She tries to smile at the man. ''Tis all feasting and gossip when the neighbours come in and 'tis difficult to get any rest.'

'That is the custom, though,' the man says, but then he shrugs. He puffs out his chest. 'My son!' he says. 'I've long waited for this.' He looks from one woman to the other carefully. 'And you're quite sure that it will be a boy this time?'

'Very sure, my lord,' the older woman says with

confidence. 'The hour the child was conceived and the potions my daughter was taking have ensured that your next child will be male. Besides, we have consulted various wise women throughout her time.'

'Quite so,' said the man. 'Because if –'

'Please!' The older woman holds up her hand. 'Please don't alarm my daughter at this time with your threats and intimidation. I can assure you, sire, that the coming child will be a boy. I'm perfectly sure of it. There will be no need for my daughter to be turned out of doors.' She looks at the man coldly as she speaks, for there's no love lost between the two of them, and then the woman on the bed lets out a sudden, piercing scream. The man hastily leaves the room, asking to be informed the moment the birth has taken place.

As his footsteps retreat the younger woman says, 'I screamed so that he'd go!'

Her mother nods, smiling. 'It was well-timed.'

'I was scared that there would be some noise from the passageway.'

'Hush!' the reply comes. 'Just forget the babe's there. All will be well.'

An hour goes by and the pains begin to come one after the other without a gap between. The older woman, knowing it is almost time, goes to the bedroom door and bolts it. Then she climbs on the bed to help her daughter, rubbing her back and murmuring endearments and encouraging words.

At last, with one final push, one tremendous effort, the child is born. Even before the cord has been cut the younger woman is struggling to sit up and look down at the baby.

'What is it?' she asks frantically. 'Is it a boy?'

Her mother shakes her head and sighs. 'No. Another girl.'

'Let me see …'

''Tis better if you don't.'

'Is there anything wrong with her?'

'Not a thing. She's a healthy size and all complete.'

The older woman swiftly cuts the cord, then wraps the child in a linen cloth, swaddling her round and round.

'Let me …' the new mother says, and the other relents and holds the tiny bundle towards her. 'So much like Maria!' she murmurs, taking the child.

'Quickly!' the other says.

'Poor little child,' says the young woman. 'Will your new mamma love you as I do? Will she tell you fairy tales?' She looks down at her daughter for the first and last time. 'Once upon a time,' she whispers, 'there was a beautiful child born in a castle …'

Chapter One

London, fifteen years later

'Come along, my pretty one. Just you come by here ...'

The voice woke Eliza but was unknown to her. It was close by, but she lay still, wanting to feign sleep until she was quite sure of where she was.

'That's it, my beauty. Go into the box ...'

Perhaps it wasn't she, then, who was being addressed? But still, best not to risk opening her eyes and being noticed. She tried to gauge what was happening without stirring herself. Where was she, for a start? Not at home, that much was sure. Home had never been this cold. Nor, she realised as her senses slowly returned, had it ever stunk quite so badly.

Eliza moved her foot slightly to try and judge on what sort of surface she was lying and felt a sort of slimy, gritty dampness beneath her. She was on the ground somewhere, then, without covering, and if her head hadn't been cushioned by her arm then her face would have been down in the slime too.

There was a sharp, sudden noise, like a box being banged shut. 'Got you, my beauty!' said the same female voice, with a cackle of laughter. There was then some crooning and whispering – it was 'Beauty' who was being addressed, Eliza supposed.

She now felt it safe to open her eyes. When she did so, however, the view before her was so disturbing that she immediately shut them again. In that instant she'd seen a long, low-ceilinged space, poorly lit by tallow candles, and some bedraggled and filthy creatures sitting around its walls, all of whom looked to be in a state of utter despair and dejection.

So, she wasn't at home – but nor was she anywhere she could ever remember being before.

So what could she remember? Dimly, the recent past came back to her: leaving her home in Somersetshire, begging lifts on carts and haywains and, once, a river craft and then, days and days later, arriving in London and quickly getting lost in its dark byways. And becoming cold and scared and hungry.

And then ... stealing a hot mutton pasty from the pieman.

There was the answer to where she was.

Eliza's eyelids flickered open again. To the left, not many inches from where she was lying, was a shallow channel which had been dug out from the hardened earth. There were neither windows nor ventilation in the room, and the stench from the channel – which was no more than an open sewer conveying filth and human waste, she realised – hung chokingly on the air of the room. Which wasn't a room at all, but a cell.

She was in prison.

Slowly, she sat up and, shuffling backwards and away from the stinking ditch, leaned against the wall.

Then she surveyed her fellow prisoners.

There were perhaps twelve in the room. All were women, and four of these looked to be chained with heavy iron fetters hard against the wall. Others sat on wooden pallets or lay on the floor, curled up – whether alive or dead Eliza didn't know. The woman whom Eliza had heard a moment before was sitting nearby, crooning softly to a brown rat in a rough wood and wire cage.

'My pet ... my sweetheart,' she was saying, 'I'll feed you and make you fat.'

Eliza shivered and instinctively crossed her arms around herself in an attempt to get warm. She seemed to have lost her bundle of possessions, her woollen shawl and her cap and shoes along with them. At least, she thought, they hadn't been able to take any money from her, because the small amount she'd possessed had already been spent on the journey to London.

Her stomach ached with hunger. She thought about the pasty she'd stolen. Where was it? How long ago had she stolen it? A vision of it came into her head: warm, crumbling pastry outside and mutton and spiced potato within. Had she actually eaten it?

She feared that she had not, for she remembered now that she'd taken it from the counter of an open shop in Leadenhall and carried it swiftly around a corner to eat. She'd lifted it to her lips, opened her mouth to take a bite – actually felt it crumble on her lips – and then the shopkeeper had raced up, red-faced, apron flapping, and, calling for the watchman, had knocked her to the ground. 'Varmint! Thief!' he'd yelled. 'Taking food from honest 'keepers! I've seen your like here before.'

And then she could dimly remember being dragged through the streets and, though she couldn't remember as much, must have been thrown into this prison cell. She felt in her pocket, without much hope. If only she'd thought to shove the pasty – even half the pasty – into her pocket for later, then at least she wouldn't die of starvation. Which, right at that moment, she felt was a possibility.

Her eyes fell on the large brown rat who was running first to one corner of his cage then the other, scrabbling, frantic to get out.

'You won't get out of there, my pretty darling,' the old woman said. 'You won't get out yet-a-while.' Her eyes slid past the rat to Eliza. 'So you're awake now, are you?' She moved the box containing the rat so that it was out of Eliza's view. 'Don't you set your eyes on him!'

'I wasn't,' Eliza said. Her voice sounded hoarse, croaky. How long was it since she'd spoken?

'Because he's *my* rat,' the old woman said. 'My own pretty rat.'

The woman seemed to be little more than a bag of bones and a handful of rags, but Eliza thought it best to humour her. She asked, 'Is he your pet?'

'No, he's not my pet, dearie,' the woman said, and her sunken cheeks creased and formed into a gummy smile. 'He's my dinner! He's my dinner as soon as ever he's good and ready. I'll feed him all sorts of pieces and soon get him plump.'

Eliza felt her stomach lurch and she shuddered with revulsion.

'You needn't look so dainty,' the woman said. 'After two months in here you'll be happy to eat your own arm.'

'Where ... where is this place?'

'Where? Why, this is Clink Prison in Southwarke,' the woman said. "Tis famous. Haven't you stayed here before?'

Eliza shook her head. 'I've not long been in London.'

'And so soon acquainted with its worthy buildings!'

'I was hungry,' Eliza said. 'I stole a pasty.'

'And I stole a whopping big pearl from a shop in Cornhill,' the woman returned, and cackled with laughter. 'A pasty or a pearl – see, we're all equal here.'

Locked up with a jewel thief, Eliza thought. How her stepmother would have laughed.

"Tis not so bad in here,' the woman said. 'Look about you.' She pointed at the stone walls which were trickling with brackish water. 'See the water laid on, just like in the big houses.' She extended her arm to include the mould and fungi growing from fissures in the stones, which had formed themselves into irregular shapes and colours. 'And the paintings and tapestries all provided for our delight!' Eliza did not reply, thinking the woman at least half-mad, and she went on, 'And here are your new friends and neighbours.' She pointed to the hunched, shabby figures crouched or lying against the far wall. 'A pretty and an elegant lot! Some in lace, some in ermine. See their jewels sparkling! Why, you might think yourself in the court of the king when you're in Clink Prison!'

Eliza regarded her wordlessly. She had a dull ache in her head and, putting a hand up to her face, felt a bump on her forehead. Her legs and arms were stiff and aching too, as if she'd been lying in the same

16

position for some time.

'How long have I been here?' she asked. 'Can you tell me?'

The woman shrugged. 'A day and a night. Two days, maybe. They threw you in like a sack of potatoes and there you stayed.'

Eliza tried to work out what the date might be. She'd left Somerset on a Monday during the latter half of April, had walked for about seven days, had two days travelling in hay carts, then walked again a good while. She'd managed to journey two days on a river barge and used up her last coins by entering London in some style on top of a post-coach. She'd then spent a day or so wandering about the city, stunned and exhausted by the crowds and the noise and the goings-on.

'Is it May?' she asked. 'And is today Sunday?'

'Not Sunday,' the woman said. 'We get meat of a Sunday. And you hears church bells then. But 'tis monstrous difficult to tell one day from the next and one month from another, for 'tis all the same in here.'

Suddenly becoming aware of some shouting from outside, Eliza bent her head to one side to listen better, causing a waterfall of dark hair to fall around her shoulders.

The woman put out her hand to touch it, and it was such a skeletal, wizened hand that Eliza couldn't help but draw back. 'Ah, don't mind old Charity,' the woman said. 'Lovely hair you've got, dearie. Black and shiny as oil. You could sell that.' She dropped her voice. 'And for a fact, you owe Charity here a favour. They would have cut your hair off while you were asleep, but I stopped them.'

17

'They were going to cut it off?' Eliza said in alarm, and, throwing back her head, wound her hair into a knot and tried to tuck it up. As she had no cap nor pins, however, it tumbled down again.

'Five silver shillings, that would fetch,' Charity said. 'Maybe more.'

'I'm not selling it!' Eliza said. She wondered if she'd been too sharp with the woman and added, 'But thank you kindly for saving it for me.' The same shouts and screams came from outside again and Eliza asked Charity what it was.

'Why, that's just the rest of our friends and neighbours!' she cawed, and Eliza looked away quickly from her gaping, toothless mouth. 'They're a-parading themselves in the yard right now, but they'll be in soon and you can meet 'em. What a grand lot they are, too!'

Eliza nodded towards the others in the cell. 'Why isn't everyone outside in the yard? Isn't it better than being stuck in here?'

'Oh, I don't care much for outside myself,' Charity said. 'And I had my pretty meal to catch. As for them over there ... they're all as lazy as hogs in mud.'

'Or too ill to move,' Eliza said, as a long sigh caused her to look over to the hunched and bedraggled figures once more. 'How long have you been here?' she asked.

'Oh, I live here,' Charity said. 'I've got no one to buy me out and they don't think it's worth transporting an old body like me, so I've made my home here. I'm street-bred, see, never had a place of my own, so whenever I'm freed, I just steal something else and come back in.'

18

Eliza looked at her in disbelief.

''Tis better than the workhouse,' Charity said, seeing the look on her face. 'There you have to work to get your food, stitching or rolling twine. Here you get bread every day and if you want a scrap o' meat you catches yourself a rat. It don't take much more than that to fill an old body like mine. If I gets hungry I go outside in the yard and beg stuffs from passers-by.'

Eliza gestured towards where the noise was coming from. 'Is that what they're doing out there?'

Charity nodded, and then bent over the rat again, whispering endearments and, finding a tiny shard of something to eat in the folds of the rags she wore, pushed it through the wire of the rough cage.

Eliza put her hand to her face again, feeling the lump on her forehead. Her head still ached, and her limbs too, and she had a longing to stretch them out and breathe some air that was fresher than the fetid stench within the cell. Carefully, for she felt weak and strange, she got to her feet and felt her way along the wall, weaving her way in and out of the women lying around. The ground beneath her bare feet was damp and gritty and, feeling something crunching as she walked, she stopped to investigate and saw, to her great horror, that the ground was covered in lice, dead and alive. She also saw a woman who appeared to be wearing Eliza's own shawl, but she looked to be such a poor, pale, stick of a person that Eliza didn't have the heart to take it back.

She passed through a doorway and, still hugging the wall closely, edged her way along a dark passageway towards the light. She would try and recover herself, she decided, and then work out how she was going to survive.

In the crowded yard she blinked and strained to see around her, for the sun was high and it was so bright compared to the cell that everything appeared blurred. As her eyes grew more accustomed to the light she could see that there were as many as two hundred men and women in the yard. They were standing in groups talking or arguing, sitting alone crying, parading two-by-two around the edge, or – as most of them were doing – gathered at one end of the yard where a barred window was set high into the prison wall.

The yard, Eliza realised, was set below street level, for suddenly two pairs of legs appeared in the opening and stopped. Immediately the group of prisoners closest to it set up a wailing and a shouting. 'Spare a coin, kind sire!' 'Six mouths to feed, sire!' 'May God bless you for your kindness, sire!'

The owners of the legs bent down, revealing heavy white lace and velvet, and a few coins were thrown. Those who were lucky enough to catch these were elbowed roughly out of the way by those behind, so that they might take their place in front of the opening.

One of the girls who'd managed to get a coin came towards Eliza, smiling and holding up a coin. 'A penny,' she said. She bit it. ''Tis not much, but 'tis real, and will buy me three good red herrings for my tea tonight.'

Eliza managed to smile back at her, though she was feeling so odd and faint – from hunger, she supposed – that she found it difficult to make her lips move. The girl seemed about her age and looked friendly, however, and, although she was wearing a dress so faded that its printed flower pattern could hardly be seen, wasn't filthy by any means.

'You're newly come, aren't you?' the girl said. 'I saw you yesterday, but you were asleep.'

'I've a lump on my head and think I must have slept a good while,' Eliza said, 'for I don't remember arriving here at all. When I woke I didn't know where I was.'

'I'll wager you know now.'

'Only too well,' Eliza said ruefully.

The girl looked down. 'They took your shoes off you for garnish,' she said.

Eliza looked at her, puzzled.

'For your keep. You have to pay to be in here, you know. And if you haven't got money then they take your clothes instead.'

'How will I get on without shoes, though?'

'Oh, you'll find some in time. Earn 'em or steal 'em!'

Eliza shrugged. At that moment she had other, more pressing needs. 'When do we get some food?'

'We had our bread at midday – were you still asleep?' the girl said, and, on hearing that she was, went to one of the several burly turnkeys standing around and spoke to him in a bold and forthright manner, pointing several times to Eliza. After a while she came back with a hunk of greyish-looking bread, which, despite it not looking at all appetising, Eliza fell upon, stuffing it into her mouth with as much relish as if it was roast goose.

The girl looked at her and laughed. 'If you stay

close I'll let you have one of my herrings later.'

Eliza smiled gratefully, but did not stop chewing.

'And … and I've long felt 'twould be good to have someone of my own age to rub along with, so if you've a mind to, we two can be friends and share what little else we have.'

'With all my heart,' Eliza said, and was mightily relieved to have found her.

Chapter Two

The girl's name was Elinor, and she thought she was sixteen.

'For I remember that about four years ago Ma had my brother George on my birthday,' she said that evening, 'and she told me that I was twelve years old on that day.'

'How many of you are there?' Eliza asked.

'Six dead and seven living,' Elinor said. 'Ma always said she'd had a baker's dozen.' She hesitated, then went on, 'She died last Mayday with what would have been our fourteenth babe. The maypoles were up and folk were wearing their Sunday best and dancing in the streets, but we were all set to crying.'

She put a hand to her eyes and turned away. Eliza pressed her shoulder sympathetically and the two girls fell silent for a while.

The prisoners had been brought in from the yard by then and locked up for the night, and the women's quarters were full to overflowing. The cell was so full, in fact, that there was barely enough space for everyone to lie down, although some tired-looking straw had been provided for that purpose. Elinor, and those others who could afford to, had hired rough bunks from a turnkey and now guarded their precious bed space jealously, not allowing anyone to sit on a corner of their wooden pallet nor even rest a bundle of possessions there. The only space that no one wanted to use was that which ran alongside the dug-out channel. Periodically, after using one of the buckets that stood in the corners, someone would dip the same vessel into the barrel of river water standing nearby and attempt to flush the channel clear. It hardly worked, however, for it seemed that the whole of the sanitation service for the prison ran through the women's cell and thence outside and down into the Thames. There was no way of washing or keeping clean, so it was no little wonder, Eliza thought, that the women stank so badly, had skin that was grey with hardened-on grime and hair as frowsy as birds' nests. To judge from the continual scratching that accompanied their every action, their bodies were running with fleas and lice.

'You haven't been in here that long, to judge by your appearance,' Eliza said to Elinor gently, when she felt it appropriate to speak. She hesitated, then made bold as to say, 'For you're far cleaner than a lot of the girls.'

Elinor smiled wanly. 'I've been here two weeks. But I've been hiring this bed to sleep on of a night, and a blanket, and have eaten well, for I knows the value of a merry smile to a gentleman and I seldom gets less than two pence a day from standing by the grille.' She patted her hair, which was tied back with string. 'I keep my hair tight to my scalp, too, and always wear a cap, day and night, for I fear that having it loose attracts the fleas.'

'But what happened to you?' Eliza asked, twisting

back her own hair again. She was conscious that she had no cap nor covering, and couldn't help but imagine a chain of fleas ascending it in a long, straggly line. 'What did you do to get imprisoned?'

'I stole from my mistress – but it was only what I was owed!' Elinor put in quickly. 'I was maid to her for two years and she paid me just once in all that time, so when she was abroad I took a bolt of cambric to sell. She has so much in the way of linens and stuffs lying around that I never thought she'd notice.'

'But she did?'

'The man I sold it to, told on me,' Elinor said indignantly. 'The double-crossing villain went straight round to my mistress and told her.' She swore under her breath. 'May the hatched-faced rogue die a horrible death!'

Eliza nodded fervent agreement. 'But how long must you stay here? Have you been sentenced?'

Elinor shook her head. 'And I don't even know when I will be, for the judge sits as and when it pleases him.'

'And what sort of punishment do you think you'll get?'

She shrugged. 'The judges punish according to whether or not their bellies are full. If I can make a case for saying I was only taking something that was due to me I may get off light. But what of you?' she asked Eliza.

'How did I come to be here? I was hungry and stole a pasty, that's all. And I was more hungry than careful, for the shopkeeper saw me and called the constable.'

'And how is it that you're here, in London?' Elinor asked. 'You have a country accent. Is it Somersetshire that you're from?'

Eliza nodded. 'From a village called Stoke Courcey,' she said, then hesitated.

'Don't tell me a thing if you'd rather not,' Elinor said. 'And take no notice of all my questions, for my brothers say my tongue runs on wheels.'

Eliza smiled at her. 'It's all right,' she said, 'I don't mind saying. I've come to London to try and find my father.'

'Did he run away from your ma?'

'No, he came to the City to get building work.'

Elinor nodded. 'London's full of tradesmen just now, since the Fire. Is he a woodworker?'

'He's a mason,' Eliza said. 'There was no work at home, so he answered the call to come to the City and help rebuild it.' She hesitated, putting her thoughts in order, knowing that Elinor was waiting for the rest of the story. 'I'm looking for him because, once he was out of the way, my stepmother told me that I was no longer welcome in our cottage.'

'Well, there's a fine thing!' Elinor said indignantly.

'I want to find him, then have him take me home and tell her she has no right to turn me out.' She looked at Elinor, who nodded at her to go on. 'Like you, I've no mother now. She died some years back ... she was swept away crossing the river. She nearly drowned, and then caught a fever and died.' She sighed. 'We managed by ourselves for a while, then our father was married again to a woman from the village. Once she began having babies of her own, she didn't seem to care about me and my brothers.'

'And did she make them leave home too?' Elinor asked.

Eliza shook her head. This had puzzled her. Still puzzled her. Why had Richard and Thomas and John, who were several years older and certainly more able to fend for themselves, not been asked to leave at the same time as she had?

'She did not,' she said.

Elinor thought for some moments. 'Perhaps you look like your mother, and your stepma don't like to be reminded of her.'

'No,' Eliza said, shaking her head again, 'it's not that. My real mother had fair hair and light colouring and was small and round. I don't look like her at all.'

'Well,' Elinor said, pondering the matter further, 'maybe you've shown unkindness to your stepmother's own babes.'

'I never have!' Eliza said, shocked. 'I've tended them with care from the moment they were born, just as though they were my own true sisters.'

'Well, then!' Elinor said. 'Having heard all about her I can only conclude that your stepmother is a selfish, vexatious and ignorant wretch who deserves to be horse-whipped!'

Eliza, astonished and rather pleased at this character assessment, forgot her surroundings and laughed. There was something else she hadn't said, of course. Something concerning the last conversation she'd had with her stepmother ... but she would think on this later.

As the girls continued to talk, sometimes straining to be heard above the shouting, singing and screaming of the other prisoners, a turnkey came in and began to distribute the food that had been sent out for: herrings, pigeon pies, hard-boiled eggs, oysters and rice puddings. As Eliza and Elinor ate their fish, the prisoners who'd had no money to order any food set up a wailing and (those who still had both shoes and energy) a stamping, and after a time a steaming cauldron was brought into the cell and hot water poured into the iron mugs which were chained to the walls. Elinor told Eliza that the water also held some oatmeal, although this was such a pitifully small amount that Eliza could neither see nor taste it.

As the women who were manacled to the walls sought to ease their aches and pains by rubbing at their chafed legs, Eliza saw that one of them, as well as being chained, was also wearing a strange contrivance on her head.

Elinor said it was a scold's bridle. 'It's fixed on her head with a spur which goes down into her mouth so that she can neither speak nor hardly breathe, just take a little water,' Elinor said. 'She's been here for six days, and will be released tomorrow.'

Eliza stared in horror at the woman, immobile in her iron head cage.

'Her husband had her put in here,' Elinor went on in a whisper. 'He said he hadn't slept for a year because of her constant grumbles.'

Eliza gasped, for she had never heard of such a thing before, and the girls exchanged glances and quickly averted their eyes.

Almost as soon as the cups which had contained the gruel were drained dry, a turnkey came around the cells ringing a bell and calling nine o'clock. Several of the tapers which lit the cell were now extinguished, leaving the place in semi-darkness.

Eliza, looking around her, began to feel frightened.

Where was she going to sleep? It looked to her as though the only space left was alongside the sewer, and who knew what rats or other creatures might come swimming along this in the night? Trying to hide her fears, however, she thanked Elinor kindly for the herring, and prepared to take her leave.

'Oh, you needn't go,' Elinor said immediately, taking her hand. 'Stay here on my pallet and share my blanket if you wish.'

Eliza hesitated.

'Really you must!'

'I've nothing to give you in return,' Eliza said, sitting down again nonetheless.

'It'll be your turn to pay another day,' said Elinor. She put out her hand to touch Eliza's hair. 'And I warrant that if you put your hair down, pinch your cheeks into some colour and go and stand before the yard grille, you'll pay your way through Clink before you know it.'

Eliza turned to her. 'Can you buy *anything* here, then?'

'You can,' Elinor asked, unfolding her blanket. 'You can buy food, warmth, clothes – you can buy a room of your own and a servant too, if you've a mind to, and if you really come into money you can pay to get out.'

Eliza's attention was suddenly taken by the threadbare blanket which Elinor was offering her a share of. It was stiff with grease and smelt of the hundred unwashed prisoners who'd used it before them. She touched it and couldn't help but recoil at its feel.

'I know,' Elinor said, pulling a face, 'it's horrid and

beastly. But it gets cold in here at three in the morning.'

Eliza, allowing the blanket to partially cover her, couldn't help but think of the feather bed and soft linens of home. Was she still able to regard that cottage in Somersetshire as *home*, though?

'And we must pray it doesn't rain,' Elinor added.

'What happens then?'

'The river rises, so the water going into it from that channel runs back into the prison. Those who haven't got themselves on to pallets will find that they're lying amongst dead dogs and offal which have floated back up here from the butchers' shambles!'

Eliza shuddered.

'But it doesn't look like rain,' said Elinor, 'so your bath can wait until another day.'

Eliza, thankful to have fallen in with Elinor, managed to smile.

Chapter Three

"Tis not begging,' Elinor said, 'but just like working.'
She looked down at Eliza in exasperation. "Tis what
you have to do in here. You'll starve otherwise!'

Eliza sat on a corner of Elinor's pallet, feeling
tearful. The previous night had been dreadful, despite
the dubious comfort of Elinor's blanket. A woman
lying nearby had sobbed the whole night through,
another had sung a tuneless and continual dirge, while
others had let out sudden piercing screams at intervals
as if they'd only just realised what a hell-hole they
were confined to. People had risen to relieve
themselves in the buckets, sometimes falling over in
the dark and swearing loudly, and the turnkeys had
walked in and out, jingling their keys loudly or calling
the time. What with the smell, the noise and the
strange and unwholesome surroundings it had been
impossible to sleep.

"Tis monstrously foul here!' she said to Elinor. 'I
don't know how you stand it.'

'You stand it because you have to,' Elinor said, 'but
– doubtless you won't believe this – you'll get used to
it a little. In time.'

Eliza burst into tears. 'I never shall!'

Elinor fumbled in her pocket and pulled out a

31

comb. 'You must start planning what you'll do when you get out,' she said. 'Now, where will you go to first to look for your father?'

Eliza shrugged hopelessly. She'd just thought to come to London; no further than that.

'As he's a mason, you can go to his trade's hall and seek him there.' Elinor removed her cap and untied the piece of string which held back her hair. 'But have you thought of what you're going to say to him?' she asked. 'And are you sure that he's not going to side with your stepma?'

'He cannot!' Eliza protested. 'He's a fair man. He's my father!' As she said this, Eliza tried to erase the memory of the busy, worried and rather remote figure her father had been and tried to imagine someone quite different. Someone who'd missed his eldest daughter most dreadfully since he'd been parted from her, someone who'd only recently realised how much she meant to him.

'But if she's the wicked shrew that she sounds ...'

Eliza thought of the final conversation she'd had with her stepmother. 'Since you've told me I'm no longer welcome here I'll go and find my father!' she'd said. 'I'll tell him what you've said to me and I warrant he won't let you treat me so.'

'Is that right?' her stepmother had said, smiling her tight smile. 'Are you so sure, miss?'

There was something about the way she'd said this which had caught at Eliza's heart. She'd tried not to show it, though, as she'd shouldered her few possessions.

'Yes, I *am* sure,' she'd said, ducking to go through the low cottage door.

Her stepmother had come out to the doorstep for a parting shot. 'You'll find out I'm speaking the truth,' she'd shouted after her. 'He no longer wants a cuckoo in his nest!'

Those words had stayed with her: *a cuckoo in his nest*. What had she meant? But Eliza had not given her the satisfaction of turning round to ask.

Elinor now pulled the small comb through her fair hair, muttering and grimacing by turn as it caught the tangles. 'Come,' she said when she was satisfied. 'Let me comb your hair now, then you and I must go and earn our breakfast. We'll get into the yard while the others are still rubbing sleep from their eyes.'

Eliza started to protest again but Elinor, ignoring this, bade her turn round so that she could comb out her hair. She made sounds of approval as she did so.

'Such curls and such waves!' she said. 'It reaches your waist and it glistens even in the glow from the candles, so 'twill look lovely in the sunlight.' She arranged Eliza's hair so that it rippled over her shoulders and down her back, then turned her round and round so she could admire her handiwork. 'There! You look good enough for a king!'

Eliza managed a smile. 'I'm sure I do not!'

'You do indeed. And your eyes are green as the leaves on the trees!'

The comb now being put away, Elinor brought out a small bottle from the pocket of her gown. 'A going-away present I stole from my mistress,' she said, carefully applying a tiny amount of the red liquid to first her own, then to Eliza's lips and cheeks and smoothing it in. She then touched a tiny smut of dirt on to Eliza's cheek to enhance the effect. 'There,' she said, finally satisfied. 'Let's see what attention we gets from the gentlemen today.'

The two girls were first outside in the yard and they made straight for the grille. Some women passed by – housewives on their way to buy produce at Borough market – and Elinor said to hold back, for a pretty face wouldn't work on them. A group of workmen came by next: builders crossing to the City by London Bridge, and Elinor turned her nose up at these, too, saying they would have no money. On seeing three tall youths approaching wearing ruffled breeches under matching velvet coats, however, she prodded Eliza into action.

'Here come some fine popinjays back from an evening spent carousing,' she hissed. 'Speak your bit and remember to smile nicely.'

As the pairs of ruffled breeches – one pair deep green, one black, the other maroon – drew level with the grille Eliza took a deep breath. 'Spare a penny for two fair maids, sires!' she called, blushing pinker than the cochineal which stained her lips. 'Oh, please help us!'

The men paused and Elinor nudged her to go on. 'We ... we haven't eaten a morsel these last days and are fair desperate for food!' she continued.

The youth in maroon velvet walked on, twirling his gold-topped cane and giving the girls no more than a haughty glance, and the one in black velvet looked hardly sober enough to know what was going on, but the other, the one in green, halted. Eliza looked up at him nervously and as their glances met he smiled at her. Such a ready smile, she thought, and a well-shaped, curved mouth and merry blue eyes. How shameful it felt to be begging money from such as he.

'Val! Do come on, man!' his friend in maroon called impatiently. 'Hang around there too long and you'll catch something.'

'If you could … could but spare a penny, sire!' Eliza said in little more than a whisper. She felt sweat begin to prickle her forehead, though the sun wasn't yet in the prison yard. 'We are nigh on starved to death in here.'

Elinor, who had been turned discreetly away, now joined in. 'Oh, sire, my sister and I are helpless with hunger,' she said, slipping her arm around Eliza and dropping her head on her shoulder in an appealing manner. 'And we are imprisoned here through no fault of our own. Our wicked father tried to sell us to a slave ship but we ran away.'

'Val! Valentine! Come on, you fool,' came from the youth in maroon.

The one in green smiled at the two girls. 'I've heard enough,' he said, reaching into his pocket. 'Any more of the tale and I shall have to call your father out for a duel.' He spun a silver coin through the bars. 'Take this and buy yourselves some food, ladies, for I cannot see such beauty be made low.'

'Oh, thank you kindly, sire!' Elinor said, nudging Eliza.

'Remember us another day, sire!' Eliza stammered, and she brought herself to glance once more at the young man and smiled.

'A silver sixpence!' Elinor said as they were elbowed out of their prime position by two or three of the other inmates. 'See how easy it is. All you have to do is act the lady, but appear down on your luck. You must seem at just the right degree of poverty. I tell you, the players at the King's Theatre couldn't put on a better performance than me when I'm hungry.'

Eliza laughed. 'If our audience were all like him I'd be well satisfied.'

'We can have oysters for breakfast every day for a week,' Elinor continued, twirling the coin between her fingers. 'Or we can buy ourselves a cell of our own for tonight and pay to have some washing done ...'

'I must have a cap to cover my head – but before that, some shoes!' Eliza said, looking down at her dirty feet. 'For I cannot bear to feel the lice under my toes a moment longer.'

Days went by and Eliza, under Elinor's guidance, managed to get along fairly well. She bought back her own pair of shoes from a turnkey, and also purchased a shawl and a cap. Elinor teased her, saying that these items were from a woman who had been hanged the week before, but Eliza said she hadn't known her, so it was of no matter. She hired her own blanket at night, but carried on sharing a pallet with Elinor, for being used to occupying a bed with younger brothers and sisters, both liked the extra warmth and companionship. After a few days in Clink, Eliza's sheer tiredness meant that she could manage to sleep for several hours at a time without waking. Every day they begged at the grille and every day too, although hardly realising she was doing it, Eliza looked for the youth named Valentine, the one in the green breeches with the merry, blue eyes, but he never came again.

On a Monday (Eliza knew it was that day because the one before, being Sunday, everyone in the jail had been given a slice of charity mutton) Elinor was taken off for trial along with twenty or so other prisoners. They went by foot, chained together, and Eliza, looking through the grille, was upset to see her friend weeping profusely as she was herded along the street. A small crowd had gathered outside to jeer at the manacled prisoners, and Eliza thought – not for the first time – about her own trial. How ashamed she would feel to be driven along, chained up like an animal going to market. What if her father saw her?

Having promised Elinor that she would beg that day for both of them, Eliza worked hard with her smiles and her 'If it please you, sires' and earned nearly a shilling. She sent out for a rabbit pie and, for a treat to celebrate Elinor's homecoming, some sugared plums.

When Elinor returned, though, her face was red and puffed up from weeping, and it was obvious that she wasn't going to be consoled with either of these things. For a moment Eliza feared the very worst, for four of those who'd gone for trial that day had been sentenced to be hanged – this news had spread back to the prison even before the prisoners had returned – but when she could draw breath through her sobs, Elinor spoke not of this unspeakable thing, but of something which she felt was worse.

'I'm to be transported,' she said, her voice broken by hiccoughing gasps. 'Six of us are to go to Virginia, for the judge said he wants to make an example of the younger ones and it would be a fresh start for us.'

'Transported!' Eliza gasped. 'Just for theft of some material?'

Elinor nodded. 'The pick-pocket before me was to

be branded on her forearm – and another thief had his hand cut off!' As Eliza gasped in horror, Elinor burst out, 'But I would rather have those punishments – both of them – than be taken across the seas to the plantations!'

For a while they cried together, and then Eliza, thinking to console her, said, 'I've heard the land is very fruitful.'

'*I've* heard 'tis a wild and desperate place, full of wolves and wild people!' Elinor said, bursting out crying again. 'And besides, nearly all who go there die on the fearsome journey!'

Eliza, who had heard the same, did not know what to say to this, and now fell silent. Neither of them slept that night.

Next morning, one of the turnkeys, after ringing the bell at daybreak, called loudly, 'Rose Abbott, Margaret Audley, Elinor Bracebridge for transportation!'

At the third name both Eliza and Elinor stopped eating their oatmeal and stared at each other in alarm.

'Surely not so soon!' Eliza cried.

Elinor ran towards the turnkey. 'Is it *now*? Are you really come for us this morning?' she asked desperately.

'Aye,' he nodded. 'You'll be taken in irons to the lighters at Blackfriars, then sail downriver to the docks. The boat is waiting there to catch the tide.'

'No!' Elinor said in a panic. 'I can't go yet – I want to see the judge again! I don't feel well enough for the journey. I'm sick!'

But the turnkey had slammed shut the iron gate and

passed on to the men's cell. 'Emmanuel Badd, Thomas Mann, Goodman Hughes,' they heard him call, and there were answering shouts and protestations.

Elinor, after ineffectually banging her tin cup on the bars and shouting for him to come back and listen to her, sank to her knees and Eliza, weeping too, knelt beside her.

'Hush ... hush ... there's nothing can be done,' she said. She put an arm around Elinor, searching for something to say which might help. 'It may not be that awful,' she said. 'Some people pay their passage to go to the Americas and start a new life. They buy land or make a lot of money working on the plantations.'

Elinor just sobbed harder. 'I shall never survive the sea trip!' she said pitifully. 'They chain you up below the decks and you don't see daylight for weeks.'

'I'm sure you *will* survive.' Eliza smoothed back Elinor's hair. 'You'll charm the sailors on the ship – and perhaps you can work out your time there and come back a rich woman. Perhaps you'll employ me as your lady's maid when you return!'

But Elinor refused to be comforted. 'I only took what was due to me – and now I shall never see my brothers and sisters again!' she sobbed, and she wrapped her arms around herself and rocked backwards and forwards. 'I should have pleaded my belly!'

'That would have done you no good,' a fat, frowsy woman next to them said. 'That will only stop you being hanged. They still sends you off on the boats whether you're with child or no.'

Eliza put her arms around her friend, holding on to

her tightly. She was scared on behalf of Elinor, and also scared almost witless at the thought of being left alone in the prison.

Within fifteen minutes the turnkey was back with two constables, and Elinor and the two other women were fitted with leg irons to guard against their running away. As these were being put on, Eliza looked through her trifling possessions and gave Elinor her shawl, an apron and all the money she had.

''Tis only fourteen pence but it may serve to buy you some small comfort on the boat,' she said.

'But I shall never survive!' said Elinor, almost bowed over with the manacles and with grief. 'Never ...'

Eliza, too devastated to give any words of comfort, merely pressed the things on to her and then looked on tearfully as her dear friend was dragged away. She went to the barred window in the yard and watched, crying all the while, as Elinor and the others were herded down the road in chains.

Chapter Four

The days went by and it grew warmer. Although she still hated doing it, Eliza took her place by the grille most days and – though her freshness was fast disappearing under layers of grime – managed to earn enough to get by. She missed Elinor very much but didn't seek to make other friends in the prison. One or two of the girls, on seeing the ease with which Eliza had made money by her smile, tried to fall in with her, but she was learning prison ways fast and knew that most of them would steal, lie, cheat and even kill to improve their lot. Twice her money had been taken when she was asleep; once she'd been kicked quite viciously when she was at the front of the grille and had had to limp back inside, doubled over with pain.

As the weather became warmer the conditions in the jail grew worse. Now the river water that was brought in was fetid and foul-smelling before it arrived in the cells, now the sewer channel was continually blocked with matter, now the stench from scores of unwashed bodies and foul clothes was so nauseating that sometimes Eliza couldn't draw in breath without choking. She kept herself to herself, trying to get through each day as best she could, planning what she'd do when she got out.

When she got out ... She spent anxious hours wondering when her trial was likely to be. And what about her sentence? Surely she wouldn't be transported just for theft of a mutton pasty? If she was, she felt, as Elinor had done, that she might as well be dead. The thought of being taken off to a strange land across the sea, of never seeing again the dear native countryside where she'd grown up, was a most horrid and terrifying one.

No, surely they'd take what had happened to her, how she'd been turned out of her home by her stepmother, into consideration. Maybe she'd be free within a few weeks, manage to get some sort of living-in job, and begin to look for her father. Perhaps she could go to a hiring fair and get a job as a maid, or go around the big houses, knocking on doors to seek employment. She rather shrank from the idea of this, though, for no one was likely to employ her the way she looked now, and she'd probably have to take some lowly and menial task like skinning rabbits or sweeping the streets to get by. If only Elinor was still here and they could seek employment together. Elinor had always known what to do ...

Early one morning there came a strange, roaring chant from the men's quarters which spread in a wave across the women's cell until they picked up the same words – a man's name – and began chanting it too.

Eliza listened, intrigued. 'Jack Parley ... Jack Parley ... Jack Parley ...' they shouted, and then they began banging their shoes or their iron cups against the bars in time to their chant. 'Jack Parley ... Jack Parley ... Jack Parley.'

Stepping through the crowd of bodies around her –

for it was so early that no one was outside in the yard – Eliza made her way towards Charity.

'What are they saying?' she asked.

'Can't you hear, dearie? They are saying the name of the highwayman.'

'Jack Parley?'

Charity nodded. 'The most famous in the country. Apart from Monsieur Claude Duval, of course.'

Eliza remained bemused. 'But why are they saying his name?'

'Because he's been sentenced to hang, my sweeting. He is to go from here today and hang on the Tyburn tree!'

Eliza gasped, for she had heard, of course, of the Tyburn tree – the famous wooden scaffold which had three great wooden arms and was capable of hanging fifteen men or women at once.

'He'll be taken out when the bell sounds to do the Tyburn frisk,' Charity said with a snigger. 'What a dance he'll do, spinning on the end of a rope!'

Eliza looked at her with distaste. If ever a woman didn't suit her name, it was Charity.

'But 'tis not all bad,' the old woman went on, 'for Jack Parley has said that his possessions are to be sold to provide a portion of meat and a sup of wine for every fellow in here, so three cheers for him is what I say!'

The chant of *Jack Parley* was kept up whilst the prisoners were drinking the water and oatmeal which passed for breakfast, and also when the gates were opened to let them out into the yard. Eliza hung back a little here and didn't rush out to be first at the grille. She liked to take a little time tidying her appearance, to go to the barrel of river water in order to cleanse her face and hands without being jostled. She'd also untie her hair at this time and try and untangle it with a small, broken piece of comb. She endeavoured to maintain some standards, for her earnings partly depended on her looking comely, but she knew she must look a fright by now. Her hair – the very feel of it made her shudder – was as matted as a mare's tail and her skin was grimy and, she thought, probably as brown as a gypsy's from being outside in the yard in all weathers. She no longer hoped to see the youth with the blue eyes – in fact, she dreaded that he would come by, for she knew that he could only look at her with disgust now.

By the time she went through to the yard that morning there was no room at all in front of the grille, for it seemed as if the whole of the prison were bunched together there, straining for a glimpse of the outside world. Those who were too far back were jostling the others for position, constantly asking to know what was happening and if Jack Parley could be seen.

'The crowds are ten deep outside!' a wiry young fellow said to Eliza. He had an eye patch and a face pitted with smallpox scars. 'They say that all the seats have been sold around the scaffold for weeks past.'

'Is Jack Parley very famous, then?' Eliza asked.

'I should say! As brave and excellent a highwayman as ever there was. And one who has evaded capture by the constables for ten years! He's the favourite of the ladies,' went on the youth. 'That is, apart from Claude Duval.'

That name again. Eliza had never heard of these

famous highwaymen before and reasoned that this was because the lanes of Somersetshire did not offer such rich pickings as those of London.

'And is *he* here in Clink, too?' she asked.

The fellow laughed. 'Never! The great Duval won't ever be caught!'

Eliza, intrigued, stayed in the yard, listening to the clamour from the citizens outside and the prisoners within. A woman beside the grille was reporting on the clothes worn by those on the other side of the prison gate, and her remarks were passed back through the crowd. 'There's a large woman wearing a Holland sprigged gown and blue satin shoes,' Eliza heard. 'A plain gentleman with a large nose wearing a heavily embroidered doublet over magenta hose,' and 'A woman, crying, wearing a cherry-coloured gown and petticoat with gold lacing.'

As well as the general noise, Eliza could also hear the sellers of food outside, crying their wares to the crowd. Once she heard, 'Fresh Somersetshire cherries! Come buy! Come buy!' and her heart contracted with homesickness. How long would it be before she walked through the orchards picking cherries again?

The bellman called ten o'clock and the chanting stopped. Eliza heard gates being clanged open and shut, and, from outside in the street, sounds of cheering and jeering in equal measure as Jack Parley and the other condemned men and women came out of the prison and, manacled together, were loaded on to the cart.

'He's wearing his best clothes, and has a white cap with black ribbons on it!' a woman at the front called back to the other prisoners, and this was swiftly passed on. 'He's been given a nosegay of roses by someone in the crowd. One of the turnkeys is shaking his hand.'

The horses being whipped into action, the cart began to trundle off and the crowd fell suddenly silent. It was quiet enough now for Eliza to hear the cartwheels turning on the cobblestones and one woman in the crowd, sobbing and calling, 'Jack my darling!' before the cart went into the distance and was swallowed up by the crowd following it to Tyburn.

'He'll be back before you know it!' the fellow with an eye patch said to Eliza.

'What do you mean?' Eliza asked. 'Is he to be reprieved, then?'

He laughed. 'No, he's coming back as city surveyor!'

Eliza shook her head. 'I don't understand your jest.'

'You're a country goose and no mistake!' the fellow jeered. 'Jack Parley has committed murder and so is sentenced to be hung, drawn and quartered,' he said, mimicking the actions of each word with his hands. 'His parts will come back here to Clink, see, and they'll stick his head atop of the prison gates so he'll be able to see right across the city!' On seeing Eliza's horrified face he threw back his head and gave a bellow of laughter, showing a mouth full of blackened teeth.

Eliza pushed past the fellow and went back inside, where she crouched on her low pallet and hugged her arms around herself, feeling sick. It was probably the subject matter, the fellow's gross words, which had made her feel bad, she told herself; it wasn't jail fever, for she knew that this started with a running cold. A cold ... leading to a swift death. The previous summer, she'd heard, the conditions in the prison had been so bad, the jail fever so contagious, that over half the inmates had died.

The following morning Eliza felt better and, having no sign of a cold, reasoned that jail fever hadn't yet crept up on her. If only she could keep clear of it, keep reasonably healthy, until such time as her case was heard. Maybe the judge would be lenient; maybe he'd say that, having already served several weeks, she was free to go. Yes, she would think that, and not think of the boy of twelve who'd been hanged for stealing a silver ring, the woman shaved and branded on each cheek for adultery, the man sentenced to be burned alive for plotting against his master. She wouldn't think about those harsh sentences, she'd just think about being free ...

Within a day or two, however, a rumour swept around the cells that the authorities weren't going to hear any more cases until the end of the summer. For with fever rife in the two major prisons, Fleet and Newgate, the judges weren't willing to be in such close proximity to the prisoners and risk catching disease. This meant, the rumour went on, that by the end of the summer the number of prisoners on remand in Clink and waiting to be sentenced would have more than doubled.

Eliza, hearing this, became quite desperate. She had never – as Elinor had inferred she would – got any more used to the prison conditions, and the thought of being crammed into that dark cell with *twice* the number of stinking bodies hardly bore thinking about.

Besides, she was finding it harder by the day to look clean and personable in order to attract a coin or two from passing gentlemen. Her hair was lank and greasy, her skin filthy, and there were dark creases on her hands and arms where the dirt was ingrained. She had rashes from flea bites all over her body, too, and couldn't help but scratch herself constantly. No wonder that the newer, fresher girls were getting all of the attention and most of the money.

To try and attract more alms – for she had a horror that one night she might find herself without money to buy a pallet to sleep on – she decided she'd devise a song, a plea for charity, which could be sung to the tune of a popular ballad. She knew she had a good voice, for she'd sung at merry-making in her village and in church on Sundays.

After several hours' thought she came up with:

'Gentlemen, hear a poor maid's plea,
If I tell my story you'll pity me.
Cast out and hopeless I'm far from home
Oh pity me, for I stand alone ...'

At first she'd felt discomfited at the thought of standing beside the grille and singing – but then, she reasoned, she'd thought this way about begging at first. Besides, many of the other prisoners devised their own cry in order to obtain aid. 'Help save a poor woman from starvation!' they'd call over and over again, and 'Aid for a soul fallen on hard times!' and really a song wasn't so much different from that.

She began to take her place by the grille much later, towards the evening of each day. It was cooler then, and most of the population of the prison had either been satisfied in their quest for alms or had given up, so the competition to be heard wasn't so great.

One warm evening, as she began yet again *'Gentlemen, hear a poor maid's plea'*, a stout woman wearing a grubby shift tied round with a length of string paused by the grille and looked down on Eliza. When Eliza finished and paused, not knowing whether to sing again or no, the woman clapped mightily.

'Yus! *Bravo!*' she said, and the foreign word sounded strange with her London accent.

Eliza looked up at her and nodded her thanks. She felt sure she wasn't going to get anything from this woman – her appearance was as disagreeable as that of any of the prison inmates – and didn't feel inclined to sing again.

'*Bravo*,' the woman repeated. 'That, I believe, is what they says on the stage these days.'

Eliza wondered whether to go inside, for there were precious few folk coming along the street now, but to do so while the old woman was trying to engage her in conversation seemed rude.

'You're a pretty one and no mistake,' the woman went on. 'Or you was, before you came in 'ere.' She bent lower, heaving with the effort, and peered into Eliza's face. 'Is those eyes of yours *green?*'

Eliza nodded, embarrassed.

'There's a thing. Such hair, too! I'm thinkin' that it's like a mermaid you are, with those long dark curls. And you have the voice of a siren to send ships on to the rocks!'

Eliza had heard enough. She bobbed a curtsy to the woman and, bidding her goodnight, made ready to go inside.

'Wait!' the woman said. 'I been watching you awhile. Take this silver shilling, my pretty.'

Eliza, astonished, took the coin that was passed through the bars and bit it to ensure it was real. 'I ... I thank you,' she said, bobbing another, fuller curtsy to the woman. She looked half-mad, Eliza thought – but maybe she was rich as well.

'Come again tomorrer and we'll talk again,' the woman said. 'You'll not be sorry you've met Old Ma Gwyn.'

Chapter Five

The following evening Old Ma Gwyn appeared at the grille and beckoned Eliza to come closer. "Tis like this, see,' she said, stooping low with difficulty, for her bulk was great. 'I likes to 'elp gels such as you.'

Eliza stared at her, thinking that in Stoke Courcey she'd have scorned to speak to such a dismal-looking object.

The old woman shifted her position. 'Look 'ere. Let me speak plain to you, my sweeting. 'Ow d'you like to come to live with me and my gels?'

'Live with ... your girls? Your daughters?' Eliza asked.

'Yers. My daughters and my gels,' she wheezed. "Ow d'you like to live with us?'

Eliza, confused, wondered what she meant. Where did she mean her to live, exactly? And on what basis? As a servant? How was she supposed to get out of the prison?

'I don't know,' she said helplessly. 'Do you mean as a maid, or –'

'A maid! Not as a maid! I means as a young lady of me 'ouse,' came the proud reply. 'There. What d'yer think of that?'

Eliza didn't know what to think.

'I shall take you in as me own – for I can see that a pretty young thing such as you is suffering mightily from being 'ere. I shall feed you and clothe you and you shall 'ave the learning and be set up fine and la-de-da.'

'But I'm not staying in London,' Eliza said. 'At least, not for long. I've come here to look for my father, and when I've sorted things out with him, then I'll be going home.'

'Yers. All in good time,' Ma Gwyn said, waving these considerations away. 'But in the meantime, my sweeting, you'll be free. Out of this place!'

Eliza stared at Ma Gwyn, hardly knowing what she was talking about. The thought of getting out, though, actually being *free* ... it was that word that shone out like a lantern in the dark.

'But how can this come about?' she asked.

The woman tapped her nose. 'That's for me to know and you to wonder,' she said. 'You just wait till tomorrer and leave it to Ma Gwyn. What's your name, my pretty one?'

Eliza told her and, the bellman calling nine o'clock, she said goodnight and went in from the yard. She looked back to the huge bulk that was Ma Gwyn, still standing beside the grille, and shook her head in bewilderment. Either she was totally mad, or she truly was a kindly benefactor who just wanted to rescue a girl in distress. Which was it? If only Elinor was still around *she* might tell her what to do ...

'*Gentlemen, hear a poor maid's plea ...*' Eliza began the following evening. All day she'd waited for something to happen, for Ma Gwyn to appear again, but eventually she'd told herself that it never would happen and she'd been a fool to even listen to her. Why, the old crow was probably newly released from Bedlam.

There were more prisoners in the yard than usual for that time of night, and the moment Eliza began her song she was roughly elbowed out of the way by a tall, thick-set woman who went by the name Annie Cut-purse. She was, Eliza had been told, the most famous woman pickpocket in London.

'Stop yer caterwauling!' she said. 'And let your olders and betters get to the grille.'

Eliza moved back quickly. She tried not to get involved in prison brawls and arguments, for she knew that cuts and sores seldom healed. As for broken limbs – well, she might as well be dead as be crippled and in constant pain from a limb that never mended. As she moved away, there came a piercing scream from outside the grille, where the bulky figure of Old Ma Gwyn had suddenly appeared.

'Eliza! My Eliza as I live and breathe!'

Eliza turned – as did everyone else in the yard, Ma Gwyn's voice having a carrying quality.

'Eliza!' came the passionate cry again. 'Is it really you, child?'

Eliza, at a loss to know what to do, stayed where she was. Some jeering began from the other prisoners, a shouting that Eliza should answer up and be quick about it.

'My poor child!' Ma Gwyn shrieked. 'She has been so brutalised by this place that she hardly knows her own kin! Her own *aunt*!' This last word was delivered in such a meaningful tone that Eliza was left in no doubt as to what was expected.

She ran towards the grille and bobbed a curtsy to Ma Gwyn. 'Yes, Aunt, it is I,' she said meekly.

'Then come 'ere so I may embrace you!' Ma Gwyn cried, pulling Eliza towards her while bending precariously over the grille. 'You was stolen away by gypsies ...' she hissed in her ear. Straightening up, Ma Gwyn fanned herself theatrically. 'Oh, my sweeting!' she said. 'I can scarce believe I've found you agin! I must go and secure your release. I'll go to the bailiff of this prison this minute and gain freedom for my precious one.'

Eliza, baffled, stayed where she was and, within a very few moments, a turnkey arrived to take her to the bailiff, a corpulent fellow wearing a most elaborate and varied set of clothes: a shirt, tunic, cravat, waistcoat, doublet and surcoat, all in different materials and clashing colours. Eliza had heard that he thought himself a dandy and that if he admired any prisoner's clothes he would confiscate them for himself, and his appearance proved this true. She bobbed a curtsy, thinking how hot he must be in all the layers of garments he wore.

'Oh, there she is, sire!' Ma Gwyn said as she entered. 'My poor precious child.'

'So,' said the bailiff, 'what happened to you, child? Did you at one time live with this woman?'

Eliza glanced at Ma Gwyn, whose great bulk was inadequately served by a small wooden chair. 'Yes, and I was ... was taken away by gypsies, sire,' Eliza replied on receiving an encouraging nod.

'Just as I told you!' Ma Gwyn butted in. 'I declares, sire, that this is my dear sister's child that I was bringing up as me own when she was stole away from me. Oh, such a shock, sire, to see her amongst the common prisoners down there in the yard.'

'And what offence have you committed to be in this prison?' the bailiff asked.

'I took a pasty, sire.'

'That's because they starved her!' Ma Gwyn said with mighty indignation. She delved into her clothes, pulled out a pocket and produced a small money bag. 'I 'ave some savings here, sire, what I was going to use to secure 'er release from the gypsies. Maybe this would go some ways ...' As she spoke she pushed the bag across the table towards the bailiff. So quickly did his hand dart out for it that halfway across it seemed to disappear.

'I think we understand each other, madam,' he said and, heaving himself upwards, he opened the door of his office and shouted something to a group of men standing at the bottom of the stairs.

Feeling dazed, Eliza followed Ma Gwyn down the wooden staircase. To the ill-smelling men sharing a jug of beer at the bottom, Ma Gwyn said, 'Kindly hescort us safely through to where me coach and four are waiting.'

'Oh, hoity toity!' said the men, making mocking bows to Ma Gwyn. Eliza heard one say, 'A coach and four? When the Thames boils!' and the rest guffawed. A different man said, 'Praise be! Another niece found!' and added (Eliza was to worry on this later), 'Set to join the other trulls in the bawdy house, I'll be bound!'

As the prison gates opened Ma Gwyn looked out and said loudly, 'Lawks! Where's me coach and four?'

and then, after making an elaborate play of looking up and down the road, proceeded to march as quickly as her bulk would allow her around the corner and out of sight of the turnkeys, who were watching proceedings with some amusement.

Eliza felt odd: elated, confused and worried all at the same time. She had, she realised, absolutely no idea of where she was going or what was going to happen to her. She'd got out of Clink; that was all that mattered at the moment.

The two of them jostled their way through the rabble of Southwarke: housewives coming back from market, apprentices running about their business, street hawkers crying their goods, messengers, sedan chairs, horsemen, carts, roped bears going to the bear-baiting. The streets were almost as crowded as the prison but Eliza, entranced and fascinated by the mob, enjoying her first fresh air for several weeks, didn't mind any of it. This was the London she'd heard so much about.

They passed music houses and theatres, bear gardens and taverns, going up alleys and down byways. Eventually Ma Gwyn stopped in front of a tall building with marble columns along its front.

'Is this where you *live*?' Eliza asked in awe, thinking that appearances were indeed deceptive, for judging by this house Ma Gwyn must be very rich indeed.

'Gawd 'elp us, no,' Ma Gwyn said, puffing from the effort of walking so far. 'These is the baths.'

Eliza looked through the pillars to sparkling stone and a brightly tiled floor. 'Baths?' she asked.

'Baths!' Ma Gwyn repeated. 'Where yer bathe! 'Ere's where I see what I've got for me money!'

An intense curiosity, plus Ma Gwyn's pokes from behind, made Eliza climb the steps up to the imposing doorway, and curiosity also led her through into a spacious, tiled area with many alcoves containing ladies and their maids and what seemed to be troughs of water. When Eliza was told by Ma Gwyn to remove all her clothing and step into such a trough, though, she declared that she would not.

'Pish, madam!' Ma Gwyn said. 'Why so modest? There are no gentlemen here!'

Eliza looked around. There were no gentlemen, true, but the ladies looked to be such terrifyingly grand creatures – all occupied in primping themselves, rubbing oils into their limbs, applying colours to their faces or having their hair dressed, while she herself …

'I feel too lowly,' she said, horribly aware of her filthy condition, from her lice-ridden hair down to her rank, sweat-blackened feet.

Ma Gwyn took in the room and its occupants at a glance. 'Hoh!' she said, spitting generously on the marble floor. 'My money is as good as theirs.'

'But I feel so … so disgusting,' Eliza said, still shrinking back.

'That, my sweeting, is why we're 'ere,' Ma Gwyn said, and she gave an impatient tug at Eliza's blouse and then reeled back holding her nose. 'If you think I'm taking you to my 'ouse stinkin' like a civit then you're mistook!'

Embarrassed at the fuss being created, for several ladies were looking across at them curiously, Eliza pulled off her skirt, blouse and undersmock – she had long ago thrown away her bodice – and discarded them without daring to look at them too closely.

A girl appeared and began filling up the bath with jugs of hot water, and then another came in and poured in some flower-scented oil. Eliza, noticing the two of them exchanging amused glances at her condition, was embarrassed all over again.

'In yer get!' Ma Gwyn said, when the bath was almost full. Eliza gingerly stepped in and, sliding down into the warmth, felt not only the luxury of clean water lapping against her limbs, but almost instant relief from the multitude of flea bites.

It was certainly, she thought to herself, the first bath she'd ever had. As a child, she'd bathed naked in the brook that ran beside their cottage, and when she'd become too old for that had washed in the mornings using a bowl of water from the well and a bar of rough soap. This was the first time her body had been totally immersed in warm water, however, and though she would have liked the leisure to enjoy the experience there wasn't time to do so, for the two bath girls were alternately scouring her skin with soap and sponges, then pummelling and dunking her. When they'd finished doing this, and the bath water, she was mortified to see, was a filthy grey, it was allowed to gurgle away though pipes underneath. More warm water was brought and her hair was washed several times over; then, as Eliza sat in the bath, jug after jug of scented rinsing water was poured over her. Squealing the occasional protest, but by and large savouring the experience, Eliza submitted meekly to all this attention. When they were finished and Ma Gwyn had inspected Eliza closely and pronounced herself satisfied, she was helped from the bath and enveloped in towels. Sweet-smelling lotion was rubbed into her limbs and her hair was combed through with rosemary water. The lack of good food inside the prison had not stunted its growth, Eliza noticed, for it was now almost long enough for her to sit on.

At last, all their tasks completed, the maids curtsied and withdrew. A set of clothes had been placed on a nearby chair: a boned bodice, undershift, plain grey linen gown and jacket, and Ma Gwyn indicated that Eliza was to put these on. She did so and finally stood for inspection, her limbs clean and pink, her face glowing, her hair sleek and shiny down her back.

'Just as I thought,' Ma said with some satisfaction. 'Of a ragged colt comes a good 'orse. You'll do very well.'

Do for what? Eliza wondered, but did not like to ask.

Chapter Six

'Ma Gwyn's coming back with a party of folk,' Susan said to Eliza late the following Saturday evening. 'She sent a message to say that you're to make yourself scarce.'

Eliza sighed. 'Why?' she asked. 'Why do I have to?'

Susan didn't reply, just shrugged. She was Ma Gwyn's grandchild – the daughter of Rose, who worked with Ma at the Reindeer Tavern next door to where they lived. She was seven years old and would, Eliza thought, have been a pretty child, except that she'd got a monstrous carbuncle on her face which puckered and distorted her right cheek from her eye to the corner of her mouth. The first time they'd met, Eliza had been unable to avoid staring at this disfigurement in fascinated horror. A little later, realising what she was doing, she'd apologised to the child.

Susan had just shrugged. 'I'm used to folk staring.'

'But ... how did it happen?'

'Don't you know that?' Susan had said. 'Haven't you seen anyone with a carbuncle before? Why, when I was in my ma's belly she was cursed by a witch and this was the result.'

Eliza nodded. There had been witches in

Somersetshire – so it was said. 'But couldn't your ma have bought a cure from the witch?'

'Dunno. But 'tis no matter,' Susan said carelessly, 'for 'tis awful good for begging. Sometimes I get two shillin' in a day!'

Now, as she looked at Susan, Eliza scarcely noticed the carbuncle, but sighed in frustration at the restrictions being imposed on her. 'Am I always to be hidden away? I might as well have stayed in jail!' she said crossly.

'Ma says you're to go upstairs to the closet and not come out until she says,' Susan reported. 'Or if she forgets to say, then you're to stay there until morning.'

She left and Eliza, grumbling to herself, climbed the ladder to the first floor of the house and went into the closet, a small room used to store linens and rough blankets. It was stuffy in there and she pushed open the high window and stood on tiptoe to lean out and breathe some fresh air. Although, she thought, you could hardly call it that. Fresh air in London was a mixture of coal, cooking smells, human waste and the rancid smell that came off the river, and not a bit like the fresh air in Stoke Courcey. There, at this time of the year, she would have been breathing in the smell of new-mown hay, full-blown roses and lavender.

Old Ma Gwyn lived in several rooms and a cellar in Coal Yard Alley, off Drury Lane. As befitting such an address, the house was dark and dank, flanked on one side by the Reindeer Tavern and on the other by a yard where coal lay in vast sooty piles and carts were loaded with the stuff at all hours. Both inside and outside the rooms of Ma Gwyn the air one breathed was loaded with the smell and dust from coal, and it was impossible to wash smocks or petticoats and have them remain white, for no sooner had they been hung in the backyard than they became specked with coal dust. Eliza, when she'd helped with the washing earlier that week, had had to carry a basket of damp linen to Hatton Garden and drape things over the bushes to ensure they dried spotless. Apart from this one errand, however, she'd hardly been out, for Ma seemed to have a fear that she'd be seen.

'Be seen by whom?' Eliza asked, and Ma would reply, 'the watch' or 'a no-good prison turnkey' and in vain Eliza would protest that she wasn't known to any of the watch and besides, hadn't Ma paid for her to get out of Clink legitimately? Ma, however, who was used to being obeyed, would sharply remind her at this point that she would be rotting in a cell had it not been for her and her kindness. Eliza thought for quite some time about this kindness and, as she got to know Ma better, wondered what she'd be called upon to do in return.

There were so many people living at Ma Gwyn's house in Coal Yard Alley that Eliza did not have a bed to herself, but instead shared with young Susan or one of the girls who worked in the Reindeer. Ma's two daughters, Eleanor and Rose, came to the house occasionally, but always at night, and though Eliza had heard plenty of tales of them, she'd not yet managed to see them. Eleanor, she knew, was an actress at the theatre, where she was known as Nell, and Rose was married to a highwayman and, when she wasn't working at the tavern next door, sold oysters in the street or went out begging with Susan. There was a family of gypsies lodging in one room of the house, and several other groups who hired rooms, or space in the rooms, and carried out what Ma called 'special work'. Eliza had no idea of what this might be, just that Ma ran a number of money-making undertakings and that a constant stream of ill-dressed fellows came and went from the house.

Eliza had got no further in her search for her father. Although Ma didn't actually lock her in the house during the day, she'd made it very clear that she didn't want her to be seen, and Eliza had so far heeded her wishes, frightened that if she didn't she might be cast alone on to the streets of London. She thought about her father constantly, though, and on the way back from Hatton Garden with the washing had gone into several places where they were rebuilding after the Great Fire and asked if anyone knew Jacob Rose, the mason. The answer each time had been no, and Eliza had since started to worry that he'd gone home. Had they, perhaps, passed each other unknowingly on the London Road? Sometimes – most times – thinking of the poor life she was leading, of the family she missed and might never see again, Eliza seethed at the injustice of it all. She shouldn't be here, in this filthy house and living in the meanest of states. It was all her stepmother's fault …

Now, sitting in the closet, Eliza could hear the kitchen filling up downstairs. Gradually it grew noisy with shouts and laughter and, sniffing the air, she could smell tobacco and ale. It was another of Ma Gwyn's private parties, she supposed, for she'd held one a few days previously. She heard a fiddler tuning up, then someone began singing one of the new ballads and a score of voices joined in; some with rough London accents, some sounding more polished. When the song finished and there was a call for more of the same, Eliza heard a lady, in refined tones, ask for 'Another, *s'il vous plaît*', which expression, she knew, was French.

After some while, greatly intrigued to see what sort of persons attended Ma Gwyn's parties, Eliza stealthily came out of the closet and made her way towards the ladder. She hadn't thought to do this at the last party. Then, newly arrived and anxious to please Ma, she'd merely fallen asleep in the closet. Surely, though, she thought, there'd be no harm in seeing what was going on?

She slipped silently along the passageway and, on reaching the opening where the ladder hung, was immediately struck with how much fun everyone seemed to be having. The room was still mean and bare, but the colour and gaiety of the party guests seemed to have brought about a vast change to it. Apart from the fiddler there were equal numbers of men and women – about eight of each. The girls were wearing silks and satins in bright rainbow hues, had elaborately curled hair and small black patches on their cheeks, and the men wore coloured shirts and be-ribboned breeches. Everyone seemed to be having a rare good time – even Ma Gwyn, sitting on a kitchen chair in the corner with a clay pipe in one hand and a jug of ale in the other, was chortling about something. People swayed to the music, tapped their feet, clapped and sung, and in the centre of all this was a girl dancing a jig. Eliza stared in admiration at the slim, pretty figure with red curls who was dancing so well – as light as a dandelion clock, twirling around and showing a froth of white petticoats, faster and faster as the fiddler played. As her feet lifted in time to the music her skirts exposed slim ankles and shapely calves, drawing the eye of every man there.

'Nell!' the party-goers called. 'Nelly, Nelly, Nelly!' and the girl twirled and kicked and finally collapsed, laughing fit to burst, while her audience surrounded her, clapping and calling for more.

Nelly, Eliza thought. This must be Eleanor, Ma Gwyn's daughter.

Eliza watched the scene for several moments, fascinated by the girls and admiring of the young men, all of whom seemed dashing, handsome and elegant. Not quite as handsome, she decided, as her hero with the curving mouth, but there were one or two who came close, and she dearly wished she could be dancing amongst them and not upstairs confined to a poky closet.

After a while one of the ladies – a small, voluptuous woman with a red silk dress – made towards the ladder, and Eliza jumped up quickly to hide herself. Reaching the room where she usually slept, she was struck by the notion that she should just go to bed. Why did she have to go into the closet? No one was going to come looking for her in her own bed, surely?

As she reached the threshold of her room she looked in and gave a little gasp, immediately aware that someone was already there. But not Susan, nor any of the tavern girls she sometimes shared with. No, this was a man, for by the light of the candle placed on the window sill she could see his surcoat hung over the door and his plumed hat resting on the chair.

But it wasn't just a man there. As Eliza hesitated,

peering round the doorway, there came the low murmur of voices and a woman crossed the room, completely naked. She climbed on to the bed where the man was lying and they both began laughing, rolling over and over on the rough wool blanket.

Eliza felt herself flush. She knew what must be going on – and hadn't she heard one of the prison turnkeys speak about a bawdy house? Here was the proof right under her nose.

The woman in red silk now arrived at the top of the ladder, closely followed by a man, and Eliza fled to the safety of the closet. Here she made herself a nest on the floor with some linens, pulled her cap over her ears and tried not to listen to what might be going on outside.

It proved impossible not to listen, however, as several couples climbed the ladder and used each of the three bedrooms as they became vacant. As she lay there trying – and failing – to sleep, Eliza's thoughts went to home. To Stoke Courcey. She missed her brothers and sisters; were they, too, missing her? Was even her stepmother missing her and regretting having turned her out? No, Eliza concluded, she thought not. Her stepmother was a plain-speaking, no-nonsense woman who'd hardly seemed to miss Eliza's father when he'd gone away. If her stepmother missed anything about Eliza not being there, it was probably her help with the little girls. Eliza thought of them now with affection: Patience and Margaret, the twins, with their blonde curls, wide smiles and own special twin-language that no one else understood, and Louise – a baby still, not yet walking, but already with the blonde curls and dimpled smiles of the other two. Her elder brothers were very fair, too, with thick, straw-like hair that was only flat and neat on a Sunday when their heads were stuck under the yard pump as part of the ritual of being made tidy for church.

Many of their neighbours had made idle comments on the fact that Eliza, by contrast with her brothers and sisters, was so dark. Once, years ago when her mother had been alive, a jolly peddler had come to the house and, after selling a dozen clothes pegs, had paused in the cottage garden where Eliza and her brothers had been playing. He'd studied Eliza for a moment, and then lifted her aloft.

'I think you're a changeling child,' he'd said, sitting her on the gate.

'What does that mean?' Eliza had asked.

'It means, my pretty babe, that when your ma and pa weren't looking, faeries came to the house and changed their own mortal child for a faerie one.'

'*Did* they?' Eliza had said, her eyes glowing. 'And is that me?'

The peddler had nodded.

'But how do you know?'

'Well, you're of the quality,' the old man had said. 'It's writ all over you. And besides, only changelings have green eyes. But you must be ready with your bundle packed in case they ever want you back!'

Eliza, thrilled at the thought of being a faerie child, had run to tell her mother what he'd said. Her mother had been annoyed, though, saying that she shouldn't have listened to such nonsense. Besides, she'd added crossly, seeing Eliza's obvious delight in the idea, wasn't her own family good enough for her? She wouldn't have that peddler at the door again, indeed she wouldn't, if he went round telling such silly tales.

Remembering it now, Eliza smiled. A changeling child indeed ...

At last, sheer tiredness overcoming both her uncomfortable surroundings and the constant merrymaking both downstairs and up, Eliza fell asleep. Before she did so, however, a dreadful thought struck her. All these girls coming and going from the rooms – was this what Ma Gwyn had planned for her? Did she intend Eliza to work in the bawdy house, too?

Chapter Seven

When, a few mornings later, Eliza rose and went downstairs, Old Ma Gwyn gave her a beaming, toothless smile and asked not only if she'd slept well, but if there was anything she needed.

Eliza shook her head, mystified at this sudden concern, then went to the conduit on the corner to draw water for washing. When she returned there was a fellow in the kitchen conversing with Ma Gwyn, and both were puffing at clay pipes so that the dim room was already half-filled with smoke.

''Ere she is,' said Ma as Eliza came in. 'What do you think to 'er?' And she bade Eliza put down the tin bowl of water on the table and walk up and down.

Eliza did so, immediately suspicious as to what was going on. Since the night of the party she'd been waiting for something like this.

'Smile at the gentleman, sweeting!' said Ma.

Eliza, embarrassed and uneasy at being shown off like a prize-winning cow at market, did as she was bid.

'And let yer 'air down, girl!' Ma Gwyn added.

Again Eliza obeyed, taking out the pins and letting her dark tresses tumble down her back. She eyed the man nervously. He was fat and ill-dressed, with a face that ran with sweat even though the sun was hardly up. If Ma Gwyn was making some sort of bargain with him, if she was planning that Eliza should …

No! She gagged at the very thought of it. She'd run away. She would! Even if she was friendless and penniless in London, she'd run away and live in the fields … in a pig sty if she had to.

'Excellent … excellent,' the man said approvingly. Even his voice was fat, Eliza thought, as if he was speaking through a mouthful of blubber.

'See the 'air,' Ma Gwyn said. 'Black and slippery as seaweed!' She beckoned Eliza to come closer. 'And the eyes on 'er! Green as em'ralds.'

'Green as the sea, you mean,' the man said, tapping his nose, and they both laughed as if he'd made a fine joke.

Eliza was dismissed then and went away. Going upstairs to turn her mattress, however, she could still hear him and Ma discussing something in low voices, and once – though maybe it was just her fearful imagination – seemed to hear the chink of money exchanging hands.

Another week went by and the weather grew hotter. The fat man didn't return, and Ma Gwyn refused to say what they'd been talking about, but other odd things happened. A woman appeared at the house, a seamstress, and Eliza was measured up for – well, for what she didn't know. A gown, or a suit, or a waistcoat? Ma wasn't saying. All she would say was that Eliza would know soon enough and it was going to be a most excellent garment.

Eliza didn't know whether she should fret. A new

gown, a brand-new gown especially for her, was an undreamed-of treat. But for what occasion was it needed? Not for a wedding, surely?

Susan didn't know either. 'Maybe 'tis something for the Midsummer Fair?' she suggested. 'I'm having a new dress for that, too – but mine will be a newly ragged one so that I may earn *lots* from my begging!'

'What happens at the Midsummer Fair?' Eliza asked her.

Susan's face grew rapt with excitement. 'Oh, there's a mighty crush of people all intent on entertainment. There's a man tightrope walking – and another eats fire! There are pageants and waxworks and clever animals who do tricks. And there are the curiosities: last year there was a woman with three arms and another with two heads!'

'There couldn't possibly be!' Eliza said, thinking how sad it was that the little girl was so disfigured that she'd never find a husband.

''Twas true!' Susan assured her. 'And there was a man covered all over in hair like a wolf – but you had to pay sixpence to see him and my ma wouldn't – and a great many peddlers and stalls and things to buy: fairings and sweetmeats and ribbons and gloves. There's a hiring fair where people go to seek positions, and apothecaries and travelling doctors. There's a mint of money to be made from begging at the fair!'

'Does everyone go?' Eliza asked, wondering if she'd be allowed there.

'*Everyone*,' Susan assured her. ''Tis on for three days and all the great ladies and gentlemen go, *and* their servants – why, 'tis even said that last year the king and queen went!'

71

Eliza looked at her, wide-eyed. 'The king and queen …' she gasped. To her the words meant some remote, divine, God-like creatures. She'd never thought of them as being living and breathing people who could actually attend *fairs*.

'But they always come in disguise,' Susan went on earnestly. 'They sometimes dress as coachmen and milkmaids and mix in with the crowd to hear what everyone's saying about them.' She dropped her voice, 'So when you're at the Midsummer Fair you must never, never say anything treasonous against the king, just in case he's nearby.'

'I would never!' Eliza promised, for she'd been brought up as a Royalist and respected the Crown, and couldn't understand how anyone would turn against the real and anointed king. Feeling some of Susan's excitement about the Midsummer Fair, she hoped desperately that Ma Gwyn would let her out of the house for such an occasion. And maybe, too, there was a chance that her father might be there for the hiring fair.

The seamstress making the outfit for Eliza came back to Coal Yard Alley with some materials to show to Ma Gwyn, the like of which Eliza, used to country tweeds, rough calico and cheesecloth, had never before seen. There were bolts of deep green brocade, shiny blue taffeta, emerald-green tulle, silver tissue and sumptuous silk that shimmered in the sunlight. Some of these were embellished with sparkling beads of sea-blue, tiny spangles of silver or buttons of pearl.

The seamstress flung different lengths of material over Eliza in turn, then she and Ma stood back to look at the results and chose which should be used.

'These are the best and finest materials in the land,' said the seamstress. 'And I think you'll agree they'll suit your purpose.'

'Indeed!' said Ma. 'Our Eliza is going to be the talk of London town.'

'But *why*?' Eliza asked, excited in spite of the frisson of fear which ran through her. 'And what exactly is it I'm to have made?'

'You'll know soon enough,' Ma said.

'Will I be wearing it to the Midsummer Fair?'

Ma's mouth gaped with astonishment and her pipe fell out. 'There's a cunning girl!' she said. 'You have worked out the very thing.' And she and the seamstress exchanged smiles and conspiratorial glances.

'Am I really to go there?' Eliza asked, suddenly very excited.

'You are,' Ma nodded.

'But what about all the people that will see me? Don't you care about that now?' Eliza asked, wondering at this sudden change in her benefactor's conduct.

Ma and the seamstress snorted with laughter.

'What is it?' Eliza asked, frowning.

'Well, it's like this, my sweeting,' Ma said. 'You'll be in disguise, you see. So you needn't worry about being seen.'

'*Disguise?*'

'Like a masquerade,' Ma explained. 'All the quality masquerade now.'

And although Eliza asked several times what she'd actually be called upon to *do*, Ma wouldn't say.

* * *

Eliza was instructed to wash her hair every other day with rosemary and thyme to scent it and make it shiny, and Susan was given the job of brushing it a hundred times a day. Sometimes when people came to the house Ma would ask Eliza to let her hair down and show it – and when she did so they'd nod sagely and say it would do very well indeed.

Eliza was pleased that they all found favour with her hair, of course, but knew there must be more to it than that. There was something else ... something else going on that she didn't understand.

On Midsummer Day Ma Gwyn came into Eliza's room very early, as soon as the sun was up. Eliza, yawning, protested that she wanted to go back to sleep, but then remembered what day it was.

'Are we to go out and collect greenery and branches to decorate the house?' she asked, for this had been the custom in Somersetshire.

'God help us – there's no time for such foolery this morning,' Ma said, pulling off the sacking from the window.

'Then why are we up so early?'

'To ready ourselves for the Midsummer Fair, of course!'

Eliza, sitting up now, saw that Ma had an outfit of some sort over her arm, a swathe of greeny-blue.

'You're to come downstairs and I'm to help you get into your new gown ready for the Fair,' Ma said. 'Now, what d'you think to that?'

Eliza looked at her nervously. 'But will you tell me now what I'll be doing there?'

'Just looking yer luvverly best, my kitling.'

Eliza hesitated. 'I'm not ... you're not giving me to that fat man, are you?'

Ma gave a guffaw of laughter. 'Indeed not. When your time comes, 'twill be to a far wealthier man than he!'

Eliza did not find this very comforting. Rising, however, she went downstairs, splashed her face with water, and then turned to Ma.

'And now am I to put on my new dress?'

Ma nodded, shaking out the material she'd been holding and displaying it before her. Looking at it, Eliza gasped, for it was a most unusual and sumptuous blue-green taffeta which shone and shimmered in the light from the window. The dress – or whatever it was – appeared to be very small, though, and hardly long enough to cover her. It was the most beautiful – yet also the very strangest – gown she'd ever seen in her life ...

Chapter Eight

An hour later, Eliza was at the Midsummer Fair. She wasn't walking around enjoying the sideshows and curiosities, however, but was inside a large, square, canvas tent. A notice above the entrance to the tent read:

See within a representation of the sea in motion with a Genuine Mermaid plucked from Neptune's Depths. Not to be confused with a waxwork. This is a Genuine Creature and may be viewed for a Limited Period Only.

Inside the tent, the mermaid wept.

'You've got to sing!' Ma Gwyn said to a weeping Eliza. 'For sixpence the people expects singing. They expects the mermaid's siren song what lures the sailors on to the rocks.'

Eliza buried her face in her hands. 'I cannot! I cannot sit here, *naked*, and sing ...'

Ma snorted. 'Oh, do not take on so,' she said, exasperated. ''Tis only for three days.'

'Oh, for shame!' Eliza cried.

'No, for money,' said Ma, and she cackled with

laughter. 'We shall all make a mint by this.'

Within the tent, an ingenious pool had been built. Constructed of wood and canvas, it was covered with undergrowth, greenery and slate, so that the general effect was one of a large rockpool on a wild seaside shore. The 'motion' advertised was caused by Susan, crouched out of sight, pulling on a piece of rope which drew a blade through the water, causing ripples and eddies to appear on its surface.

Eliza was sitting on a rock with her feet in the pool of water, through which glided some small ornamental fish. From the waist downwards her body was encased in shimmering blue-green material which had been painstakingly covered in tiny oxidised metal spangles sewn in an overlapping fashion like fish scales, finishing in a spectacular silvery-blue tail. Her bosom was naked apart from a narrow length of material tied around and only partially concealing it; her tumbling black locks were intended to hide the rest.

Outside the tent which enclosed Eliza and the pool, the fat man stood on a box and shouted to be heard above the crowds.

'Come and see the gen-u-ine mermaid in all her glory!' Eliza heard him call. 'Her like has not been seen at any Fair in this country before! A sixpence to view this fantastical creature! Roll up! Roll up!'

Eliza wept on. 'My family would be shamed – they would disown me,' she protested, forgetting for the moment that such an unfortunate fate already seemed to have befallen her.

Ma coughed and spat. 'For a lass who was running with lice in Clink prison a while back you're talking mighty dainty! Would you rather be there amid the filth and the fleas than here at Midsummer Fair, sitting on a rock as pretty as a picture?'

Eliza didn't know what to answer to this.

'Just you say the word, my little Miss Hoity Toity, an' I'll take you back there straight and find another girl. Why, most poor jades would give their maidenheads to be dressed up so fine.'

Eliza rubbed at her wet cheeks. 'So you wish me to sit here, near-naked, while all the world comes and stares?'

'Of course yer must be naked!' Ma Gwyn said. 'Mermaids do not sit on rocks in their gowns and flannel petticoats. And you 'ave yer 'air and a ribband to 'ide your privities.'

'I shan't stay!' Eliza looked wildly around the tent. 'I shall run off.'

'You can try,' Ma said reasonably. 'But 'ow will you run with no legs and your fish's tail a-flapping?'

'I shall get out of this costume!'

'If you do, we shall all 'ave the pleasure of seeing your bare arse a-running across the field. I shall charge double for a view of that!'

As Eliza burst into fresh tears, Ma leaned towards her conspiratorially. 'Better to stay, lass, and pay off some of your debts.'

Eliza looked up. 'What debts?'

'Why, what you owes me. There's the cost of gettin' you out of Clink, plus your board and keep for three weeks – that's a tidy packet I'm due. All you've to do now is sit 'ere as nice as a nosegay for three days, and you'll 'ave gone some ways towards paying me back.'

Eliza fell silent. Had she really thought that a person such as Ma Gwyn would have rescued her out of the goodness of her heart? In Somersetshire, maybe, that might happen. But not in London. She gave a long, resigned sigh.

'So, my sweeting – about yer singing,' Ma said, sensing victory. 'Just a plainsong or a nice ballad would suffice. Or even just a tra-la-la such as a mermaid might sing to get 'erself a sailor boy.'

Eliza said nothing.

'Nothing too modern, mind,' Ma went on. 'Some o' the old stuffs.'

Defeated, Eliza gave a slight nod. She would do it, she would *have* to do it. Sighing again, she looked down at her bosom and adjusted the ribband as well as she could, then threaded her fingers through her hair and spread it over her shoulders to try and hide herself even more.

Ma Gwyn smiled so that the wrinkles on her face, engrained with coal dust, went into a spider's web of lines. 'Get that pool movin', Susan,' she called over. 'The customers are waitin'.'

Obligingly, the pool began rippling. As it lapped gently up the side of the rock on which she was seated, Eliza moved her tethered legs and made her tail flick across the surface of the water and back again, twisting slightly like the live fish she'd seen on market stalls. If she was going to be a mermaid, she decided, she may as well try and be a convincing one.

As Ma Gwyn went outside ready to take money from the customers, Susan's face appeared above the foliage to stare at Eliza.

'Are you a real mermaid now?' she asked wonderingly.

'Of course I'm not,' Eliza said, flicking her tail

again. 'I'm Eliza! You've been sharing a bed with me these past nights. And you saw me being dressed in my tail just a bit earlier.'

'But you look so like ... just the same as the mermaid in the window of St Mary's Church,' Susan said wonderingly.

'Of course I do,' Eliza said, 'for the seamstress must have copied that very one.'

From outside they suddenly heard the words, 'If you please, my lords, ladies and gentlemen – the genuine mermaid awaits!' and Susan ducked down again behind the rock.

Eliza's stomach knotted with fright as the tent flap was drawn open and Ma Gwyn was silhouetted in the doorway. Behind her could be seen perhaps forty people, jostling each other, pushing, nudging and peering over shoulders, each anxious to be first to see the wondrous sight.

'Mind your manners,' Ma exhorted, spitting on the floor. 'Step up nicely to see the genuine mermaid! And gentlemen, for a few extra coins thrown into 'er pool, the mermaid will be obliged to sing for you.'

Eliza lowered her head modestly. Not for anything was she going to look up and see those who were staring at her with such intent. This wasn't really her ... she wasn't truly there ...

'The Genuine Mermaid' was the hit of the Fair, that much was certain. From eight in the morning until eight at night a procession of people paid their sixpences, queued outside the tent for up to an hour and entered in groups of twenty or so to stare at Eliza. Grand ladies came and marvelled, threw coins into the pool, then told their equally grand friends about this fabulous creature. Drabs, cinder-pickers and tub-women arrived too, screeched with fright and wonder at the sight, and spread the news. So popular was the curiosity that when Ma Gwyn's party arrived on the morning of the second day of the Fair, a hastily contrived rival, 'King Nepture and his Court of Sea Creatures', had appeared.

Susan was sent to spy on this, and returned to say that it was but a shabby imitation of their own spectacle: a roughly painted backdrop featuring an old man with long beard, sitting amid a host of fishing nets and holding a trident. This was dismissed as of no import.

Ma gave Eliza, as a further enhancement to her role, a hairbrush and mirror fashioned from a conch shell. She was instructed to brush her hair, slowly and languidly, whilst admiring her reflection in the mirror.

'And with yer first lot of customers this morning yer must be sure to brush and sing with extra refinement,' she said, 'because Claude Duval is waiting in line.'

Eliza frowned. She knew she'd heard the name before, but couldn't remember where.

'Monsieur Claude Duval – 'e's French, you know – is the very best, most genteel gentleman of the road.'

Eliza nodded, remembering now what she'd heard at Clink.

''E 'as an eye for the ladies,' Ma added, and she took out a dingy handkerchief and rubbed it over her face, wiping away the sweat which had gathered in the fine hairs of her top lip. She winked at Eliza. 'Ladies of all ages!'

'How shall I know which is he?' Eliza asked.

'You shall know soon enough,' Ma said, 'for when you catches sight of 'im your breath will catch and your 'eart will go to thumping, for 'e's the most comely man that ever could be looked upon.'

And when Claude Duval entered, a foot taller than any man there and twice as handsome, Eliza's heart did indeed miss a beat. He was accompanied by a richly dressed, masked woman, however, and though he smiled at Eliza and blew a kiss, he and the woman – who was clinging to him like ivy – did not stop in the tent for more than a moment.

In spite of herself, Eliza found that she was almost enjoying her time as a mermaid. Her life had been drab, sour and unpleasant for weeks now, but for the last two days she'd been transformed into this truly fabulous, glittering creature, marvelled at and admired by everyone who attended the Fair. Of course, she reasoned, she wasn't a *real* mermaid, and those people who flocked to see her wouldn't have been interested in the ordinary Eliza – but wasn't that just what those in the London theatres did all the time: pretended to be other people? And there was no doubting how much *they* were admired.

The curious continued to pour into the tent. They leaned across the pool to try and touch her, walked around the rock pool to see her from the back and called across to ask questions, wanting to know where she was caught, how she had been transported to London and if she ate fish to keep herself alive. Many threw extra money into the pool to hear her voice and several men made lewd comments or asked questions of a sexual nature which Eliza pretended not to hear.

Whenever she sang, a hush came upon the tent, no

matter how many people it held or how riotous their mood. Eliza devised a ditty about the 'wild, stormy sea' and also amended slightly the prison song about being 'far, far from home' and these went down well with those who crowded in. Whether they actually believed that she was a real mermaid or not, Eliza didn't know. That didn't seem to matter much.

On the third and final day of the Fair, Ma Gwyn's daughter Nell appeared with a group of youths and young actresses – a party of perhaps twelve persons who paid extra to have the tent to themselves. They seemed so gay and happy when they appeared in the doorway with their feathers, furbelows and exaggerated mannerisms that Eliza, who'd grown bolder over the last two days, immediately dropped her head so that her face once again became almost entirely hidden by her hair.

The young men were obviously well-born and dressed very fine, and the ladies were arrayed in silks of all colours and carried favours which had been purchased at the Fair: ribbons, hair ornaments and silvery trinkets. One auburn-haired beauty had a nightingale in a cage, another a pet monkey which ran continually backwards and forwards across her shoulders.

Despite their apparent sophistication, however, everyone was entranced by the novelty of a mermaid.

'Where did you find her, Mother?' Nell asked, bending across the pool to try and lift a lock of Eliza's hair.

'Why, in the ocean, of course,' Ma Gwyn replied.

'Really, Mother!' Nell reproved her.

Eliza looked up and into Nell's eyes and the two

girls smiled at each other conspiratorially.

'She has lovely green eyes – and such excellent dark waves,' Nell said, and she held out her own gingery tresses and gave an exaggerated sigh of disapproval, whereupon all the young men present immediately cried that they adored and admired red hair and no other shade was bearable. 'But I don't think she came from the ocean!' Nell added.

'As I hope to be saved, that's just where we found her!' said Ma.

Nell indicated a plump man in clerical attire. 'Mother,' she said warningly, 'we have a minister of the church with us.'

'If I tell a lie, may I go to bed a woman and wake up a donkey!' Ma said, looking wounded.

One of the men gave an *ee-aww* bray and the party laughed.

'Oh, someone throw some money into the pool!' a girl in green satin cried. 'I want to hear her siren song.'

Several other female voices rose to say that they, too, wanted to hear the mermaid sing, and then a youth's voice called, 'Valentine! Have you some change? Throw it in, there's a good chap!'

At the mention of the name Valentine, Eliza grew hot, then cold. *It was he* – the first person she'd ever begged money from! And his companion, the one who'd just spoken, was the same friend he'd been with outside Clink – the one who'd seemed so arrogant.

A coin was flicked and splashed into the pool and Eliza gasped as she saw the gold angel sinking to the bottom. Susan, making the waves, saw it too, and the turbulence in the water suddenly became greater as she increased her efforts in line with the amount given.

Ma Gwyn's sharp eyes had also caught the glint of gold. 'The mermaid will give you a lovely song for that!' she said. A moment went by and, no song being forthcoming, she crossed to stand in front of Eliza and frowned deeply at her. 'A luvverly song such as she sings on the rocks far out to sea,' she confirmed. 'Yers, she will for certain.'

Eliza sat still as a statue, her face hidden under the veil of her hair. She feared being exposed as a convict and a trickster in front of all these fine people, but more especially she feared him – Valentine – recognising her, perhaps laughing with derision when he realised that this so-called mermaid had actually been in Clink. Surreptitiously she glanced at him and saw the same merry eyes and ready smile. He was *very* comely. Claude Duval was handsome and magnificent, of course, but he was perhaps twenty-six or twenty-seven years old, a fully grown man and in a different league. Valentine, although vastly more sophisticated and elegant than she, was perhaps only two or three years her senior. And there was something so vastly compelling about his blue eyes and wide, curved mouth.

'Dammit, but the jade won't sing!' the first man said crossly.

'Give her a chance, Henry,' came the more reasoned voice of Valentine.

'Yes, give the girl a chance,' Nell said, laughing. 'If you were a mermaid plucked out of the ocean perhaps you wouldn't always feel like singing.'

'She'll sing if she knows what's good for her,' Eliza heard Ma mutter in an undertone.

'She *must* sing!' said the girl in green. 'We've given her gold and if she doesn't then she'll have to be chastised for her insolence!'

Eliza knew she'd have to perform. She swallowed hard and, remembering *not* to sing the adapted prison song, began the ditty about the 'wild, wild sea'.

As she sang, her audience became still and attentive, and when she finished a smattering of applause broke out.

'That was very lovely,' Eliza heard Valentine say. 'And let's go now for a glass of sack and a pigeon pie!'

Eliza breathed a sigh of relief. She would have liked him to have stayed there longer; she would have liked to have looked at him again. But it was better that he went away.

Arguing and taking bets amongst themselves as to the authenticity or not of the mermaid, the small group began to move off. One remained behind, however.

'She has a damn fine figure for a mermaid!' the arrogant youth called Henry said, staring at Eliza.

Eliza did not react to this comment, but looked at him under her lashes and through her hair. She saw a man of average height, with pale blue eyes and fair, almost blond lashes and eyebrows. His long curly periwig was fair, too, and he wore a soft blue coat, heavy with gold lace and braiding. He wasn't unpleasant-looking as such, but she did not like what she saw: the lips were full but over-red, the eyes hooded, the skin too pink-and-white.

'A fine figure!' he repeated. 'And ... and yes, I think I should rather like to lie with a mermaid. What a novelty *that* would be.'

Eliza felt herself flushing with shame and embarrassment.

'Novelty, indeed!' said Valentine, who had come back for his friend. 'But Henry, remember that he who bulls the cow must keep the calf. How would you like to breed a child who was half fish?'

They stared at Eliza while she, horrified, kept utterly still. Susan, behind the rock, was so rapt at their conversation that she forgot to pull the blade to stir the water, and the ripples in the pool ceased.

'I shouldn't mind it if I'd had the pleasure of lying with its mother,' Henry said.

'But not today!' countered Valentine. 'Come on, my friend. The others are waiting.'

'Let them!' Henry shrugged off the arm which Valentine had placed around his shoulders. 'Let them wait.'

He approached Ma Gwyn, who was standing at the side of the tent ready – just as soon as she'd removed the gold coin from the pool into her pocket – to let in the next crowd of customers.

'I want,' he said grandly, 'to make you an offer for the mermaid. I presume you are her bawd.'

Eliza began to shiver, in spite of the closeness of the air within the tent.

Ma shook her head. 'Oh no, sire,' she said. 'She's rare and beyond price.'

'I don't want her for ever,' Henry said. 'Just for the one night.'

'She'd still be awful expensive,' said Ma.

'Come now. I'm sure we can arrive at some arrangement.'

Ma considered this, taking deep puffs on her pipe.

'Just the one night, you say?'

'Quite.' He gave an affected wave of his arm. 'You can name your price.'

A small cry escaped Eliza, but neither Henry nor Ma Gwyn took any notice. Ma's old, creased face broke into a broad smile as she beckoned him outside the tent.

'Well, sire,' she said, 'I think you and I will talk business.'

Chapter Nine

'Oh, do not take on so,' Old Ma Gwyn said to Eliza as the Fair closed on its final evening. 'You'll make your eyes red and nose run and you'll end up looking like a boar's backside.'

Eliza, hunched in a corner of the kitchen in Coal Yard Alley, carried on weeping. As she did so she reflected on the fact that, since coming to London, she'd probably spent part of every day in tears. She'd thought that once she got to the city her problems would be solved, but London, in fact, contained more troubles than she'd ever known existed.

'Don't you want to 'ave a rich admirer?' Ma said in disbelief. ''Tis what every wench dreams of! You give 'im what 'e wants and 'e'll keep you more than the one night, you see if 'e don't. 'E might even rent you a nice little room and give you an allowance.' She sniffed and spat. 'You'll be made, then. A kept woman. And just you be sure to remember Old Ma Gwyn when you is.'

'I ... I cannot just lie with him,' Eliza began, her breath catching in her throat. 'I don't know what to do, and besides I –'

'Don't you worry about not knowing what to do!' Ma said cheerfully. 'I warrant that young man will know all right. And don't you be fretting about losing your maidenhead, neither. We can fix it so that any man who comes after this one thinks you still 'ave it! Why, some of my girls lose their maidenheads regular – like whenever there's a customer who wants a girl who's new to the game!'

Eliza refused to be comforted. Apart from the fact that she had no idea of what might be expected and feared that the experience might be painful, she hated the idea of being sold off like a penny loaf. She'd known, of course, from quite a young age, that one day she'd marry and sleep with a man, but had always thought that this act would only happen when there was some love between the two parties. But now – well, money on one side and fear on the other didn't seem the right combination at all. And besides, she had no wish to have a child, and surely that was what happened when you slept with someone.

'Now, 'e wants you to be dressed as a mermaid,' Ma went on, 'so you stay wearing that tail.'

Eliza looked round the room hopelessly. She would have to stay wearing it, for her own clothes seemed to have disappeared.

Ma stuck her head out of the door and squinted at the church clock. 'Let's just hope he gets here before he's too drunk to remember what to do. A carriage and four, 'e's coming in.'

But Eliza thought of his round face with the bleached eyebrows and lashes, and the over-red, moist lips, and was revolted. She couldn't bear him kissing her with those lips, or touching her with those delicate, manicured hands. She would bite him if he came near her!

''E's jest come into a title, too,' Ma went on. Eliza did not look impressed by this and she went on, 'Most wenches would sell their own arms to lay with a man with a title! A Monteagle, and a lord! Now, what do you think to that?'

Eliza did not think anything to that – in fact it just made her feel more desperate, for she knew full well that those with money and power always got what they wanted in life. What hope was there for her? She'd be ruined by sleeping with this man. No decent man would ever want her.

Ma went across to the fire and lifted down a heavy black kettle of boiling water from the trivet. She poured a quantity of water into a cup, then added a teaspoonful of something from a lidded pot. She stirred the mixture and handed it to Eliza, telling her to drink it up quick.

Eliza looked at the mixture suspiciously, thinking that she wouldn't put anything past the devious old hag.

''Tis a recipe given to me by a cunning man,' Ma said. 'Camomile flowers and St John's wort. 'Twill make you settle down and enjoy the experience ahead.'

Eliza took the cup from her, although she had no intention of drinking its contents – for all she knew it was a sleeping draught and she'd wake up some hours later to find that the deed had been done – while at least if she had her wits about her she might be able to run off once her fishtail had been removed. She looked round the kitchen desperately. *Where were her clothes?* If she knew they were nearby, then she might possibly be able to roll herself on to the ground, wriggle out of her sequined tail, get into her smock and run away. But that would only be possible if Ma were occupied elsewhere – and it was clear that, until Eliza was safely inside the carriage, she wasn't going to be left on her own. If Susan was around maybe she could have been persuaded to help – but she'd gone off to prison to visit her highwayman father, and besides, like Ma she did little to help anyone without being paid.

Dusk was falling when they heard a carriage clattering on the cobblestones outside. Eliza began weeping again, but swiftly stopped when a ferocious Ma rounded on her.

"'E's paid good money for you and 'e won't want tantrums. Take care you don't get a beating from 'im as well as a good tumbling.'

Eliza, terrified, bit her lip hard to stop herself crying. Steps were heard coming across the cobbles and Eliza braced herself, but, to her enormous surprise, it was Nell Gwyn who came in. Her hair was bedecked in jewels, and she wore a vast taffeta dress of cobalt blue with a hooped skirt and looked magically out of place in such mean surroundings.

'I've not much time, I've come straight from the theatre,' she said, glancing at her mother.

'There!' Ma said, nodding at her daughter with satisfaction. 'See the dress, Eliza? See the jewels? That's what you gets when you 'as admirers!'

Eliza felt too overawed to speak. She knew Nell was only Ma's daughter and thus from a humble background, but at that moment her dress, jewels and deportment said otherwise. Why, she'd heard that King Charles himself had noticed Nell and admired her.

'Have you come to collect Miss?' Ma asked, indicating Eliza. 'I thought His Lordship was coming to the 'ouse 'imself.'

'I'm collecting her all right,' Nell said briskly, 'but not for him.'

Eliza and Ma Gwyn stared at her. 'You what?' said Ma.

'I've not much time, Ma,' Nell said breathlessly. 'Henry Monteagle is even now trying to gather his ale-addled wits together. When he does he'll straight away call the carriage and come to collect his mermaid.'

'As was agreed and paid for very nicely,' Ma said. She frowned. 'But what are you to do with anything?'

'I'm here to take her away,' Nell said, and Eliza shrank back.

'Lord above!' Ma said. 'What d'you mean, girl?'

'Where are her clothes?' Nell asked swiftly. 'She can't come to my lodgings wearing only her tail!'

Ma gave a roar of dismay.

'Listen out, Ma,' Nell said, 'I am determined to take her. I won't let Henry Monteagle bed her and spoil her!'

'*What?*' Ma lowered her bulk on to a chair. 'What are you going to do? I shall be ruined!'

'No, you won't! You'll find more girls – you always do.'

'But this is a special girl that I can earn fair money by. A mermaid –'

'Anyone can play a mermaid and most girls can play a whore,' Nell snapped, 'but this is a girl new to London who's as green as a gooseberry. 'Tis not right that she should be given to Henry Monteagle as a plaything.'

Ma began to rock in her chair. 'Oh, Lord! I'll 'ave to give 'im 'is money back.'

'Where are her clothes, Ma?' Nell said, looking around the room.

'No, I shall not give it back,' Ma said decisively, while Eliza looked from one to the other of them, speechless. 'I shall tell 'im that the little wretch stole the money!'

'Her clothes!' Nell cried impatiently. 'Tell me this instant.'

'They're all in a bundle in the privy,' said Ma. She waved her hand dismissively. 'Yers. I shall tell 'im she stole the money and ran away!'

Eliza sat on the corner of a rough chair in Nell's rented room by the Cat and Fiddle in Lewkenor's Lane. It was a poor dwelling, the room containing just a bed, a table holding a washstand and jug, and two chairs. Several nails had been knocked into the walls and there were clothes hanging on these, and the floorboards were bare apart from a grimy rag rug upon which, if one looked carefully, some of the original colour could be detected. Nell's room, Eliza thought, looking around her, didn't seem to go with her at all.

Nell turned and asked to be unbuttoned from the blue satin dress, then carefully stepped out of it, revealing pristine white petticoats edged with lace.

'The whole outfit, right down to my undersmock and hair ornaments, belongs to the theatre,' she said, seeing Eliza's admiring glances. 'It's the costume of an Italian Countess.'

'Where are your own clothes, then?' Eliza asked.

She glanced up at the nails as she spoke, thinking that these did not appear to hold any gowns worthy of a girl such as Nell.

Nell, putting on a muslin smock, said, 'I'll tell you all that in a moment.' She poked at the fire and made one or two coals glow, then lit two stubby candles and set them to stand upright on the table. She turned to smile at Eliza. 'You needn't look so rabbity-scared,' she said. 'I'm not going to hurt you. I know your name's Eliza, and mine's Eleanor – although they call me Nell. And that's not all they call me when they've a mind to!'

Eliza returned the smile. She wondered, however, if she could trust this girl, this Nell. There must be *some* reason why she'd been brought here.

'Most of my clothes – my good clothes – are at Charles Hart's house,' Nell explained. 'He's a playwright.'

'Susan told me that he's your ... your admirer,' Eliza said.

Nell laughed. 'That's the polite way of putting it,' she said, beginning to take down her hair. 'I live at his house in St James's some of the week, but I keep this room rented for when he wants me out of the way.'

Eliza looked at her enquiringly.

'For when he's entertaining his playwright friends or the nobs. They get girls in from a brothel then and he doesn't want his everyday whore around!'

Eliza felt herself going red. 'Don't you mind that?'

'Lord, no!' Nell said. 'Two can play at that game.' She winked. 'When the cat's away the mouse dances!' She looked at Eliza consideringly. 'It's a shame, but we must cut your lovely hair,' she said, 'and I'll get a wig from the theatre wardrobe for you to wear.'

'But why?' Eliza asked, and she instinctively pulled her hair back and wound it around her hand. Was this why she'd been taken? Just for the cost of her hair?

'Why? So that Henry doesn't recognise you again, of course. He'll be fair furious that he's been done out of his mermaid!' Nell came closer to Eliza, close enough for Eliza to see that her pretty face was covered in freckles which no amount of whitening could hide. ''Tis a pity we can't do anything about your green eyes,' she went on, 'but half the time Henry can't remember what colour his *own* eyes are, so that's no matter.'

Eliza sighed. She looked around at her bleak surroundings and felt that she'd have given anything to be back in Somersetshire in her little bedroom. She'd felt safe there.

Nell sat down in front of her on the rag rug. Her hair was free of false curls and ribbons now, and she ran both hands through it and shook her head as if taking pleasure in the freedom. 'You're wondering why I've got you here, aren't you?'

Eliza nodded, waiting.

'To tell the truth it was but a whim,' Nell said. She shrugged. 'My ma has caused the ruin of so many young girls, though – girls fresh from the country – and I didn't want to see it happen to you.' She smiled at Eliza. 'I suppose you'll tell me now that you've already turned tricks with a man and are as hot as a sow on heat!'

'No. No, indeed,' Eliza stuttered. 'I've never lain with a man.'

'I thought not,' Nell said. She smiled at Eliza.

"'Twas different for me, see. I was drawing ale in a tavern when I was eight and working in Ma's bawdy house by ten. I took my first tumble when I was twelve.'

Eliza gasped, shocked. The way Nell just came out with such things! And she didn't appear at all shamed.

'But besides all that, Henry Monteagle is not the right man to take any girl's maidenhead.'

'Why is that?' Eliza asked timidly.

'Because he's a good-for-nothing fop. He affects to be a gentleman but has the manners of a pig farmer.'

Eliza, puzzled, wondered aloud why such a man could have any standing in society.

'Because's he's devilish rich,' Nell explained, 'and newly titled since the death of his father. Besides, he's a friend of the king's son – of James, the Duke of Monmouth. They study together.'

Eliza shook her head wonderingly. 'I didn't think the king and queen had any sons.'

'Oh, Monmouth is not the queen's son, but a natural child of the king,' Nell went on, 'although no less loved by him for all that. His Majesty enjoys the company of the young men who surround him. He calls them his merry gang – his gang of wits.' She laughed. 'Those loved by him can do no wrong. Why, last week Monmouth and his drunken friends pissed on the crowd from the balcony at Whitehall Palace, and the king just laughed. And as for the Earl of Rochester – why, he writes such scurrilous poems that even I blush to read them!'

Eliza stared at her, wide-eyed. Such goings-on were undreamed of in Somersetshire. But were they *all* as bad as that?

'The friend of Henry Monteagle's – the one named Valentine,' she asked hesitantly. 'Is he as dissolute?'

'Valentine?' Nell asked, frowning. 'Oh, you mean Sir Valentine Howard.'

'He's a *sir*?' Eliza asked. She felt cast-down for a moment, and wondered why, for it could be of little matter to her whether he had a title or no.

Nell looked at her and laughed. 'I can see where your fancy's heading,' she said. 'And he's a fine young man and I might try for him myself if I hadn't set my sights higher.' She sat down on the bed and began to put her false ringlets and hairpieces carefully into a box. 'I'll tell you a secret,' she went on. 'I already have one Charles, but would have myself another.'

Eliza looked at her enquiringly.

'I would have Charles the Second!' Nell said. 'Although he would be my Charles the Third – for I've already been mistress to Charles Hart and Charles Sackville.'

Eliza stared at her with amazement. Nell was hardly older than her, but obviously had ten times the experience. 'But I thought –'

'You thought the king's mistresses would all be high class!' Nell kicked off a pink, high-heeled shoe. 'Oh no, the king will pay court to any shapely body who'll throw up her petticoats for him.' She went across to poke the fire again. 'And he loves play-going and adores actresses, so I think I've as good a chance with him as has Mary Davis. Besides, *her* legs are quite fat!' she added peevishly.

'And has he ... have you and the king ...?' Eliza asked.

'Not yet!' Nell said. She smiled at Eliza and her eyes

sparkled. 'But things grow warm between us!'

'And so ...' Eliza began, widening her eyes.

Nell nodded. 'The king has long-term mistresses – high-born ladies who bear his children and receive titles – but he also has other girls, just for fun.'

'And you will be of the fun kind?'

Nell laughed. 'Indeed I will!'

Eliza took off her own dress and hung it from the hook; then, wearing just her undersmock, went outside to use the latrine in the back yard.

She stood outside for a moment, thinking about all that had happened to her. The riotous clamour of London was dying away now and little could be heard but the heavy wooden wheels of carriages turning on the cobbles and the shouts of link boys as they lit the way home for late revellers. A bellman cried eleven of the clock and called that there had been an accident on the river and a woman had drowned, making Eliza think about her poor ma. If *she* hadn't died she herself wouldn't be in London now. How strange life was ...

When she went back inside, Nell was sprawled on the iron bedstead. She patted the near side.

'Hop in,' she said. 'We'll top and tail it tonight.'

Eliza went to the other end of the bed and wriggled under the blanket and Nell wished her goodnight. She replied likewise, remembering to thank Nell for her kindly rescue.

'But what's going to become of me?' she couldn't resist asking. 'What will I do now?'

'What do you want to do?' Nell asked.

'I want to find my father,' Eliza said. 'All I know is that he's working somewhere in London.'

'He has money of yours?'

'No, it's not that. It's because my stepmother threw me out and I need to appeal to him to allow me home.'

'Well, then,' Nell said, 'you must search for him.'

'And in the meantime I can stay here with you?'

Nell murmured that she could. 'I don't spend many nights here,' she said, 'and when I'm elsewhere you can have my bed to yourself and welcome to it. But you must work and earn your keep.'

'Willingly,' Eliza said. 'But what can I do?'

'You can help me with my clothes and hair – if I'm to rise in the world I must have a maid! And you can work in the theatre as an orange seller.'

Eliza gasped inwardly, but said nothing. Orange sellers: weren't they just trollops and trulls, girls who'd sell their bodies for a pint of tuppeny ale? Had she been rescued from one man only to be put at the mercy of a whole legion of others?

Chapter Ten

'Eliza! Surely it can't be you? You look such a fine lady!'

'Yes, it is me, Father! I've found you at last.'

'But what are you doing here in London, and so far from home?'

'I came to find you, Father. There's a wrong that you must put right.'

'I will, of course I will. Oh, bless you, my child,' said her father, breaking down into sobs. And he held out his arms and Eliza ran into them ...

Three days later Eliza lay on the bed in Nell's lodgings, newly wakened, going over the details of the dream in her head. Since coming to London she'd had several versions of it. They all featured her father, but in one her real mother also appeared, monstrous angry that her daughter had been thrown from the house, and in another her stepmother showed herself, weeping profusely and saying that she bitterly regretted her hasty words to Eliza, whom she now loved as dearly as her own flesh and blood.

I must find my father! Eliza thought fiercely and, the dream having filled her with a new determination, made a vow that she would go to find Mason's Hall that very day and make enquiries. Her employment as an orange seller had not yet started, for the King's Players, the theatre company to which Nell belonged, was currently still in rehearsal. The new play, a comedy by Wycherley, was due to open in a few days.

Sitting up in bed, Eliza caught sight of her reflection in the window and was momentarily shocked. She'd forgotten all about her hair! She'd forgotten that the day after she'd arrived at Nell's she'd gone to a hair dealer recommended by Nell and her long, lustrous curls had been cut off to within two inches of her scalp.

She'd wept throughout the process, but the dealer had pronounced the hair most excellent and, after weighing and giving her eight shillings for it, said it would make a fine wig for a gentleman.

Nell had shrieked with laughter when Eliza, that same evening, had taken her cap off to reveal her shorn locks. 'You look as if you've been treated for the pox!' she said, and then, seeing Eliza's crestfallen face, told her that she'd straight away go to the theatre and borrow a wig for her.

The wig she'd brought back was of short auburn curls and had been made for a boy playing a girl on stage. Pulling it on to Eliza's head, Nell said that it looked well.

'And by the time your real hair grows again Henry Monteagle will have forgotten all about the sea creature he bought at the fair.'

'My hair has always been long,' Eliza had said wistfully.

'And 'twill be again!' Nell said. ''Twill grow quicker than a weasel jumps.' She adjusted the auburn wig so it reached further down the nape of Eliza's neck and teased out a curl or two in front of her ears. 'There,' she said, standing back to admire her. 'No one would ever know you for the mermaid. Besides,' she added, 'he hardly saw your face.'

Eliza had shaken her head. 'No. It was the notion of lying with a mermaid that intrigued him.'

'And it could have been any mermaid!' Nell said.

Eliza smiled. 'Is he still railing at your mother?'

Nell nodded. 'Yes, but 'tis no matter,' she said. 'Ma's used to dealing with the likes of him.'

With the money from her hair, Eliza had visited the rag fair in Cheapside and purchased two sets of clothes: a brown linen skirt and waistcoat for every day, and a flower-printed gown for Sundays. The Sunday gown reminded her of the one Elinor had worn in Clink, and now, as Eliza lay on the bed in Nell's room, she wondered to herself where her friend was and how she was faring on the seas. She sighed as she thought of her, for she still missed Elinor very much. She determined that, even though it wasn't Sunday, she'd put on her new gown when she went to seek out her father, and maybe the wearing of it would bring her luck.

There was a sudden noise downstairs in the house and a pattering on the stairs, and a moment or two later Nell's face appeared round the door. 'Not still abed?' she asked. 'What a lazy goose it is!'

Eliza smiled. She'd not seen Nell the night before, for she'd stayed at Charles Hart's house after attending a private party. She was still wearing the clothes she'd borrowed for it from the theatre costume department: a fine embroidered cambric gown in primrose yellow, with a blue velvet cloak lined in the same colour.

Nell now slipped off the cloak and took a leap and a skip on to the bed to sit beside Eliza. 'What do you think – the king was at the party!' she said excitedly. 'And we danced together and he held my hand very tightly and asked me when I was next appearing on stage.'

'And what did you say?'

'I said next week in the new musical entertainment, and if I knew he was in the audience I would be dancing especially for him.'

Eliza looked at her, enthralled. 'And then ...?' she asked breathlessly.

'Then he said he would come to the tiring room after the play and maybe ask me to do a very *special* jig!' Nell gave a sudden scream of joy. 'He desires me – I know he does! He tires of Castlemaine at last.'

'Which is Castlemaine?' Eliza asked, for Nell spoke of so many people with so many titles that she often felt completely confused.

'His mistress: Lady Barbara Castlemaine. She had no title at the start; she was plain Mistress Palmer – so he titled her Lady Castlemaine and then made her a duchess. Now I hear that she's demanding to be a countess. She's borne him children, of course – but then so have many others.'

'But what will you do about Charles Hart?'

'Oh, a pox on Charles Hart!' Nell said carelessly. 'If the king wants me then *he'll* have to step down.'

'But tell me more about the king. Did he look very regal? What did he wear?' Eliza asked eagerly. 'Does he sit on a throne?'

'He wore a purple satin suit with gold lace at the neck,' Nell said, 'and had an ermine-lined cape which he flung over his shoulder like a cavalier. But there wasn't a throne in the room so he couldn't sit upon it.'

'And is he very handsome?'

'He's the king,' Nell said, looking astonished at the question, 'of course he is. He's tall and dark of skin, has a long, curling moustache and all his hair is his own – it's so long and wavy that he doesn't need a wig. He's most elegant and cultured,' she went on, lifting her nose into the air in pretend hauteur, 'and can speak in French whenever he chooses.'

'And do you speak French to him?' Eliza asked, wide-eyed.

Nell laughed. 'I can say *oui* when the time comes,' she said. 'That will be all that's needed.'

On entering the City later that morning, Eliza discovered that Mason's Hall, where all practitioners of that trade were required to be registered, had been burned down in the Great Fire and had not yet been rebuilt. She was told that there were records being kept at Guildhall of all registered masons, but finding the right room there was difficult enough, and then she couldn't find the appropriate person and he couldn't find the proper register, so the fond father/daughter scenario which she'd visualised still seemed a long way off. The only way forward was for a note to be left at Guildhall for her father in case he called there, but though Eliza could read quite well, she couldn't write much beyond her name, so a letter setting out her precise circumstances and how she came to be in London was quite beyond her. A clerk, sensing her dilemma, suggested that she might leave her address and also one of her precious silver ·shillings with him so that a messenger could be sent to Lewkenor's Lane to inform her when and if he appeared. Eliza thought a moment about this, wondering what would happen if the messenger should fail to find the right house, or came for her when she was out, or simply took the shilling and ran away with it, but finally decided it was the only thing she could do.

Walking back through the City to Nell's lodgings, she was astounded at the amount of building going on everywhere for, after the Great Fire, shacks and tents had quickly been thrown up on the ash-and-rubble-strewn earth, then been replaced by makeshift taverns and foodshops to house and feed the incoming builders. Brick-built houses were swiftly replacing these now and Eliza could see for herself that the new lanes were wider than the old, so that the facing houses wouldn't be able to catch fire from each other. They would be safer, too, now that they weren't allowed to be built from wood and thatch.

Eliza lingered long at the market stalls and shops, marvelling at the number of them and the selection of goods on offer. One could, it seemed, buy anything one desired in London, and most shops held a large variety of the particular item they specialised in. One sold painted and enamelled bird cages, another perfumed gloves, yet others beautiful leather shoes, decorated candles, satin girdles, glass ornaments or pewter plates.

Eliza pressed herself first against one shop window, then the next, her mouth almost watering with desire as she went across the lane from side to side, exclaiming and gasping by turn. So much to buy if you had the money. How different it was from Stoke Courcey where there had been just two shops: a butcher and a baker, and everything else had to be purchased from travelling peddlers or be sent away for.

It was nigh impossible to come away from these shops empty-handed so, after deliberating at length, Eliza bought a length of dark green velvet ribbon to decorate her white cap. She couldn't help being pleased when the shopkeeper, measuring to determine the amount of ribbon needed to go around the brim of the cap and tie under her chin, remarked, winking, that the green would bring out the colour of her eyes and cause the lads to come a-running.

The following week the cap was trimmed with the ribbon and Eliza, again wearing her best flowered dress, was nervously standing in front of the stage at the King's Theatre carrying a basket of oranges over her arm. Looking around at the glittering chandeliers, the gold plaster cupids decorating the walls, the colourful scenery and the rows of gilded seats ascending until the topmost ones became almost lost from view, she thought it all quite amazing. The good folk at home would be astonished if they could see it!

It was nearly one o'clock, and the theatre doors were about to open to let in the public, but all was not well. Nell had arrived at rehearsal two hours late that morning because she'd been out all night at a party, so her role as Sylvia – a faerie character required to dance and sing – had been taken by her rival, Mary

Davis, who apparently had danced it rather well and was now reluctant to relinquish the role. Eliza, at first surprised and fascinated by the shouting match which ensued between Mary and Nell, was then shocked to see them almost come to blows. There were greater things at stake here, she realised, for Mary had also been noticed by the king and, rumour had it, had already lain with him.

A break in proceedings had been called, food and ale sent out for, and both girls had gone into separate tiring rooms in the hope that they would calm down. Nell had used this time to speak to Mol Megs, in charge of the orange sellers, and asked that Eliza be allowed to take the position she, Nell, had recently vacated by becoming an actress.

Mol Megs, universally known as Orange Moll, had neither teeth nor much hair and was, at first sight, terrifying. She spoke kindly enough to Eliza, however, telling her that the oranges were to be sold for sixpence each and there was to be no haggling over the price. 'An' if you give a special smile to a gentleman and p'raps a kiss on the cheek, then you might find yourself earning extra,' she added. Eliza nodded as she dropped Orange Moll a curtsy, privately thinking that she certainly didn't intend to give any gentleman this encouragement.

Eliza had gone to join the line-up in front of the stage. There were six other orange girls – although not all of them sold oranges. One sold apples and lemons, and another sweetmeats: sugared almonds, marzipan shapes and frosted rose petals. All had very low gowns, Eliza noticed. One girl's was cut so deep, in fact, that when she bent over both bosoms obligingly appeared at the top of her dress. This, of course, didn't go unseen by the boys lighting the candles on the chandeliers that hung across the stage or by the musicians, who kept throwing pennies at the girl and making sure that they landed on the floor.

As two o'clock approached, Eliza glanced up at the stage, wondering what was going to happen between Nell and Mary. They were both dressed in the sylph-like costume that the role demanded and, standing one each side of the stage, were studiously ignoring each other. The musicians were tuning up, the stage manager was wringing his hands and the musical director, a fop named Fortesque, seemed unable to make a decision about who should dance on this most important opening performance.

From outside the theatre there came shouts and noises from people hammering on the doors.

'It's well past one o'clock!' came the nervous cry from the stage manager. 'We must open the doors or have them broken in.'

Nell and Mary each gave an uncaring shrug.

'Ladies ... ladies ...' said Fortesque, flapping his hands. 'The public are about to be admitted and this matter must be decided between you without more ado!'

'Mistress Gwyn cannot care for the play or she wouldn't miss rehearsals the way she has,' Mary said disdainfully. She was a tall girl, no older than Nell, with a froth of fair hair which had been fashioned into tiny ringlets. 'And besides, Mr Fortesque, you said this morning that I was more suited to the role.'

'That's treason, Fortesque!' Nell said, looking daggers at him. 'You said you wrote the role with me in mind!'

'I didn't actually say –' Fortesque began nervously.

'And besides, the king is coming specifically to see me dance!' Nell added.

'He said the same to me,' said Mary. She fingered a gold chain around her neck. 'And has already given me this as a token of his great esteem.'

Nell gave a short scream. 'What lies! You got that from a peddler and 'tas already turned your neck black!' She approached Mary, arms outstretched, but whether to strangle her rival or view the love token Eliza couldn't determine. At that moment there was a banging and a crashing as the doors of the theatre finally gave way and a score of apprentice boys ran in, shouting and whooping to each other. They were followed, at a more sedate pace, by a body of well-dressed merchants, some businessmen, a party of sailors and an assorted crowd of London's high- and low-born. Several daringly dressed women with patches on their faces, holding masks on sticks, made their way into the pit area beside the stage and, even from some distance away, Eliza could smell their sweet, cloying perfume.

The orange girls began to wander around the theatre calling, 'Fine, sweet oranges! Who'll buy my oranges?' and Eliza followed their lead. She wasn't comfortable doing this, for she knew with what disdain everyone viewed orange girls, but she decided that she would treat it just as an acting job. Those on stage would play their parts and she would play an orange girl, just as she'd played a mermaid.

'Fine sweet oranges! Sixpence, my oranges!' she cried, turning it into a refrain, even though she feared little could be heard above the continual noise of the crowd and the tuning-up of instruments.

A group of gallants swaggered in and were cat-called by the apprentices and addressed in effusive, honeyed terms by the masked women who, Eliza now realised, must be prostitutes. As the gallants circled the theatre, speaking to whoever they chose and once or twice kissing the hand of an attractive woman, Eliza looked at them more closely and all at once caught her breath as she recognised Henry Monteagle and Valentine Howard.

Monteagle would recognise her, she thought in a sudden panic. He'd recognise her as the mermaid and Valentine Howard would further remember her as a beggar in prison, and then she'd be made a laughing stock in front of all the crowd, dragged through the streets in chains and returned to Clink.

With a hand that was shaking slightly she adjusted her cap so that it sat a little further over her face and pulled at the wig so that some auburn curls showed. Then she tried to avoid the parts of the theatre which they were in.

'Come buy my oranges!' she called, a slight nervous quaver to her voice. 'Juicy, fine oranges …'

Fifteen or so minutes later most of the gallants, having tired of their socialising, had climbed up on to the stage where a special section had been boxed off for them by means of a low wooden partition. Having settled themselves, they removed their swords, flicked back their capes and began smoking, drinking and calling to their friends in the audience.

There came a shout from one of them to Nelly, still poised prettily at the side of the stage. 'Mistress

Gwyn! You look very fine this afternoon.'

Nell glanced at the man who'd spoken. 'My Lord!' she said, and Eliza knew she was pleased to have been addressed before Mary was. 'May I return the compliment and say you look most handsome in your magenta waistcoat?' And she dropped a mock curtsy, sinking very low.

'Come and join us!' one of them called to Nell. 'There'll be more fun to be had with us than play-acting on stage today!'

'And the king won't be in – he's to Windsor for the races,' said the first.

Nell hardly paused. 'Of course!' she said. 'He told me so earlier. And I don't care to dance without him here to watch me, so I shall ask Mistress Davis to entertain you. She can dance for us on those sturdy legs of hers!'

Eliza heard this speech with some admiration. Nell had not only inferred that she was privy to the king's movements, but also that she was responsible for deciding who would dance. Smiling at the gallants now, and lifting her dress to show her small feet and trim ankles, Nell stepped across the stage to join them.

The performance began at half past two, although Eliza didn't discern much difference in the audience's behaviour either before or after curtain-up. They still talked, laughed, shouted and flirted – once there was even a stand-up fight. The orange girls carried on circling around – occasionally being shouted at for standing between the audience and the action – and their goods were either eaten and the peel tossed on to the stage, or thrown whole to attract the attention of someone in another part of the auditorium.

Nell stayed with the gallants, drinking and laughing, and studiously turned her back and affected complete disinterest when Mary Davis was doing her final solo.

By the end of the performance Eliza had sold all her oranges and was just reflecting, relieved, that her disguise had worked, when suddenly someone jumped down from the stage and made straight for her.

'I see a new orange girl!' Henry Monteagle said, his voice slurred with drink. 'I've found a new girl and would have a kiss!'

Eliza, shocked and alarmed, didn't know whether to run for it or stand her ground. She saw Nell stand up swiftly. 'Oh, someone do get Henry back before he paws that girl to the ground and gets himself banned,' she called.

Another youth jumped down and pushed through the crowd after Henry, catching him just as he reached Eliza.

'A lovely new miss with auburn hair!' Henry said, standing foursquare in front of Eliza with a ridiculous smile on his face, swaying backwards and forwards. 'A del ... delishous ... new miss.'

'Henry!' It was Valentine Howard who'd come after his friend. 'There's a gaming table at the Two Magpies and the carriage is outside. Come on!'

Henry, ignoring him, put an arm around Eliza. 'First I must have a kish ... a kish from this lovely new orange girl.'

Eliza froze as his fleshy lips moved closer. And then he suddenly halted.

'But are you really new, my pretty?' he asked drunkenly. 'Haven't I seen you somewhere before?'

'No, indeed, sire,' Eliza said, deliberately thickening her accent. 'I arrived from Somersetshire on the coach only two days ago.'

'Let's away, Henry!' Valentine Howard said, pulling at his arm.

'But Val, don't we know this girl?' Henry began, lifting up Eliza's chin.

'How could you, you blaggard?' came the reply. 'She's just told you she's off the coach from Somerset,' and he gave Henry Monteagle a friendly shove to send him on his way back to the others.

As Monteagle lurched off, Eliza managed to murmur her thanks to Valentine, turning away from him slightly and lowering her eyes.

'It was nothing,' he said.

'But meant much to me,' Eliza said, her voice shaky.

With a finger he lifted her chin, making her look into his eyes.

'You're welcome to call on me at any time,' he said, 'for Valentine Howard will always help a mermaid.'

Chapter Eleven

'But what if Henry Monteagle comes to the theatre again?' Eliza asked Nell as they left Nell's lodgings and began to push their way through the market crowds.

'*What if?*' Nell asked with a smile. 'Oh, he'll come to the theatre again for certain, for now the king comes everyone wants to be there.' She was in a good mood that morning, for she'd had a message from the king to say he was sorry that he'd missed her performance and would make arrangements to see her as soon as he arrived back in London.

'And suppose Monteagle suddenly remembers where he first saw me ...'

'He won't!' Nell said dismissively. 'For his brain is already half-turned into brandy. He may recall that he saw you somewhere, but he won't remember where. Besides,' she said, looking at Eliza in mock innocence, 'you have Val Howard on your side now, have you not?'

Eliza began to blush.

'Sir Valentine Howard. There's a noble name,' Nell teased.

'Yes, he seems ... seems a fine youth,' Eliza stammered. She waited until she felt her blush had subsided. 'I expect he is betrothed?' she asked, for she knew that the nobility often had their marriages arranged while the potential bride and groom were still in their cradles.

'I should think so,' Nell said. 'I'll wager that when his studies are over he'll be married to some ugly foreign bride to secure his overseas investments. Or he'll try his luck with some old dowager who'll leave him all her money.' She glanced at Eliza, amused. 'But you don't think of *marriage*, surely?'

'No! Oh, no,' Eliza said. 'I know I'm much too young.'

'Not so,' Nell said, 'for Anne Fitzroy, the king's bastard daughter, is set to be wed when she's thirteen.' Then she added, 'What I mean is, you surely don't think of marrying so high?'

Eliza, embarrassed, didn't know what to reply. Of course she didn't. Or only in the most childish, make-believe way.

'The nobility may bed us, and they may even kidnap us, as Rochester has just kidnapped Elizabeth Malet – but they will never marry us,' said Nell.

'No, indeed,' Eliza said, pulling herself together. She brushed down the pleats of her skirt and tried to hide her discomfort. Of course she didn't – wouldn't – ever dare to think that Valentine Howard harboured the least interest in her. Even though he'd begun to fill her thoughts when she lay awake on hot nights, she knew that the interest must all be on her side.

'Instead you must aim to become his mistress!' Nell said brightly. ''Tis not beyond you. I can teach you some artful tricks ...'

'Indeed I would rather not,' Eliza said quickly, 'for I

couldn't bear to be a mistress and see the man I loved marry someone else.'

'How strangely you speak,' Nell said, beginning to laugh. ''Tis certain you are from the country!'

The two girls continued through Covent Garden towards the theatre, walking carefully on their pattens for, after a heavy fall of rain, the cobbles were thick with muck and debris.

Fortesque's musical had run its short course and the company had begun readings for another play. Nell, however, despite her many other undoubted skills, couldn't read, so Eliza was accompanying her to the theatre to help her with her lines. She was happy to do this for, apart from being a small way of repaying Nell for her kindnesses, all the while there was no play being performed at the theatre she had no work selling oranges. Instead she ran errands for Nell and acted as her maid and companion, and enjoyed being employed like this very much. She'd even devised a way to tame Nell's hair: dowsing it in sugar water and tying it into rag curls overnight meant that in the mornings it was a mass of glossy ringlets instead of a bird's nest frizz, and Nell was very much taken with these hairdressing skills.

Life with her was much nicer than it had been with Old Ma Gwyn, for Nell didn't take life seriously and was always telling amusing tales about the nobility or finding things to laugh about. It was true there wasn't much space in her lodgings, but certainly the food was better. At Ma Gwyn's Eliza had inevitably dined on the pottage that was always bubbling over the fire, or oysters that Rose hadn't managed to sell, but Nell loved to eat and would send out for food from eating houses and taverns: rabbit pies, lobsters, buttered asparagus, a dish of roasted pigeons or a chicken fricassée. Eliza noticed that often she didn't have to pay for these things; innkeepers were pleased to have her custom. They knew her credit was good and that sooner or later one of her gentlemen admirers would settle her bill.

As they walked through Henrietta Street, Eliza noticed that a small crowd had gathered on the pavement outside a bootmaker's shop and was endeavouring to see through the bowed glass window. She pointed this out to Nell, wondering what was going on.

'Oh, 'tis the shop where the king buys his riding boots,' Nell said, beaming. 'Perhaps he's inside. If he is I shall go and speak with him!'

She crossed the muddy lane and Eliza, vastly excited at the thought that she might meet the king of England, followed a pace behind, fervently wishing that she'd worn her best dress that day.

On seeing Nell, the people melted back from the doorway, for she was becoming increasingly well known – especially there, in the theatre area. Eliza heard two people say, ''Tis Nelly!' and a woman reached out to touch her dress, as if it might bring her luck.

The tall man within the shop was having his feet measured by a harassed and excited shopkeeper. Hearing the stir outside, he turned, saw Nell and, flourishing his plumed hat, gave a low bow.

'Mistress Nelly!' he said, and he came up, bent low over her hand and kissed it.

'Monsieur Duval!' Nelly said, curtsying.

Eliza, close behind her, bobbed a curtsy too. She was disappointed that it wasn't the king, but nonetheless quite excited at seeing the dandy highwayman again.

'May I present Mistress Eliza Rose,' Nell said, 'my companion and also my reader – she's helping me learn my lines.'

Claude Duval took Eliza's hand and kissed it, looking deep into her eyes. 'Your servant, Mam'selle,' he said with the faintest trace of French accent, and so handsome and charming was he that Eliza knew immediately why so many girls had lost their hearts to him.

'I'm to appear in a new play at the King's Theatre next week,' Nell went on. 'You'll come, won't you, Claude?'

He smiled. 'Will the nobility be there?'

Nell nodded. 'They will.'

'Then I won't!' He paused, smiling. 'But maybe I shall see them on their way home from the theatre and relieve them of their spare jewels.'

He winked at both girls as he spoke and Nell laughed. 'You, sire, are outrageous!' she said. 'And now tell me what brings you to the king's own outfitters.'

Claude Duval smiled. 'I was in need of a new pair of riding boots and thought that a place which was good enough for the king would be good enough for me.'

'Please, sire!' the shopkeeper said, for those outside were being slowly pushed into the shop and it was now half full of gawping onlookers. 'May I have your other foot to measure?'

'Of course. My apologies,' Claude Duval said genially to the shopkeeper and, after bowing extravagantly once more to Nell and Eliza and kissing their hands, he returned to having his feet measured and they pushed their way out of the shop.

'Such an excellent man!' Nell sighed as they continued towards the theatre.

Eliza nodded, deep in thought. 'I've been wondering about him – about Claude Duval,' she said. 'He has a great price on his head and everyone knows who he is, so why is it that no one turns him over to the constables?'

'Because the people of London love him!' Nell said immediately. 'They love him for holding up the coaches of the nobles and stealing from them, and also because he's gracious and mannerly when he takes their money. Even the gang of wits admire him – I know that he plays the occasional hand of cards with them. And did you hear the tale of the coach he stopped at Turnham Green?'

Eliza shook her head.

'He stole four hundred golden guineas from the couple within – and then offered a hundred guineas back if the man would play the lute whilst Claude danced with his wife.'

'And did the man allow it?' Eliza asked, delighted.

Nell nodded. 'He did. He played a coranto while Claude and the woman – who was very beautiful, apparently – danced together on the grass verge beside the coach. They say that she's now quite lost her heart to him.'

The writer of the new play was a friend of Nell's, a

dramatist named Aphra Behn, and the play was called *Secret Love*.

''Tis a handsome piece – a romance and a comedy,' Nell said as they entered the theatre, 'and what's more, the playwright is female.'

'A woman!' Eliza said, much surprised. 'Aphra Behn is a woman?'

Nell nodded. 'And I think the first to write plays and books and have them published. The clergy are scandalised,' she said, giggling with delight. 'Just think: first women are allowed on the stage, then one of them produces a play. To their mind, the only thing a woman should produce is a child.'

Eliza was introduced to Aphra, who was a small, serious-looking woman. She had hardly a penny to her name, Nell told Eliza in a whisper, and was living entirely on borrowed money, but all that would change if her play was a success.

Nell was to act the role of a woman named Sophia. This was a part which called for Nell to disguise herself as a youth wearing short breeches and tights, a disguise calculated to please the men in the audience. While Eliza and Nell sat with the script at the side of the stage, other members of the cast were being put through their paces, several pastoral landscapes were being painted on the scenery boards behind them, and some people were singing accompanied by a lute. All was disordered, a pleasant muddle, and Eliza, looking around her, thought that she had seldom felt herself quite so content as on this day.

Into all the chaos a young man strode down through the seats and leapt up on stage. He was accompanied by what appeared to be a girl, though she was so heavily cloaked and hooded that neither her face nor form could be seen, just some pale green kid leather shoes which protruded from under her cloak.

The youth looked dishevelled but was handsome, with dark eyes and high cheekbones. He appeared vaguely familiar to Eliza, but it was only after a few moments that she realised he was the third youth – the one who'd been with Valentine Howard and Henry Monteagle the first day she'd ever begged money in Clink. She didn't fear that he'd recognise her, however, for he'd hardly glanced at her that first time and was brusque and impatient now, seemingly anxious to do what he'd come for and be on his way.

One of his arms supported the girl, while the other held his feathered hat. 'Mistress Gwyn. Mistress Behn,' he said, making bows in different directions towards the two most important women there.

'William Wilkes!' Nell said. 'What brings you to the theatre so soon? You are – what? – some five days early for my next performance.'

'I beg your indulgence, madam,' William Wilkes said to Nell. 'If we may speak in private …'

Eliza saw Aphra give Nell a weary look, and Nell smiled and shrugged. She beckoned the youth and the mysterious, cloaked person over to where she and Eliza were sitting, two chairs were called for and they sat down. The cloaked girl's dress, Eliza noted, was of delicate watered silk, green to match her shoes, and there was a broad border of expensive lace around the hem.

'You may speak in front of Eliza, my companion. She's but recently arrived from Somersetshire and knows nothing of intrigue,' Nell said, but neither of the two figures even glanced at her.

William began to speak earnestly to Nell as, in the centre of the stage, Aphra clapped her hands for the rehearsals to continue.

'Briefly, the case is this,' he began. 'I've formed a strong attachment in which my own family rejoice, but which my lady's family think unsuitable. The consequence is we've been forbidden to see each other.'

'Oh, how very romantic, William!' Nell said, and Eliza looked at her curiously, thinking she'd heard an ironic tone in her voice.

'Possibly. Although my lady's father would rather run me through with a rapier than wish me the time of day. And so we've eloped and intend to hide out in London for a while and then buy our passage on a boat set for overseas.'

Eliza, thinking of the enormity of what the girl had done and how scared she must be, tried to see under her hood and give her a reassuring smile, but could make out no more than a few wispy fair curls and the tip of a delicate nose.

'I fear my lady's father and brother will pursue us,' William went on, 'so I wish to hide her away here in the theatre until the time is right for us to take passage. If her family come to seek me out, they'll find me alone in my house and presume she's gone elsewhere.'

'I see,' Nell said. She addressed the girl. 'And do you wish this too – to be taken away from your family?'

The hood of the cloak nodded. Eliza heard a girl's

voice say fervently, 'Oh, with all my heart!'

'And is marriage your intended aim?' Nell asked William, somewhat sternly.

He nodded. 'Of course.'

'And you wish me to find her lodgings?'

'I'll give you a sum of money to cover her expenses; just keep her hidden while I work out what's to be done for the best,' William said. 'She has an excellent speaking voice and can read and write, so maybe she may take some small part in a production and earn her keep.' He looked down into the face of the girl and gave her an encouraging nod, and after a moment the girl raised a trembling white hand and pushed the hood back off her head, revealing a pretty face framed with silky blonde hair.

'And your name is?' Nell asked.

'Lady Elizabeth Jemima –' the girl began, but William interrupted hastily, 'I think we may just call you Jemima here. 'Tis best.' He bent and kissed her on the cheek. 'I leave you in good hands, sweeting. Mistress Gwyn will see you want for nothing.'

'Darling William!' the girl said, and Eliza saw her eyes fill with tears. 'Please don't go.'

He took her hand and kissed it. 'I must. I'll return soon – and in the meantime keep close within the theatre and don't go abroad much. The fewer people who see you, the better.' He bowed to Nell. 'Your servant, madam,' he said, and then he was gone.

Jemima – as she was to be called – promptly burst into tears.

Nell sighed. 'Take her into the tiring room, Eliza. I'll come in a while.'

Amid the chairs and dressing tables, Jemima wept for

some time, until Eliza almost wept in sympathy. Then, her breath catching in her throat, she told Eliza her story – how she'd met William at church when he'd been visiting his family home, and how they'd fallen desperately in love, and how her father had forbidden her to see him because she was set to receive money and lands from her grandfather's will and he thought that William was after her inheritance.

'But indeed he isn't!' she said. 'He says he'd love me just as much were I as poor as a rag-picker.'

Eliza listened, enthralled.

'I'm sure he loves you for your sweet self alone,' she said, and thought to herself how romantic it would be to have a man willing to leave his home and country for you …

'He's after her fortune for certain,' Nell said when she and Eliza were on their way back from the theatre that evening.

'Surely not,' Eliza said, dismayed.

Nell nodded. 'His father has gambled most of the Wilkes money away, and William's drunk the rest. An heiress in the family is just what they need.'

'But Jemima cannot suspect any of this. She truly loves him!'

'And he truly loves her money! A marriage made in heaven, don't you think?'

'But it *may* work out, surely?'

'It may,' Nell conceded. 'But I'd feel more confident if William Wilkes hadn't already deflowered two such maidens and left them by the wayside.'

'He has scandals against his name already?' Eliza gasped.

Nell nodded. 'And he's only eighteen.' She gave a shrug. 'It would be nice to think that this time might be different, but I wouldn't wager my petticoats on it.' She smiled wryly. 'She seems a delicate little thing – keep an eye on her will you, Eliza? I've too much already on my mind what with the king, the play and how to bid a fond fare-thee-well to Charles Hart.'

'So where will Jemima stay?' Eliza asked.

'With Mrs Trott: one of the theatre seamstresses. She'll be safe there – her father will never think of looking in a dingy hole like that. And then we'll see if William comes and takes her away, or just robs her of what he can and leaves her.'

Eliza sighed. 'Poor Jemima.'

'Poor Jemima indeed.' Nell slipped her arm through Eliza's. 'So be sure not to fall in love with one of the king's gang of wits, for it can only lead to heartbreak.'

'I won't,' Eliza promised, and vowed that she'd forget – or at least make some small effort to stop thinking of – Sir Valentine Howard.

The two of them stopped in a tavern to eat a plate of pork and roasted potatoes on their way home from the theatre, so it was almost dark by the time they approached their lodgings. When a little, grimy figure jumped out at them from behind a pile of rubble, Eliza screamed in fright.

'Is it Eliza Rose?' the figure piped, and Eliza saw that it wasn't any sort of foul fiend at all, but a little boy of about eight.

She nodded, her heart beating fast.

'I got to tell you that yer father come to Guild'all today and will be there tomorrer,' he said.

For a moment Eliza was too overcome to speak, then she asked him to repeat what he'd just said.

'Yer father come to Guild'all today and will be there tomorrer.'

'Is he well? Did anyone tell him that I was looking for him? Does he lodge nearby?'

'Yer father come to Guild'all today and will be there tomorrer,' the boy said stubbornly.

Nell laughed. 'He's learned that as the parrots do,' she said. 'Best to go there tomorrow and see for yourself.'

'Oh, I shall!' Eliza said fervently, and didn't sleep a wink that night.

Chapter Twelve

There were two reasons Eliza didn't sleep. One was that she was excited because she might soon be able to go home; the other was that she didn't actually *want* to go home at that moment.

One part of her thought longingly about the security and safety of her dear Somersetshire, about the pleasant, peaceful greenness and about being amongst her brothers and sisters, but the other part thought of the tedious life she'd lived there – of the sullen ways of her stepmother, of endless hours spent carding wool, minding children or helping with the washing at the big houses. She also mused on the fact that, living in such a small village with very little choice of beaux, she would probably be required to marry a red-necked farmer's son; someone who wore rough wool clothes and worked on the land. Most people in Somersetshire never strayed far from the village where they were born, much less to London. As for the theatre – well, she doubted if they'd even heard that women were now allowed on the stage.

Here in London she'd long ago stopped crying every day. She loved being part of theatre life, found Nell excellent company, enjoyed the shops even if she couldn't afford to buy much and looked forward with great excitement to being at the opening of the new play when the king might be in the audience. And there was also Valentine Howard, of course …

Perhaps, she thought, she might ask her father if she could return home within a month or two. Or perhaps a little longer. But wouldn't that sound strange? How could she make him understand that she *wanted* to go home, but not quite as desperately as she had done before. Could she ask, maybe, that her role as eldest daughter be left open, so that she could return when she'd had enough of London?

Sleepless still, she resolved to let her father's reaction to her dictate what she said and did. If he was overjoyed to see her, said that he'd send a message forthwith to her stepmother to say that she must be allowed home – then go home she would. Very soon.

Dressing the next morning, Eliza decided to wear the second-best gown. Her father was, after all, a country man, and he might think the flowered one – which had a low neckline – improper. She'd have to wear the wig under her cap, of course. Suppose he thought what Nell had joked of, that she'd lost her hair when being treated for the pox? She'd get over that by telling him quickly that she'd sold it to enable her to buy food. Which was true, in a way. And it was best that he didn't know about Clink prison, or about the mermaid, or discover that she was working in the theatre as an orange girl. He'd be bound to think the worst.

Reaching Guildhall, she was told that her father was now working with a score or more masons on the rebuilding of St Columbus Church, which had gone down in the Fire. She couldn't find out if anyone had told him that his daughter was looking for him, however, so didn't know if he'd be prepared for the meeting.

St Columbus Church was, as yet, little more than an odd-looking collection of walls and pillars, for the roof had not yet been put on and the windows weren't in place.

Her father was within the shell of it, loading up a wheelbarrow with stone blocks as she approached. She called 'Father!' first and, when he didn't turn, used his full name, 'Jacob Rose!'

He turned and saw her, and she saw shock writ large on his face. He *didn't* know of her mission, then, for he was rubbing his eyes as if he couldn't believe what he was seeing.

'Yes, it's me, Father!' Eliza said joyfully. Whether or not she wanted to go home, it felt wonderful to see the long-familiar face and have that dear reminder of her childhood.

'Eliza?' he gasped. 'Is it really you?'

Eliza nodded, smiling, taking in his every feature. Although pale with shock then, he had the same blue eyes and strong, straight nose as her brothers, the same golden thatch of hair, now mixed with grey.

'How did you get here?' he asked, looking at her as if she'd been transported by witchcraft.

Eliza shrugged. 'Cart and boat and on foot. All sorts of ways!'

'But why did you come?' he asked urgently. 'Is your stepmother ailing?'

Eliza shook her head. 'No, no, indeed. She's well.'

'The children, then. Who is it? Is one of them –'

Eliza put her hand on his arm. 'None of them are

130

ill, Father. They're all perfectly well and happy. They send you their love.'

'Then I cannot believe nor understand why …'

His voice trailed away and Eliza took a deep breath. She'd rehearsed this speech many times and had decided that it wouldn't do to blame her stepmother too much nor speak disrespectfully of her, in case her father thought it was a mere case of them disliking each other.

'I came to find you to ask you to intercede between me and my stepmother,' she began. She coughed nervously. 'As your oldest daughter –'

Here, she couldn't help but notice how he suddenly started, as if he'd been stung.

'As your oldest daughter,' she repeated nonetheless, 'I feel a special obligation towards you and my stepmother. I know it will be me who'll tend you in your old age, and who'll oversee the running of the house should any illness befall either of you.'

Her father didn't speak, but a strange expression came over his face.

'But my stepmother,' Eliza continued, 'seems not to want me to take this role in the household, nor indeed wants me at home at all, for she's forbidden me the house. She told me to leave!'

Still her father didn't speak, although when Eliza had rehearsed the speech to herself she'd always thought he would query things here, ask her if there had been an argument between the two of them which had caused her stepmother to say such a thing.

Slightly discomfited, Eliza went on, 'And so I resolved to come to London and find you, so that you could send a message to her that I must be allowed home again and ... and must be ...' She faltered and stopped, because her father's lips had formed themselves into a straight, grim line and he was shaking his head.

'I'm sorry to have to tell you this,' he said gruffly, 'but your stepmother spoke to you on my orders.'

Eliza was struck dumb.

'She spoke as I had requested. She carried out my instructions.'

'No! You can't mean that!' Eliza cried.

''Tis true and I'm sorry for it, but there it is.'

He went to turn away, but Eliza held on to his arm. 'You must tell me why ... why you no longer want me in the house!'

He looked at her solemnly. 'I've my reasons.'

'But Father, *why*?'

'*Why*?' He hesitated, then said abruptly, 'Because you've been a cuckoo in my nest since the day you were born and I no longer see any reason to let you lodge there.'

'A cuckoo?' Eliza repeated stupidly. 'But Father –'

His eyes suddenly burned with fire. 'Do not call me that!' he said, stressing every word with terrible emphasis. 'I am not your father and never have been!'

Eliza stared at him uncomprehendingly, then shook her head and burst into tears. Running beyond the confines of the church, she went to a corner of the churchyard, threw herself down and sobbed out her misery.

'Well, then,' Nell said later that evening in their lodgings, 'at least it's made things easy for you. You were undecided about whether you should go home;

now you know you won't.'

'But where is my home?' Eliza asked with a sigh. 'I've no home to go to.'

'Your home is here for the time being, but you'll make another home for yourself soon! Some rich young man will set you up in a house and you'll be a made woman.'

'I don't want –' Eliza began, and then sighed again and burst out, 'And who's my father?'

'Who's mine?' Nell retaliated calmly. She picked up a bowl containing sugar water and moved to sit on the chair before Eliza. Dipping a comb in the water, she held it up to her.

Eliza stopped crying. 'You don't know your father either?'

'No,' Nell shrugged. 'And I never felt the lack.'

Eliza dabbed her eyes on a corner of her gown, then took up the comb to begin wetting Nell's hair.

'At least you had a happy childhood … did you not?' Nell said.

Eliza nodded. 'I believed so. I believed I was loved – but maybe I wasn't! Maybe my father always resented my presence there.'

'But if you didn't know he resented you, then it's as if he didn't! I'm sure you had a cheerful time with your brothers – I've always longed for brothers. Tell me about them. What are their names?'

'Richard, Thomas and John,' Eliza began, now twisting a strand of hair around a strip of rag.

'And are they like you?'

Eliza shook her head. 'They're not. And that's why,' she gasped with sudden realisation. 'They aren't my brothers, are they? I have no brothers!'

'They're your half-brothers. As Rose is my half-sister – and none the less for being that.' Nell smiled ruefully. 'It's said that Ma lay with a whole army of men before having us, so there was no way of telling whose *we* were.'

'So my mother ...' Eliza murmured, struggling to work things out as she rolled the hair, '... gave birth to Richard, Thomas and John, and Jacob was their father. Then she lay in another man's bed and bore me.'

'That's right,' Nell said matter-of-factly.

'So I wonder if he, if Jacob, knew about this cuckoo in his nest as soon as I was born, or if he didn't learn of it until my mother died?'

'Maybe there was a deathbed confession.'

Eliza tried to think back to that terrible time just after her mother had fallen into the flood-swollen river. Had her father's attitude towards her changed after that?

She couldn't remember. She'd only been eight and it had been hard enough to accept that she had no mother; that she'd never again see that dear, care-worn face. She hadn't really thought about anything else.

Nell poked her to carry on with her hair. 'Can you remember any man in particular – someone in the village – who was a friend to your mother? Someone who took a special interest in you?' she asked.

Eliza shook her head slowly. 'No one at all. And our family moved from south Somersetshire to the north of the county after I was born, anyway.' She thought on; she could remember Richard talking about their old cottage, describing it, and saying that they'd been very poor then, and she – on the rare occasions when she'd ever thought about it at all – had presumed that they'd got more money from somewhere and gone up in the world, to a better cottage. But perhaps they'd gone solely to get away from *him*, the man Eliza's mother had lain with. Her real father.

'You must make a new life for yourself now,' Nell said, breaking into her thoughts. 'You must make up your mind what you want, and think well on how you may get it. As I am doing with His Majesty,' she added. Her eyes sparkled. 'I yearn to be invited to court, Eliza, and live amid all that lavishness and luxury and treasure! I want to see the fops and gallants fawning around His Majesty, and the queen and all her ladies-in-waiting in their jewels and fine dresses. I even want to see the king's mistresses at close hand so I may admire their fashions and their manners and see what I've to compete with.' She patted her head, which was now full of rag curls. 'Although none of them have got my lovely ringlets!'

Eliza managed a smile.

'And at least that sort of life is possible for me and you, for we are blessed with – well, perhaps it is immodest of me to say we've more than our fair portion of attractiveness – but 'tis certain we have!'

'I suppose we're lucky not to be born like poor Susan,' Eliza said after a moment's thought. 'For surely she will never secure a husband.'

'Susan?' Nell enquired.

'Your sister's poor child with the disfigured face.'

'Ah!' Nell said. And then she began laughing, but would not be drawn on why, just said that Eliza might find out one day. Eliza didn't dwell on this, however, for her mind was set completely on her father – her real father – and she couldn't sleep again that night, this time for wondering desperately who he might be.

Chapter Thirteen

'So are you hiding away here as well?' Jemima asked a week or so later when she and Eliza were alone in the tiring room of the theatre.

Eliza hesitated. 'Not really. At least, I'm not hiding from my family, as you are.'

'I asked because you wear a wig, do you not?' Jemima said delicately. 'And I wondered why you would want to change your appearance.'

Eliza scratched under her wig. The weather was very hot and the wig made her itch; she was almost sure that whoever had worn it before her had had fleas.

'I could probably take it off now, for my hair has grown somewhat,' she said and, suddenly making up her mind, she removed her cap, pulled off the wig and ran her hands over her scalp, fluffing out the short curls. 'How do I look without it?' she asked Jemima. 'Am I like a shorn sheep?'

Jemima shook her head. ''Tis very pretty – all over curls like a young boy's. But tell me why you needed to cut your hair and wear a wig.'

Eliza shook her head from side to side, enjoying the feeling of freedom. 'I used to wear my hair very long,' she said, 'but 'twas my undoing.'

'How was that?'

''Tis a desperate story. By some unfortunate circumstances I ... I found myself confined to a prison.'

Jemima opened her blue eyes very wide.

'I was merely hungry and stole a pasty,' Eliza filled in hastily. 'But then I was begging at the prison grille one day and Old Ma Gwyn happened to come by.' She looked around to make sure Nell wasn't near. 'You've heard of her?'

Jemima nodded. 'Nell's mother – and she's said to be the madam of a bawdy house.'

'I didn't know that then,' Eliza said. 'She offered to get me out of prison – and she did, too. She paid good money for me.'

Jemima's jaw dropped. 'She wanted you to be a bawd?'

'Not exactly,' Eliza said. 'I had very long black curly hair all down my back, you see – 'twas like seaweed, she said – and she wanted me for a mermaid at the Midsummer Fair.'

Jemima gasped, and then laughed. 'I am sure you were a very good one.'

'I was! And Ma Gwyn made a deal of money out of me. After the Fair, though, she sold me to a drunken and moneyed youth who had a wish to sleep with a girl with a silvery tail. It was then that Nell came and took me away.'

'Who was the youth?' Jemima asked.

'Henry Monteagle,' Eliza said with a shudder.

'I know him!' Jemima said immediately. 'He's a friend of William's. A not very nice friend.'

'And he's seen me since, here in the theatre, but

didn't know me. So I think perhaps I can come out of my disguise now.'

Jemima looked cast down for a moment. 'You are lucky that your disguise can be so short-lived. I must stay hidden from my family for the rest of my life.'

'Is it really as bad as that? Your father will be angry at your elopement, but perhaps he'll come round in time. Your mother may talk him into being more agreeable.'

Jemima was shaking her head before Eliza had even finished the sentence. 'My mother is frightened of my father – we all are,' she said. 'He has a fierce temper and has vowed to kill William for taking me away. I was set to marry an old cousin of mine, so it's a matter of the family honour, you see.'

'An *old* cousin?' Eliza asked, picking up on this one word.

'Cedric is sixty,' Jemima replied, screwing up her nose with distaste. 'I was to marry him to ensure that our titles and property stayed within the family. Of course I refused! And then I met William ...' her eyes softened, 'and he and I fell in love and there was no solution but to run away together.'

'And will you marry soon?' Eliza asked.

'Oh, of course,' Jemima said. 'William is making the arrangements and 'twill happen quite shortly. And then we'll go to the Americas, William will buy some plantations and we'll live out there very happily for the rest of our lives.'

'And does William ... is William very rich that he can buy all these lands?' Eliza asked, thinking of what Nell had said about him.

'I believe so – although I, happily, have enough for

both of us. I inherit my grandfather's estate when I am eighteen.'

Eliza nodded. 'You're very lucky to have your own fortune,' she said, thinking privately that she was glad that she had not, for then how could you trust any man – be he father, cousin or lover – and believe that they loved you for yourself, and not your money?

At least, she thought, there was going to be no feuding over her, for without a family name she had little hope of ever being married at all. But she must be *someone's* child! Would her father – the man she'd thought of as her father – tell her the truth if she asked him outright? Did he even know the truth? Her thoughts went to and fro, to and fro, wondering how she could find out what she so longed to know, and she finally determined to write to her Aunt Thomasina, her mother's sister, who might have been told the truth if anyone had. Surely her mother must have confessed to *someone* whose child she was carrying?

That same afternoon the tiring room was filled with people coming and going. Aphra Behn had not managed to get enough funding for her play so it had been withdrawn at the last moment. Now a meeting had been called and actors and actresses were demanding money for attending rehearsals – as were the scene-painters, seamstresses, dressers and all other behind-the-scenes workers.

In the midst of all this, Mary Davis was lying full length on a chaise longue at one end of the tiring room. She was wearing a loose muslin gown, cut very low and designed so that it would best show off a heart-shaped locket which she said was a gift from the king. Nell, similarly attired in a long silk wrap with two lustrous strands of pearls sent by an admirer, was lounging at the other end of the room. Both of them, Eliza noted with some amusement, were talking animatedly to their own select circle and appeared not to be in the least aware of each other. Some refreshments had been sent for and, after they had been consumed, a little black-skinned messenger boy in a turban and velvet suit appeared with a letter who, after bowing uncertainly in several directions, was called over to Mary. After speaking to him in a low voice, Mary swung herself upright, then prised off the seal to read it.

'I shall read this to everyone,' she called over to Nell. 'Unless, Mistress Gwyn, you wish to –'

'No, by all means,' Nell said, 'for I've never found it necessary to read! In fact, I think reading dulls a woman's brain.'

'Ah, those who cannot read oft say that,' Mary retaliated. She held the paper aloft and, after glancing swiftly at it, said, 'It asks for all those who have a charge against Aphra Behn to submit their requests for payment to her accountant in the Strand.'

There was a general groan at this, for no one had much confidence that they would ever receive their money.

Mary crumpled the letter and tucked it under the bolster cushion. 'So those of us who know our numbers and can reckon as well as read, are at an advantage,' she said, looking down her nose at Nell.

'I can reckon,' Nell said quickly. 'I can reckon within moments what a man's worth!'

There was laughter at this. Eliza, though, was wondering why, when Aphra Behn had been at the theatre only that morning, she hadn't delivered this message to the Company verbally instead of going to the expense of having it written and delivered by messenger. This led her to question if, despite Mary's boasting, she couldn't read after all – or alternatively, whether she'd read the message and decided to keep its real contents to herself.

As people drifted in and out of the theatre bearing gossip, scandal and general news about what was happening in the City, Eliza reflected that even when the theatre was closed it was an exciting place to be. Sitting in the tiring room helping Jemima sew beads on a costume, she heard about a case being brought between two noblemen for defamation of character, about what Barbara Castlemaine, the king's mistress, was wearing that day, of a duel fought, a highwayman caught and how the queen *still* wasn't with child. She also heard of a new hairstyle just arrived from Paris which consisted of twisting the hair aloft with coloured ribbons to match one's gown, and resolved to try this on Nell.

At five o'clock Mary Davis arose from the chaise longue, saying she couldn't sit around gossiping for a moment longer as she had – here she glanced at Nell – a *very* important engagement for that evening.

Nell, deep in conversation with a wardrobe mistress about costumes for a possible new role, affected not to see her departure. Eliza jumped up, however, and swiftly moved to where Mary had been sitting. Pretending to plump up the cushion, she obtained the letter which had been delivered and tucked it into her sleeve. Going outside to the yard she unfolded it and read:

From Will Chiffinch, Keeper of the Closet
To all ladies of the King's Players
I am commanded by His Gracious Majesty King
Charles II
To invite you to a musical evening and reception
at Foxhall New Spring Garden
This evening at 9.00 pm
*

'Are we going?' Nell asked Eliza in mock amazement a little later. 'Of course we're going! And won't little Mistress Bitchington get a surprise when she sees me there.'

'Will you tell the other girls?'

Nell shook her head. 'We'll tell Jemima, but I don't want anyone else competing for the king's attentions. As it is I expect Will Chiffinch has asked the girls from the Duke's Theatre.'

Eliza frowned. 'Who *is* Will Chiffinch?'

Nell's eyes gleamed. 'A gentleman I'm hoping to see a lot more of soon.'

Eliza, puzzled, said she couldn't think what she meant.

'Will Chiffinch is a procurer for King Charles,' Nell explained. 'He arranges for girls to be smuggled into the palace for His Majesty's pleasure.'

'Really?' said Eliza, blushing and reflecting that she was still not used to Nell's frank way with words.

Nell nodded. ''Tis said that there's a special backstaircase in Whitehall built just for that purpose.' She thought for a moment, then said, 'But you and I must go down to Tower Hill market straight away.'

'To buy something special to wear?'

Nell shook her head. 'We'll visit the costume department for that, for I've a notion that we should appear in disguise. No, I was thinking of going to buy something special for Mary.'

'For *Mary*?' Eliza asked, startled. 'But why?'

Nell smiled. 'You wait and see.'

It was a good walk from the theatre in Bridge Street through New Gate and around the City walls to Tower Hill, but Nell kept up such a constant stream of chatter about the king and his current mistresses that it didn't seem at all wearisome to Eliza. The people on the streets, too, were so varied and their conditions so different – lame beggars, masked ladies, street-sellers, music men with their monkeys, city merchants, farmers come to sell their wares – that Eliza was constantly amused and diverted from thinking about her aching feet.

Arriving at Tower Hill and first of all marvelling at the size and antiquity of the great Tower of London, they crossed on to a long, grassy bank where a motley collection of stalls and sideshows was erected. Each of these was supplied with its own montebank or quack doctor, shouting their wares and extolling the merits of the product they were there to sell.

Eliza gazed around, bewildered.

'I am ninety-eight years of age and yet by taking my Elixir Vitae am as strong as anyone of forty!' shouted one.

'There is no disease under the sun which I cannot cure! In certain circumstances I can even revive the dead!'

'I've saved arms, legs, toes and fingers from being

cut off when they have been ordered for amputation the vulgar way!'

'I sell a true and certain prolonger of life and can make the deaf to hear and the blind to see!'

'What is it you want here?' Eliza asked Nell, stunned by the multitude of promises and declarations of genius going on all around her. Only once before had she seen a montebank – at a hiring fair in Stoke Courcey, but he'd only sold pills for ague and headache.

'I don't seek to bring someone back from the dead,' Nell said, 'but something more modest altogether. Come,' she said, taking Eliza's arm, 'let's walk down the length of them and you must read their bills and tell me what they say.' She looked at Eliza mischievously. 'I'll tell you now that I'm looking for a purge.'

'But why?'

'You'll see soon.'

'For *Mary*?'

Nell just smiled. 'And it must be but a small amount which can easily be put into liquid undetected.'

And so they walked through the stalls, with Eliza reading their posters and blackboards.

'*A powder for the greensickness,*' she read out. '*An infusion for three-day ague. A water for sore eyes. An elixir for gravel in the urine …*'

Nell shook her head and moved on.

'*Friendly pills, being a tincture of the sun, giving relief and comfort to those ladies who have dull complexions …*'

'*I make the hair to fall out where it is growing in unnatural places, and make it grow again where it is too little …*'

'I've cured a man whose body was swollen so big that his clothes would not come together, and drawn from him a worm of four yards long ...'

The two girls shrieked in horror as she read this last.

'I set artificial teeth and can cure the deaf and dumb. I also cure the hare-shotten and cut out carbuncles.'

'Cut out carbuncles!' Eliza repeated, stopping in front of the poster. 'Couldn't Susan come here and be changed?'

Nell burst out laughing and Eliza looked at her in surprise, for it seemed a strange thing to be laughing about.

'Is it not a sad affliction?' she said. 'Shouldn't we tell Susan that it is possible that she can be made well?'

Nell pulled at Eliza's arm to come away. 'These montebanks are not capable of doing one quarter of all they profess to do.'

'But all those cures! There must be something to try for Susan.'

Nell shook her head. 'Not now,' she said. 'I'll tell you another time what's to be done about Susan, but *now* we are here for a purge. Go on reading, do ...'

'*An incomparable medicine which speedily, safely and infallibly cures all sorts and degrees of melancholic passions ...*'

'*A powder which disperseth all female distempers ...*'

'*A useful wax which takes away itching so violent that it causes persons to scratch until their skin is striped like tigers ...*'

At last Eliza read out a bill which promised, among

other things, that Doctor Vernantes's powder would *'Cause a purging of the stomach when the bowels have not been proficient for several days.'*

Nell nodded towards it. 'That's it!' she said. 'That's what I want.'

Doctor Vernantes bowed low before them. He was wearing a royal-blue wool coat which had once been grand, but was now threadbare and had its buttons hanging by strings. He smiled at them with a quantity of ill-fitting false teeth, which Nell said later certainly came from a cow.

'Ladies!' he said. 'Great ladies, both!'

Eliza bobbed a curtsy but Nell didn't.

'Do you wish a private consultation with me?' he asked. 'I've a house by the postern gate in Little Tower Hill where the quality may park their coaches and not be seen. I treat ladies for all distempers and can bring down their courses when that time of the month has passed and –'

Nell held up her hand. 'Please,' she said, 'I only wish for your stomach powder. I've not been regular this past two weeks and would have a purge.'

'My special elixir will preserve the fineness and delicateness of your skin so that you keep your beauty till you are seventy years of age and beyond!'

'Thank you kindly and I'll let you know,' Nell said. 'But for now, just the purging powder, please.'

Chapter Fourteen

'I think we look very handsome,' Eliza said to Jemima as they approached Swan Steps on the Thames. 'Although neither of us looks quite as dashing as Mistress Gwyn.'

'*Master* Gwyn, if you please,' Nell said, giving a sweeping bow to her two companions.

The three girls were attired as boys and wearing dark velvet doublets slashed with gold, short breeches and velvet-lined capes. The breeches worn by Eliza and Jemima were quite modest, but Nell's were cut daringly high to show as much of her shapely legs and silken hose as possible. Each girl carried sword and scabbard, and wore a plumed hat with a curled brim.

On reaching Swan Steps, Nell put her fingers to her mouth and gave a piercing whistle for a boat. Foxhall Garden, being on the Southwarke side of the river, could only be reached by water.

It was a while before a craft came across to them, for the Thames that fine evening was as busy as any street and it seemed that most of London's quality were upon the water already: some picnicking and accompanied by musicians or singers. When, however, Nell called to an approaching waterdog and he realised that the three youths waiting at Swan Steps were, in fact, three pretty wenches showing a lot of leg, his intended passenger was ignored and he rowed swiftly towards the girls. A price was settled and he helped them on board.

'Do you think my darling William will be there?' Jemima asked Eliza eagerly as they settled themselves down.

'Nell said she thought so,' Eliza replied. What Nell had actually said was that William would be there for certain, 'possibly drunk, probably with a whore' but of course she didn't repeat this. Eliza, fearfully excited at the evening ahead – for although she'd heard much about such places of entertainment, she'd never thought she would visit one – had already been speculating about the events on her own account. Her first thought had been about Valentine Howard: was he going to be there and, if so, would he speak with her? Her second was altogether wilder and, she knew, quite absurd, but, since she'd been disowned by her father and because Nell often spoke of the king's many and varied natural children, she sometimes allowed herself to speculate that she might possibly be a child of the king.

No, she chided herself, it was just too nonsensical.

But the king *was* very dark and tall, as she was, and everyone knew that when he'd been young and on the run from Cromwell he'd spent time in Somersetshire. So wouldn't it be an astounding thing if she discovered that he had green eyes?

Foxhall Garden was a short trip along the river and before Eliza could see their destination she could hear music, singing and laughter coming across the water towards them. On arriving at the wooden pier Nell paid the waterdog and they jumped ashore, smiling to each other, knowing that if they'd been attending as girls they would have been lifted carefully by the attendants from boat to pier as if they'd been made of porcelain. Eliza found some elements of being dressed like a man rather tricky, however, for her sword was long and ungainly and *would* keep twisting itself around her leg as if trying to trip her up.

Nell led the way through the trees. She had, she told them, been to Foxhall before, and Jemima had attended outdoor balls at home, but this was the first time that Eliza had ever been to such a place and she couldn't help but gasp and stare around her – so much so that Nell had to beg her to remember she was in costume.

'You're supposed to be a young court gallant, not some Tom-pudding just off the coach from Devonshire!' she hissed.

But Eliza wouldn't be quietened. 'Oh, but 'tis all so amazing and done most excellently,' she continued to exclaim as they passed arbours of trees lit with candles, mossy grottos, sparkling fountains and little wooden eating places hung with lanterns. 'I've never seen anything so pretty.'

In an open glade, people were dancing to a fiddler's tune, and in another a small group of musicians was playing to people seated on the grass. The flowerbeds contained pink and white blooms hedged around with purple lavender, and there was even, Eliza was amused to see, a cow being led around by a milkmaid who was calling that she would milk it there and then and provide a jug of milk as refreshment for the revellers.

'See, Eliza, there's a cow,' Nell said, pointing. 'So it's not so different from your home!'

'Oh, it is,' Eliza said, laughing, 'for *this* cow has a white skin and is scrubbed clean. Besides, the cows in Somersetshire don't have flowers around their necks nor wear straw hats!'

Quickly surveying the whole place, they ascertained where the king was, for a silken awning had been erected and he and a group of his courtiers were within this, beside a small lake on which floated strange boats which Nell said had been sent from Venice. Eliza, eagerly looking in the tent for the king, could see a tall, well-shaped man with an assortment of little dogs playing at his feet and Nell confirmed that this was he.

Mary Davis was sitting with some other girls on a low branch of a tree to one side of this courtly arrangement, and Nell approached her with much friendliness and affability, bowing low, flourishing her plumed hat and saying she was sorry to be rather late and she hoped she hadn't missed anything.

Mary, not recognising her at first and taking her for a gallant, returned the greeting with a curtsy, but some laughter from Eliza and Jemima prompted her to look more closely at the young man and discover who it really was. In view of the proximity of the king she must have thought it best to pretend friendship, however, and Nell and she made a show of kissing each other with delight.

Eliza, although fascinated by this little play-act, moved to a spot where she could see the king in greater detail, and now had eyes for no one else. She thought his face very like his portraits, although he wasn't handsome by any means, but striking, with coal-black hair, an aquiline nose and long moustaches. Disappointingly – although she wasn't close enough to see the colour of his eyes – there didn't appear to be any clear resemblance between His Majesty and herself, however. The king had one arm around his son's shoulders – for she knew Monmouth from Nell's description – and was surrounded by a pack of brown and white spaniels, and the group of friends Nell had referred to as his gang of wits. Among these she spotted William Wilkes, Henry Monteagle and then Valentine Howard, and she felt herself blushing.

But she wasn't going to let Valentine see that he affected her in any way. Adjusting her sword slightly, she stared around her, adopted what she hoped was a manly pose and waited to see what was going to happen next.

Nell was still a little way off, talking animatedly to Mary. Eliza saw her pause for breath, then take a sip of Mary's drink and call for some of the same. Almost immediately a tray holding golden goblets of wine came around and was passed among the company. When the tray reached her, Eliza took a goblet and sipped its contents cautiously, for she had heard much of the effects of strong wine and didn't wish to fall unconscious – for that, apparently, could happen if one was unused to it – and miss the evening's entertainment.

Her eyes still on the king, she felt Jemima, beside her, give a start.

'I think William's recognised me!' she said, and she gave a bow in his direction. A moment later William came over. He *had* recognised her and wasn't pleased to have her there.

'May I remind you, madam, you're supposed to be in hiding,' he said in a low voice, neglecting to make a formal greeting to either her or Eliza.

'Darling William,' Jemima's voice trembled. 'I thought you'd be pleased to see me.'

'Well, I'm not.'

'But we *are* here in disguise,' said Jemima.

'Don't be ridiculous,' he snapped. 'A child of two can see that you're not men. Unless you want to incur my wrath, madam, you'll cease this silly play-acting and go home immediately.'

'But William –' Jemima started.

William took Jemima's elbow. 'My dear,' he said, and Eliza could see that his jaw was set and his lips tight. 'I'm only being harsh on you because I don't want our love for each other jeopardised. If your family find out where you are, your father will have you kidnapped and me killed. Is that what you want?'

Jemima shook her head. 'No! No, of course not. Darling William, I'm so sorry. I didn't think.'

'You must go home now. Back to your lodgings.'

'But when will I see you? I've not set eyes on you this past week!'

'I'll send word soon,' William said, and Eliza noticed that his eyes were sliding past Jemima towards where two girls dressed as milkmaids were dancing. 'You must be more patient, my sweeting.'

A boat was called for and Jemima, looking desperately sorry for herself, went away. Her sweetheart, Eliza noticed, didn't go with her to the pier at the river's edge, saying it was best if they were not seen together.

Seeing Eliza now standing alone, Nell beckoned for her to come over to where she and Mary were gossiping with some players from the Duke's Theatre. The talk was light and superficial, with no one taking much interest in what anyone was saying, for the attention of everyone was fixed upon the king and they were watching every move, every glance, every gesture he made.

Nell, still playing the gallant, put a loose arm around Eliza's shoulders and clinked their wine goblets together. 'Keep your eye on Mary Davis,' she hissed in her ear. 'She may, unfortunately, have to leave us very soon.'

Eliza gave a start, for she'd almost forgotten the powder which Nell had purchased from the quack doctor. Just a few moments after this, however, Mary Davis gave a little groan and clutched at her stomach.

'My dear, are you ailing?' Nell asked solicitously. 'Have you had too much wine?'

Mary shook her head wordlessly.

'Let me send for some water,' Nell said with pretend alarm. 'You have gone very pale.'

'No. No, I shall be ...' She gave a strangled cry. 'I fear I must take my leave,' she said urgently.

Nell signalled to one of the girls standing nearby. 'Do come and take care of Mistress Davis,' she said in a low voice, 'or I fear she will disgrace herself in this fine company.'

As Mary was led away, groaning, Nell raised her eyebrows at Eliza. 'I cannot think *what* she must have consumed.'

Eliza gazed at her friend with admiration. 'But how

did you get her to take it?'

'Oh, 'twas easy – I pretended to try her drink, and slipped it in then.' She gazed after Mary with feigned sorrow. '*Such* a pity that she'll miss the company of the king tonight.'

'Indeed,' Eliza agreed, stifling her laughter.

A short period followed during which everyone continued drinking, and the king and his merry gang, Eliza concluded, fully lived up to their reputations. The two milkmaids were caught, rolled down a grassy bank and reduced to dancing in their undersmocks, a fiercesome-looking man without a nose (Nell said it had been cut off in a duel) threw someone else up a tree, and a knave who turned out to be the Earl of Rochester removed all his clothing and ran around the company utterly naked. Finally, a couple disappeared into a tent and were seen entwined there, the shadowplay being thrown by the candlelight leaving little to the imagination.

Eliza scarcely knew whether to be shocked or amused by all these antics, and finally decided to be a little of each. She was very aware of Valentine Howard nearby and couldn't help but wonder what he thought of her. If he thought of her at all, that was.

'At last!' Nell said, after glancing once more to where the king was. 'Chiffinch is on his way to us.'

Eliza looked over to see a stout man approaching them, formally dressed in black velvet with gold trimmings. He bowed low and Eliza and Nell bowed back to him, flourishing their hats.

'Mistress Gwyn,' Chiffinch said smoothly.

'Oh,' Nell said, pretending to pout. 'You have seen through my disguise!'

'Not many men have such a figure, madam,' said Chiffinch.

Nell nodded graciously at the compliment. 'And this is my companion, Eliza Rose.'

Chiffinch gave another short bow but only glanced at Eliza. 'I'm commanded to say that the king wishes to speak with the ladies of the King's Company.'

Eliza felt her heart give an enormous leap. It was enough to be here, see such sights, be in such company – but now actually to meet the King of England ...

'Alas, sire,' said Nell, 'there are just two of us at present. But Mistress Rose and I will be delighted to attend upon His Majesty.'

Chiffinch bowed again and Eliza had just enough time to exchange an agonised, excited look with Nell before he began to lead the way towards the king in the silk tent. It was only a short stroll across the grass towards him but Eliza, feeling every eye upon the two of them, felt it to be of an immeasurable length. She was aware that she should be taking manly strides, yet feared being tripped up by her sword – and moreover had neglected to put down the goblet she'd been holding and so was forced to flourish this along with her hat. She began to wish she was in a woman's garb (and it was mere vanity but how she would have loved having her own long hair) for curtsying came more easily and surely looked more charming.

Following close behind Nell, she realised that it was customary to stop every few seconds and bow again to His Majesty, and that as you got closer each bow should be deeper than the one before, each flourish of the hat a grander gesture, until, at last, Eliza stood before the king with knee bent, hat touching the floor and body bowed so low she was feared she might overbalance. Terrified into immobility, she was relieved at last to hear manly laughter.

'Do rise, Nelly, for I know it's you!' said the king.

There was a moment's pause, Eliza heard some girlish giggles from Nell, and then the king called, 'And you may arise, too, my dear,' and Eliza finally straightened up and looked into the eyes of the King of England. It was the most thrilling moment in her life, and her only disappointment was that his eyes were brown and not green.

A little later, Valentine Howard strode up and stood before Eliza, looking amused.

'So is this – what? – your fourth incarnation?' he asked.

Eliza bobbed a curtsy and then, remembering her disguise, turned it into a bow. 'I don't know what you mean, sire,' she said, meeting his eyes boldly.

'Tonight you are a young rake. Yesterday you were an orange girl. Before that you were a mermaid, were you not?'

Eliza dropped her gaze.

'And before that?'

Eliza drew in her breath sharply. Surely he didn't …

'Before that, I believe you were staying in one of His Majesty's finest' –'

'Please, sire!' said Eliza, looking around to make sure no one had overheard. 'No one but Nell knows of my background.'

'It's all right,' he said, amused. 'Your secret is safe.'

'I didn't think you had … I mean, how can you possibly remember seeing me in Clink?' Eliza asked.

There was a pause. 'Could any fellow forget those green eyes?' he said, and Eliza, for one brief second, smiled up at him with surprised delight. Swiftly reminding herself, however, that such compliments were merely part of the ritual undertaken by those of the male sex when they were seeking to bed a girl, she took a step backwards.

'That is as maybe, sire,' she said stiffly. 'I ... I've put that time behind me now and don't wish anyone else to know about it.'

He smiled at her. 'And what will you give me for my silence?'

Eliza felt her face flush. 'It may surprise you to know, sire, that not all girls are to be bought and sold.'

To her discomposure he burst out laughing. 'My apologies. Your servant, madam,' he said, flourishing his hat and bowing low.

They were interrupted by Nell, her eyes sparkling and her colour high.

'Eliza, the king wishes me to dance,' she said breathlessly. 'Will you accompany me by singing? There are musicians waiting and we've some ballad sheets.'

Eliza gasped. 'Sing? I ... I've not practised for some time,' she stammered.

'Possibly not since you were seated on a rock in the ocean,' Valentine Howard murmured.

Eliza, choosing to ignore this remark, turned away from him. 'But of course, Nell. I'll do my best ...'

Chapter Fifteen

'I wish I could have stayed to see you,' Jemima said in the tiring room of the theatre the following day, 'for I'm sure that you looked very fine singing before the king.'

Eliza glowed as she thought of it. She'd been a little off-key sometimes, she was sure, and once or twice could barely manage the complicated roundels which sought to twist her tongue, but by and large she'd been pleased at her performance. Even the drunken wits had seemed to appreciate her voice.

Of course, she knew she'd only been secondary, an accompaniment to Nell's dancing.

'Nell was magnificent!' she told Jemima. 'Everyone was cheering and bravoing her as she whirled around. Why, she had the king clapping and whooping like a schoolboy. "*Nelly!*" he kept shouting – for that's what he calls her – "Nelly, dance and never stop!"'

'And *after*?' Jemima asked meaningfully.

'After ... she went back to Whitehall Palace with him!'

The two girls exchanged conspiratorial smiles.

'She's got what she longed for, then,' Jemima said.

'It seems like it. But I've not told you the most exciting news, Jemima, for when the king commended my voice, he also gave me leave to attend singing classes with his daughter. He said she has a music teacher newly arrived from France, and he thought she and I would sound very pretty harmonising together.'

'That's excellent!' Jemima said. 'For the king's daughter will be sure to have the best teacher – and besides, you'll have to go to the palace and see all the finery and fashions!' She thought for a moment. 'I wonder which daughter he referred to.'

'Is there more than one?'

Jemima nodded. 'There's Catherine Fitzcharles – she was born of Catherine Pegge. And Barbara Castlemaine has a child a year by him as regular as clockwork. I believe that at least two of those are girls.'

'A child a year!' Eliza said. 'So Nell will never be his one and only.'

'She won't,' Jemima said. 'Even the queen doesn't have exclusive rights to the king. But I suppose if you set your sights on Charles II for your lover, then that's what you must expect.'

She smiled at Eliza somewhat sadly. She looked paler than ever, Eliza thought, her complexion almost matching the white-blondness of her hair.

'And how was my darling William after I left?' she enquired after a moment.

'He was …' Eliza bit her lip. It had been William, she'd discovered, who'd been performing so athletically with the girl in the tent. 'He wasn't much with the others,' she said with diplomacy. 'Indeed, I hardly saw anything of him.'

Jemima sighed. 'I must be patient, for we'll be together soon for the rest of our lives. I just have to keep reminding myself of that.'

They fell into silence for a while, each busy with their own thoughts, then Eliza said, 'I've a favour to ask you. I want to write to someone and I don't know enough of my letters to do so. Will you help me?'

'Of course,' Jemima said. 'And teach you to write too, if you like, for I've much time on my hands.' She smiled wanly. 'Is it a love letter?'

'No, indeed not!' Eliza said. 'I don't have a sweetheart here or at home. In Somersetshire, I mean,' she corrected, for she wasn't sure where home was any longer. She hesitated. 'Do you remember that I told you about my father disowning me?' As Jemima nodded, she continued, 'Well, I've decided to write to my aunt – my mother's sister. If anyone knows the truth about this, it'll be her.'

Some paper, a quill and some ink being sent for, Eliza – with Jemima's help – wrote the following:

Lewkenor's Lane, London

My Dear Aunt Thomasina,
You will be surprised to see from my address that I am in London. To be brief, I came here to find my father, who is at present working on the rebuilding of churches following the Great Fire of four years ago.

I came to find him due to the fact that my stepmother told me I was no longer welcome at the house and requested that I leave. Be assured that I didn't do anything to cause this rift between us, but do believe that I have always acted as a loving and dutiful daughter.

On finding my father here, I was much cast

down to hear him say that it had been he who had told my stepmother to send me away. He also said that I was a cuckoo in his nest and that he wasn't my father. You can imagine that this was a great shock to me.

Here is a delicate matter, Aunt. As my dear mother's sister, it is possible that you know the identity of my real father. If so, I beg you to let me know his name, be he dead or alive, so that I may satisfy myself as to my rightful heredity. Without knowing this, I feel at a loss as to who I am.

If you feel you can answer this question I would be grateful for your reply to the above address. I send my greetings to my uncle and my cousins and remain your affectionate niece,
Eliza Rose

'I'm sure she'll tell you if she knows,' Jemima said reassuringly. 'Your own mother would wish you to know, surely – and your aunt is the closest you can get to her on this earth.'

Eliza nodded and sighed. 'I hope you're right.'

Jemima stood up. 'I've a letter of my own to send to William,' she said, 'so I'll take yours down to the agent with it.' She yawned. 'I need a walk, for I'm feeling very slothful and dull.'

She took up the hooded cloak she habitually wore when going out, and swung it around her. As she did so, Eliza's eyes were on a level with her stomach, and what she saw surprised her very much. Gasping, she looked up at Jemima, but she was fastening the tie at her neck and didn't see.

162

Eliza, embarrassed, looked away. She'd seen too many women with stomachs protruding like that not to know what it was. Of course, she thought, *that* was why Jemima had gone to change in private the previous evening, and why she usually kept her shape hidden under loose smocks. She was with child, and judging by the size of her, the pregnancy was considerably advanced.

'Here she is ... here she is!' A murmur ran through the girls in the tiring room as, very late that afternoon, Nell came in. She was dressed in the same young gallant's garb she'd worn the evening before, the only difference being that around her neck she was now wearing a gold chain upon which hung a man's ring set with a massive ruby.

Against the dark velvet this ruby showed up very well, but in case anyone hadn't noticed it, Nell began casually swinging it backwards and forwards on its chain.

She sat down in front of a make-up mirror and studied her reflection with interest. 'Do I look different?' she mused, moving a candle nearer to the glass. 'Am I changed?' Then, pretending not to notice all the curious and interested eyes upon her, she asked Eliza to send out for a pigeon pie and some cordial, saying she was fair famished.

Eliza gave a coin to Thomas, the boy who ran errands for them, then sat down beside Nell, looking at her expectantly. Jemima did likewise.

Nell looked around, waiting until the eye of everyone in the tiring room was cast in her direction. 'Well, it is official,' she said then. 'I am now the king's whore.'

There was a sharp intake of breath from those around her, and several girls looked over towards where Mary Davis was pretending to learn some lines from a play script.

Nell went on, 'I say whore, for I won't presume to say mistress after just one calling. However,' she swung the ruby along the chain, 'I think I may say that His Majesty was very pleased with my performance.'

There was a pause before Mary got to her feet and approached Nell. Eliza waited nervously, thinking she was going to unleash a torrent of fury on their heads, but she merely said, 'Was that your first time at Whitehall, then, Mistress Gwyn?'

Nell nodded.

'It's very beautiful there, isn't it?' confirmed Mary. She patted her neckbone, as if to draw attention to the gold locket, and, smiling sweetly at Nell, drifted towards the door. 'I am often there,' she said before she went out.

Eliza longed to know more about Nell and the king. There was, though, much to ask, and she wouldn't have known where to start or what words to use. It was just too delicate a matter. It did seem that Nell had achieved what she'd set out to do, however, and Eliza was happy for her. How Nell would manage to order things thereafter with regards to the queen, and Barbara Castlemaine and Mary Davis and whoever else the king might choose to sleep with, Eliza couldn't begin to think. How difficult being someone's mistress must be. And even worse to be just one of a number of mistresses.

But Eliza felt she couldn't worry about Nell at the moment, for all her concern was centred on Jemima. She'd twice tried to say something to the girl about her condition, but each time Jemima had pretended not to know what she was talking about. Eliza deliberated whether to tell Nell or not, and couldn't decide what to do for the best. It was Jemima's secret, after all, and it was obvious that she didn't want even Eliza to know. Perhaps she hoped to be on the high seas before she gave birth ...

Nell spent several nights at the palace during the week that followed. She'd receive a message from the king late in the afternoon, then travel to Whitehall by carriage under cover of darkness and be met by Chiffinch in a certain courtyard. She told Eliza that behind a locked door in this courtyard was the secret staircase which she'd climb to spend the night in the king's private apartments.

She also told Eliza that the king had promised her an apartment of her own, perhaps near to Whitehall Palace, so that he'd easily be able to visit her. Eliza wasn't sure if this new housing arrangement would extend to her, and didn't like to ask for fear that it wouldn't. She'd found things rather dull lately, for Nell wasn't around much and there was no play currently at the King's Theatre, nor any rehearsals to attend. She was resigned to the fact that she wouldn't hear from Aunt Thomasina for several weeks, but hoped daily that she might have word from the singing master at Whitehall about the promised lessons. How she'd have loved to have proper tuition to develop her voice! Sadly, no such message arrived, so Eliza spent her time doing odd jobs at the theatre, practising her writing, or attending to Nell's washing and cleaning. She tried not to think too much about Valentine Howard, for it seemed to her that he knew the effect he had on her and enjoyed seeing her discomposed. Besides, what girl in her right mind would spend time thinking about one of the king's gang of wits? It was more certain than rain that they were all the same ...

On Sunday, Nell came back to Lewkenor's Lane proposing an outing. For a moment, Eliza thought she meant them to go to church and was very surprised, for Nell always had a hundred different reasons why they couldn't go to Sunday service: they had too much mending, she had an appointment, she'd no clean smocks, she'd promised to call on someone.

But it wasn't a church service she was suggesting.

'You asked me about Susan and her carbuncle, did you not?' she said to Eliza. 'You suggested that one of the quack doctors might be able to do something for it.'

Eliza nodded.

'Well, we are going today to see this surgery performed!'

'On little Susan? Today?' Eliza gasped, thinking of how scared the child must be.

Nell nodded.

'But ... is it in a doctor's house or will it be performed at home?'

'Neither,' Nell said. 'The quack who's doing it is Doctor Daniel and he works outside the coffee house by the Angel and Crown.'

This, to Eliza, didn't sound very ordered or safe, but not knowing how these things were usually carried out, she didn't comment further.

Nell, with her new-found status as king's mistress, had hired a glossy pink-painted coach pulled by two white horses, and this was employed to take the two girls to the Angel and Crown. It was an enjoyable ride for, far from pulling the curtains across and travelling incognito as did most of the well-to-do, Nell sat full in the window, waving gaily and calling out to those passers-by who recognised her. Eliza waved at people too and enjoyed the trip immensely, for it was the first time she'd been in a private carriage and this one was very grand, the interior being padded with fine upholstery and filled with embroidered cushions.

The two girls arrived by the coffee house at midday to see that a broad stage had been erected on the pavement outside. A crowd of perhaps a hundred persons had gathered and Doctor Daniel, in sombre black suit, cloak and battered top hat, was walking amongst them inviting them to throw money into a bowl.

A board to one side of him read:

See the Amazing Doctor Daniel perform a miracle!
A child whose mother was cursed by a witch and
thus was born grossly disfigured will be cured this day!

On stage, sitting on a kitchen chair, sat Susan, smiling to the crowd with her strange little twisted face.

'Isn't she frightened?' Eliza asked, looking at Susan in surprise. 'She'll be having her cheek cut most horribly, surely?'

'Oh, he may not use the knife,' Nell said rather

carelessly, looking around her to see who was there.

'But what will he do, then? Is he going to rub a salve on it, or make her drink a special cordial or something?'

Nell smiled and raised her eyebrows. 'You'll have to wait and see.' She patted her side. 'Take care that no one steals your pocket in this crowd,' she added.

Nell, Eliza thought, wasn't taking the matter at all seriously. 'And is the child's mother here ready to dress the wound and carry her home?' she asked, looking for Rose.

'Oh, no – we'll take Susan home in the carriage,' Nell said.

Eliza looked at her in dismay, visualising tears and upsets and maybe blood all over the pristine embroidered cushions, but Nell said no more.

Doctor Daniel, on regaining the platform, removed his top hat and bowed low to his audience. As he did so, they – unlike those at the theatre, Eliza thought – fell to a respectful silence. The doctor moved to stand behind Susan and placed one hand on her head.

'Cursed by a malevolent witch, this child has been hideously disfigured from the moment she was born! I will now attempt – with necromancy and my incredible medical skills – to lift the spell and cure her. Those of you in the audience who suffer likewise, are hare-shotten or have other disfigurements, may book a private audience with me afterwards at a cost of one shilling.'

There was a murmur from several of the audience.

'You need not be hasty, my friends!' the doctor said. 'See first what can be achieved at my hands, and then judge whether you wish to avail yourself of my services.'

Doctor Daniel now moved to stand before Susan and covered them both with a vast black cloak. He screamed, 'Curse, begone!' and the cloak fluttered, as if he was passing his hands across the girl's face. Then he stood motionless for several moments while the audience waited, rapt with anticipation.

When he whisked the cloak away and staggered to one side of the stage, seemingly exhausted, a new Susan was revealed, smiling at the audience with a perfectly formed face. There was absolutely no trace of the carbuncle.

The crowd gasped and Eliza's own mouth dropped in amazement. She hadn't really thought that Doctor Daniel would be able to do it. And certainly not instantly. She'd thought – as was usual with these things – that he'd send Susan home with some salve, saying that she must be patient and that it would work within a few weeks.

This, though, was beyond all expectation.

'That is excellent!' Eliza gasped to Nell. 'I've never seen anything like it! How does he do such things?'

Nell shrugged, smiling. 'He said by necromancy and sympathetic magic, did he not?'

'You may come and inspect this child at your leisure,' Doctor Daniel boomed, 'and, finding no trace of her former affliction, I will leave it to your discretion as to how much you think my performance is worth.'

He stood beside Susan, holding out the bowl again, and the audience began to file past, shaking their heads in wonder and dropping in a coin or two.

'It *is* a miracle!' Eliza said in the carriage going home,

staring at Susan as if she couldn't believe her eyes. 'It is the most wonderful cure I've ever seen.'

'Do you think so?' Susan said pertly.

'Don't you? Have you yet seen yourself in a mirror? Why, your face is very prettily shaped now. There's no trace at all of the growth.' To Eliza's bewilderment Nell and Susan just exchanged amused glances. 'Your Aunt Nell must look to her laurels,' she went on, 'for I believe you'll be a great beauty when you're grown!'

Nell began laughing.

'What?' Eliza asked. ''Tis true!'

'Will you show her, Susan?' Nell said.

Susan turned away, hiding her face for a moment. When she looked back at them, her cheek was once again disfigured by the monstrous carbuncle.

'No!' Eliza cried out in disbelief. ''Tis horrible! It cannot be.'

Nell and Susan laughed so hard they could barely speak.

'You're right, it cannot be,' Nell said eventually, through giggles. ''Tis but a trick – a stuck-on plaister. Ma had it made for her.'

''Tis for me to go a-begging with,' Susan explained. 'And then, every few months, I arrange with one of the quack doctors that he should cure me, and we go half and half on the day's takings.'

Eliza was speechless, but, reflecting on the matter later, decided that it was probably no worse than the subterfuges she'd used in prison to beg money, and that, indeed, in London one had to make one's way however one could.

Chapter Sixteen

Now that Eliza had noticed Jemima's stomach, she couldn't stop herself from sneaking a glance at it at every opportunity. Even though Jemima always laced herself tightly into her gown and wore a loose jacket or smock, the bulge of her belly was quite discernible. She was with child, Eliza was certain of it. Either that or she had some malignant disease which had caused her to swell up.

She wished someone else would notice, but Jemima was such a reticent creature that she hardly ever came to anyone's attention. Even Nell didn't notice anything untoward for a time, for she continued her evening visits to Whitehall Palace and only came into the theatre to rehearse her lines, have Eliza curl up her hair or have a costume fitting. The new set of clothes being stitched were for Aphra Behn's play which, now that she'd borrowed some money from a rich noble, was at last going ahead. The emphasis of *Secret Love* had been changed somewhat, Eliza realised as she helped Nell with her lines; it now reflected Nell's higher status as one of the mistresses of the king. It was a rags to riches story which partly mirrored Nell's own life; a romantic comedy about a woman who left her faithful but boring husband to live with a lord.

Nell's role as Sophia was a much more important one now, and as well as the scenes where she had to dress as a youth in tights, included an opening view where she was revealed asleep, only partially dressed, on a grassy bank. This first scene alone, it was thought, would get the audience flocking in, for everyone wanted a glimpse of the king's latest mistress, especially without her gown and bodice.

One afternoon following rehearsals, Nell didn't rush off as she usually did, but sat around in the tiring room gossiping with the other actresses. It was then, at last, that she noticed Jemima's shape.

'Hell's teeth, Jemima!' she said suddenly. 'I do believe you've got something to tell us!'

Jemima, seeing where Nell was staring, went scarlet. She shook her head, though, and said in a low voice that indeed she had not, that Nell and Eliza knew all her secrets.

'But I don't think we know *this* little secret,' Nell said with feigned coyness.

Jemima didn't reply and Eliza held her breath.

'For you seem to have a certain happy event planned.'

'I have not!' Jemima said, all in a fluster. 'I ... I am merely putting on a little weight.'

Nell looked at her. 'Are you sure?'

Jemima nodded vehemently.

Nell shrugged. 'Just as you please,' she said. 'Although I wonder what William is thinking of to leave you in such a condition.'

Eliza shot Jemima a sympathetic glance, for William – darling William, as Jemima always referred to him – had hardly been by to see her of late. Instead he'd sent notes to excuse himself, assuring Jemima that he was working hard to earn money to secure their passage to the Americas. Eliza repeated these excuses to Nell, who'd replied that if working hard meant he had to visit every gambling den and whorehouse in London, then he was certainly doing his best.

'I regret that I spoke to Jemima as I did,' Nell said to Eliza a little later that same afternoon, 'for she's taken it badly, hasn't she?'

Eliza nodded, for Jemima had broken down in tears, then gone off to hide herself backstage somewhere. 'But she *is* with child and I'm glad you brought up the subject.'

'I fear she is,' Nell said. 'And what will happen to her when she's saddled with the child I don't know, for she's lived such a molly-coddled life up to now with her servants and maids that she's hardly capable of looking after herself, let alone bringing up an infant.' She sighed, exasperated. 'Curses on William Wilkes!'

'He's nothing but a worthless oaf!' Eliza chimed in, thinking of all the times Jemima had sat crying over him.

''Tis terrible: a woman without a protector in her situation …' Nell's voice trailed away and Eliza, learning fast about London life, had no doubts about what would happen to Jemima. She'd be sent to a poorhouse, or – worse still – to Bedlam with the mad people, for anyone who had a child out of wedlock was perceived to be of dangerously weak morals.

'Go and buy some sweetmeats for me, will you, Eliza?' Nell said. 'I'll give them to Jemima and say I'm sorry for having brought up the subject. No doubt she'll tell us about it in her own good time.'

Eliza made her way on foot towards the Royal
Exchange, the very grand trading exchange in the City
which had been rebuilt after the Fire. Here there were
not only facilities for the rich merchants to trade
wholesale, but a multitude of little shops and stalls
selling delicate and flavoursome things. At a shop
calling itself The Sugared Plum she purchased some
frosted rose petals and a quantity of dainty crystallised
fruits and, after looking in every other shop window,
crossed the courtyard of the Exchange to make her
way back to Drury Lane. She was rather preoccupied,
wondering when she'd hear from Aunt Thomasina,
when she saw William Wilkes, grandly dressed and
seeming rather drunk, talking to several other young
gallants. She hesitated, nervous about approaching
him, yet anxious to take the opportunity to say
something about Jemima's condition.

Quickly ascertaining that Valentine Howard wasn't
amongst the young men surrounding William – for
much as she wanted to help Jemima, she didn't intend
to be embarrassed in front of him – she went over
and, curtsying low, asked if she might speak with Mr
Wilkes for a moment in private.

'Not another of your girls, William!' the cry went
up from his cronies. 'I swear you have already laid a
dozen wenches this year!'

Eliza gave the group what she hoped was a cold
look and one of them said, 'Ah, no! 'Tis the pretty
songstress from Foxhall,' which rather made her want
to smile.

William stepped away from the group. 'What is it?'
he asked irritably.

'Sire,' Eliza began somewhat nervously, 'I'm maid to Nell Gwyn and friend to Jemima – as we call her.'

He narrowed his eyes. 'Yes? And so?'

'Excuse me for being so bold as to approach you, but Jemima is pining and also … also …' she reddened and couldn't bring herself to say the words that Nell would have uttered without a qualm, '… she seems to be soon … soon … that is, she is not quite herself at present.'

Wilkes puffed out his cheeks, rolled his eyes. 'That's too bad.'

'Sire!' Eliza said, shocked at his seeming callousness.

''Tis not at all what I wanted. It has all gone wrong!' he said, making a drunken, throwaway gesture with his arms.

Eliza felt a great desire to kick him. 'It has all gone wrong for Jemima, too, then,' she said, suddenly emboldened, 'and her misfortune is much the greater, for you may go on just as you please, but she has to bear an added burden.'

Wilkes looked at her again and then gazed into the distance, appearing to be considering, in an ale-sodden way, what was to be done. 'Oh, I suppose I shall think of something,' he said eventually.

'May I tell her that?'

'If you wish.' He gave her a half-nod, turning again to his cronies, and Eliza made her way back to the theatre. At least, she thought, she could tell Jemima that she'd seen him, and give her his message, such as it was.

The following day a sealed document was delivered at the theatre for Jemima. She tore open the parchment and read down the lines quickly, then flushed pink, swayed and staggered backwards.

'What is it?' Eliza asked anxiously, putting a chair in position for her to sit on. 'Not bad news?'

'No, not bad news,' Jemima said, sitting down heavily. 'Most excellent news.'

She passed Eliza the letter. It read:

I've secured the cleric and he is willing to marry us this evening at nine. The utmost secrecy must surround this matter and I ask you to tell no one and to arrive alone, apart from one maidservant.
I shall send my carriage at eight-thirty and remain, my dear,
Your William

'There!' Jemima said. 'Darling William. I knew he wouldn't let me down.'

'No. No, indeed,' Eliza stammered, rather taken aback at this seeming display of chivalry on his part. He really did mean to marry her, then.

Jemima grasped her arm. 'You'll come with me, won't you? You'll come with me as my maid?'

Eliza nodded. 'If you wish, of course I will. But what will you wear for your wedding?' She looked Jemima over doubtfully as she asked, for she'd been appearing in the same drudge-grey gown and oversmock for some days now and she suspected it was the only outfit she could get into.

Jemima sighed. 'I'd thought to have a lovely dress for my wedding, and a bouquet of flowers and bride-maids in attendance – but no matter, as long as darling William has arranged this, I'll be content.'

'But your *gown*. Does ... does nothing else fit you?'

Jemima looked down at herself. 'I've rather increased my size, have I not?' She smiled brightly. 'But no matter. I shall find something to wear in the costume department. You can help me look.'

At eight-thirty that evening they were both ready and waiting. Eliza was wearing her best gown and a hooded cloak, and the bride was wearing a dark blue silk dress that was much too big in every place except around her midriff. She had a circlet of the customary myrtle and rosemary around her head and carried a bunch of yellow roses, as well as yellow silk garters to hold up the stockings, tied in bows above her knees as was the custom.

Nell hadn't appeared in the theatre all that day. If she had, Eliza would have sought her advice about the marriage, despite William's plea to keep things secret. She had odd misgivings about it, for it all seemed much too rushed. She didn't dare say anything about this to Jemima, however, for the girl was half-hysterical with a combination of happiness and terror – concerned that her father would find out at the last moment, or her brother would rush in and challenge William to a duel. Only once during the day had Eliza gently referred to her condition, asking her if she knew when a certain happy day might occur, but her question had been met by a wide-eyed stare and a shrug. 'My life will consist entirely of happy days once I'm married!' she'd said, and Eliza couldn't decide if she genuinely didn't know she was with child, or was just being awkward.

William Wilkes's carriage and four was waiting

outside the theatre at the appointed time, the painted coat of arms on its doors deliberately obscured by large banners hanging from its windows. Eliza helped Jemima in, and then asked the coachman if he was taking them to Mr Wilkes's house. He didn't reply, however, and Eliza climbed in after her and spent the journey holding on tightly to Jemima's hands, for the girl was seemingly scared out of all speech.

After driving for fifteen minutes there came a 'Whoa!' from the coachman as he reined in the horses and, as the coach came to a standstill, Eliza peered out. She had no idea where they were, for it was pitch black and there wasn't even a link-boy around to illuminate the scene. Her heart began to pound, for she feared they were about to be kidnapped. She'd heard that there were lawless parts of London ruled entirely by the underworld, where girls were taken away for years at a time and used for the pleasure of rich madmen. Was *this* what William Wilkes intended for them?

A torch appeared by the carriage window but it was impossible to see who was carrying it. As the door was opened Eliza and Jemima clung together, with Jemima making little mewing noises of distress. These only stopped when they heard William Wilkes's voice, its tone rather bored, say, 'Come, my dear. Are you prepared?'

The carriage steps were lowered and, after some moments spent composing herself, Jemima was helped down. Eliza, noticing that William had a small group of friends standing in the darkness behind him, followed nervously, wondering who they were. She saw Monmouth, the king's good-looking son, then with a shudder noticed Henry Monteagle and the Earl of Rochester. The one she really sought wasn't there, and she didn't know whether to be pleased at this or not.

Eliza lowered her eyes and pulled the hood of her cloak further over her face, praying that Henry Monteagle wouldn't recognise her and that the ceremony would be quick so that she could get away. She'd attended weddings in Stoke Courcey where the fiddler had played merry tunes as the bride and groom arrived and the guests called their good wishes, but here there was no fiddler and Wilkes's friends didn't seem inclined to call anything at all, merely stood around talking amongst themselves.

Eliza couldn't think where they were. They'd not come to Wilkes's house, that much was certain, for she knew he lodged at a fine dwelling at the river end of Whitehall, and *this* was a dank and shabby area, with a laystall of filth to one side of the street and a pile of rotting market garbage on the other. There was no church visible either, so it didn't seem as if the wedding would be a church one.

'Where are we?' she asked the nearest youth, for Jemima was all of a dither and didn't seem about to ask anyone anything.

'Fleet,' he answered. 'We're outside Fleet Prison.'

'No!' Eliza cried in alarm.

He laughed. 'Don't mind the name, mistress. The Fleet is the place for secret marriages, haven't you heard?'

Eliza shook her head.

'Oh, many a fine couple have been married in Fleet!'

'Many a fine couple – and now we two,' William said with a coarse laugh, and with Jemima clinging to him, he pushed open a stout oak door and the wedding party went in.

'But it was the strangest wedding I've ever heard of, for no one made merry or seemed happy or even *smiled*,' Eliza reported to Nell the following morning. 'And I felt desperately sorry for Jemima, because she looked for some signs of love from William, but none were forthcoming. And no one threw petals or took off her yellow garters and tossed them or had any sort of fun.'

'And what of the reverend gentleman? The one who took the service?' Nell asked.

'He didn't look like someone who was in holy orders, for I'm sure he was drunk. And his robes were smeared and nasty and he seemed to forget what he was saying halfway through.'

Nell nodded. ''Twas all a play, I'm sure of it.'

'What do you mean?'

'Well, if a girl won't suffer to be bedded without a wedding, or if she's someone with a lot of money on her head, often the man will take her off to Fleet Prison and undergo the ceremony there. 'Tis happening more and more.'

Eliza looked at her, worried. 'Isn't it a lawful marriage, then?'

'It all depends if the reverend gent is genuine.'

'But …' Eliza thought about it, confused. 'Has William done it to give his child a name?'

'I doubt that! He's done it to put her family off the scent. He'll send word that they're married in the hopes that they'll give up the hunt for them, then he can play the fop and live off her money for the rest of his life.'

Eliza sighed. 'Poor Jemima.'

The two were silent for a while. 'But did she not have any bride-feast afterwards?' Nell asked.

'Not a thing. They went straight off to a tavern to stay the night, but she'll be back later this morning, for he told her that it still wasn't safe for them to be seen together.'

Nell swore under her breath. 'I've a mind to tell the king of his behaviour,' she said, then added after a moment, 'but of course that won't do a bit of good, for the king is in every way just as wayward.' She paused thoughtfully. 'He's the *king*, though. He's allowed to do as he pleases.'

'Is there nothing we can do to help Jemima?' Eliza asked.

Nell shook her head. 'Only give her a bride-feast when she returns,' and she sent to a tavern for a pastry case to be baked and the dish filled with live singing birds. On Jemima's return to the theatre and the pie being cut, these fluttered out and flew all round the room, eventually disappearing out of the topmost windows. Jemima laughed and seemed charmed by this, but Eliza could see the sadness in her eyes and knew that she must be deeply unhappy.

Chapter Seventeen

As Nell took her final curtsy on the opening night of *Secret Love*, the theatre erupted. Flowers were thrown on to the stage, gallants jumped up and down on seats, apprentices roared, prostitutes waved their masks in the air and the whole building shook with bellowing cheers and cries of 'Bravo!'

Eliza, from her place with the other orange sellers in the pits, glanced up at the stage and tried to catch Nell's eye to smile at her, but Nell had eyes for only one place: the king's private box. And the king's private box was empty.

Later, in her dressing room, Nell angrily tore off the fancy costume she was wearing and kicked it to one side. She'd received Aphra Behn graciously enough, had tolerated a collection of ardent lords, ladies and playgoers anxious to offer their congratulations on her performance, but was now venting her fury on her costume and anyone around her.

As a dresser scuttled to retrieve the items before hastily leaving the room, Nell said peevishly, 'He didn't come! The king didn't come. I gave my all and he didn't see it!'

'Maybe ... some affairs of state,' Eliza said uncertainly, holding out an Indian-style loose garment for Nell to put on.

'Affairs of state!' Nell punched her arms into the baggy sleeves. 'They've never stopped him before. Affairs of the bedroom, maybe.' Nell's delicate face grew red with fury. 'I've heard the queen has a new lady-in-waiting! She's a Frenchwoman and *supposedly* most devastatingly beautiful.' She kicked off a shoe and sent it flying across the room. 'He's after laying her, I'm sure of it! He probably has one hand under her petticoats even as we speak!'

Eliza didn't know what to say to this. Indeed, she thought, Jemima had had the right idea for – after ascertaining that darling William wasn't present in the audience – she'd gone home. Eliza began to wish that she'd done the same.

There was a gentle tap on the door and Nell screamed at whoever it was to go away, then sat down in front of her make-up mirror and scowled at herself. Eliza, quietly brushing Nell's red leather shoes, didn't hear any retreating footsteps so looked out of the door a moment later to see the little black-skinned messenger boy in the corridor. He carried a cushion on which rested a letter.

'I've a message for Nelly Gwyn,' he said in a timid voice. 'But someone shouted at me to go away and now I don't know what to do.'

Eliza opened the door wider. 'It's all right,' she reassured the child. 'You can give it to Nelly yourself. She won't shout at you.'

He tiptoed in and Nell, seeing him and seeing, also, the king's seal on the back of the folded parchment, let out a scream of joy. She snatched up the letter.

'Quickly,' she said, thrusting it at Eliza. 'Read it and

tell me what he says!'

Eliza dutifully read out:

My dear Nelly,

Our compliments on the beauty and success that we are certain you brought to the role of Sophia today.

We, being overrun with foreign ambassadors, must provide them with entertainment, therefore the queen is holding a musical event this evening and we would be glad of your presence from nine o'clock.

Your Charles

Nell let out another scream and the child scurried for the door holding on to his turban.

'Tell His Majesty we'll be there!' Nell shouted after him.

Eliza gasped with excitement. '*We?*' she asked.

'Of course *we*,' Nell said. 'If the king's wife has twelve ladies-in-waiting, the king's whore must be allowed at least one!'

'But do you think the velvet, or the satin?' Nell asked, holding first one then the other gown in front of her.

Eliza considered the matter carefully. The burgundy velvet gown was stately, grand and elegant, having a low neckline encircled by pearls which continued down to form a sharp V just below the waist. The skirt of the gown was full and swept out at the back in a train, showing an underskirt of pearl-white satin. By contrast, the sapphire-blue satin was more informal, had its bodice embroidered with red roses and its full skirt ruched up about the hem to show a crimson underskirt.

'I think ... the velvet,' Eliza said at last. 'And then I can do your hair in pearls and white ribbons to match.'

'Excellent!' Nell said. 'And you must wear the other gown.'

'Indeed I could not!' Eliza said, overwhelmed by such an idea.

'No. I insist,' Nell said. 'It mustn't be thought that the king's mistress can't afford to dress her companion decently.'

It took several hours to get prepared for the occasion, for Nell was insistent that every part of her that was on show should be as perfect as possible. Eliza thus had to run to the shops three times: once to the apothecary's for a muslin cloth impregnated with a lotion which made the complexion clearer and whiter, next for a dressing for the hair to make the ringlets immovable, and finally for the latest innovation from France: a small brush to cleanse and polish the teeth.

Both girls being ready at last, they set off in Nell's shiny pink coach for the short ride to Whitehall Palace. Their progress through the streets was unimpeded, for the usual traffic jam of hackney carriages, sedans and horses had cleared from around the theatre. Eliza was rather sorry about this, for, resplendent in Nell's gown, she would have loved them to have drawn the eyes and curiosity of the passing crowds.

'But tell me,' she asked Nell nervously, for she was anxious about how they would be received at

Whitehall, 'does the queen really know about you?'

Nell shrugged. 'Of course! She knows the king has women friends.'

'But a certain *sort* of woman friend?'

'Oh, yes. 'Tis expected of a king,' Nell said robustly. 'Imagine a king who didn't avail himself of whatever woman he wished! That wouldn't be considered at all kingly.' She thought for a moment. 'Although King James, of course, loved men. They called him good *Queen* James. Did you know that?'

Eliza, smiling, confessed that such tales had not spread to Somersetshire. 'But Queen Catherine really doesn't mind?' she persisted.

'If she does she keeps quiet about it. And indeed she cannot care overmuch, for Barbara Castlemaine is allowed to keep her own apartments at Whitehall with a nursery for all her royal bastards.' Nell paused and thought a little. 'But it must be a sadness for the poor lady queen that she can't have an heir, when Castlemaine drops them like kittens.'

The two girls were silent for a while, looking out of the carriage on to the darkened streets of London, then Nell said, 'And speaking of kittens, what of Jemima?'

Eliza shook her head and shrugged. 'There's nothing to say. I tried to talk of it again yesterday, asked if she had things laid by and her childbed linen prepared, but she changed the subject by saying that the summer had flown and autumn would soon be upon us. When it comes to her condition, I can't get any sense out of her at all.'

Nell tutted. 'I must try and speak to William,' she said, and then both girls forgot about Jemima because they were driving through the magnificent Holbein Gate and into the grounds of Whitehall Palace.

The carriage entered a grand square lit with flaming torches and drew up beside a flight of stone stairs leading up to large carved oak doors. These were open and allowed light from the myriad candles within to reflect off the pale silk walls and spill on to the shiny marble steps. Alighting from the carriage, Eliza stood for a moment looking around her. How she wished that she had some family to tell about this moment. Her mother – her real mother – would have been so proud to tell the neighbours that her daughter had been to Whitehall Palace and met the king and queen!

'This is just one of the squares within the palace,' Nell said. 'There are – oh, I don't know how many others, for the buildings stretch down Whitehall and in all there is said to be over two thousand rooms.' She spun round, pointing in all directions. 'Over there are the queen's apartments, and that is the banqueting hall, and there's the privy garden and that's the gallery and the chapel and the great hall ...' She paused for breath and wrinkled her nose. 'Pooh! And *those* are Barbara Castlemaine's private apartments. They say she has forty rooms of her own!'

Eliza gazed about her, entranced, trying to take it all in.

'*Mesdames!*' cried the flunkey on the door. 'Please to come through where the entertainment awaits!'

He spoke in a heavy French accent and Nell smirked at him as they passed. 'He's no more French than you or me,' she said, 'for I swear I've seen him selling chicken livers down Smithfield market.'

Another manservant began to lead them along a

seemingly endless corridor. 'I've never been in this part before,' Nell confessed to Eliza in a whisper. She assumed an aristocratic accent. ''Tis verry faine, eh, what?'

Eliza giggled, but was too consumed with awe and admiration to speak. The carpet – well, she'd been in a house with a carpet before, but this one was thick and soft, like walking on grass. The walls were covered in paintings and there were little tables holding small statues, shiny bowls, a huge shell, a clock or a carved head. Each of these tables was illuminated by a flaming torch on the wall above and Eliza longed to stop and examine the treasures more fully, but the manservant was proceeding at a good pace and Nell was keeping close behind him, so she had no option but to follow them both.

They were led up a sweeping staircase, along another corridor and finally joined a large group of people in an antechamber.

Eliza, nervously looking at what the other females were wearing, was thankful that Nell had lent her the sapphire gown, for everyone was most exquisitely dressed in satins and silks and sarsenets and her own best dress would have looked shabby and old-fashioned in comparison. The young men, too, looked very fine, dressed in the latest French fashion of gaily coloured silk shirts under tight doublets and ballooning breeches festooned with ribbons.

'Oh!' The exclamation escaped Eliza's lips before she could stop it, for the youth whose breeches she'd been studying so intently had turned and she found herself looking straight into the eyes of Valentine Howard. He gave her a distinct wink – which, to her vexation, made her blush – and then the double doors opened and the assembled company went through into the queen's music room.

Eliza's first impression was of a dazzle of light, for candles in glass holders stood on every surface and a vast chandelier hung from the ceiling, illuminating the white flowers massed in silver containers. Colourful tapestries hung from the walls, and the floor held a deep carpet patterned all over with blue and white flowers. The whole effect was very fresh and pretty, making Eliza gasp with pleasure.

The company already in the room had just come from the dining hall, and had evidently wined and dined most agreeably. As everyone swarmed about, the king and queen took their places on a little dais at the top of the room, sitting on grand chairs with a canopy over them. Around their feet were four or five baskets each containing at least two small brown and white spaniels. The rest of the guests arrayed themselves either close to the royal couple or further off, according to their social standing.

'That man there is Doctor Deane, the royal astrologer,' Nell said, nodding in the direction of a dusty-looking middle-aged man in the garb of an Oxford scholar. 'The king does nothing without consulting him. And *those* are the ladies-in-waiting,' she continued, seeing that Eliza was staring at the eight or so girls who were smoothing the queen's dress, passing her a fan or bending to whisper in her ear. 'What do you think of them?'

'They are all very pretty,' Eliza said, fascinated by their butterfly-like fluttering around the queen.

'The king thinks so too and he can't keep his hands

off them. Although I can't see the new French one there,' Nell muttered. She sniffed. 'If I were queen I'd have the greasiest old hags from Dog and Bitch Lane for *my* ladies – certainly not beauties for my husband to ogle.'

'But who is the tall and haughty woman?' Eliza asked suddenly, noticing a woman standing apart from the others.

'Ah,' Nell said. '*That* is Barbara Castlemaine.'

Eliza's eyes lit up with interest as she stared at the woman standing there resplendent in red satin, her rich auburn hair tumbling about her shoulders and her large, dark eyes taking in the scene. She appeared arrogant and aloof, Eliza decided, yet somehow decadent at the same time. She could quite see how any man might be in thrall to her.

''Tis rumoured that she's had half the male servants in the palace,' Nell hissed. 'If there's one can match the king in lust, it's her.'

'I thought you said he was tiring of her?'

Nell shrugged. 'When he starts looking elsewhere, she gets herself with child. He likes women who're having his children.' She looked up at Eliza questioningly. 'But are the pearls and ribbons in my hair still in place? Do I look as fine as she does?'

Eliza assured her that she did indeed, for although Nell lacked Barbara's handsome demeanour she had a pretty vivacity which few could match.

'We'll be presented to the queen soon,' Nell said. 'You must tell me what you think of *her*.'

Queen Catherine, Eliza noted on getting closer to the woman, was not really the king's equal in either presence or appearance. She was short and rather plain, with ears that stuck out slightly and an elaborate hairpiece that seemed to swamp her. She was also French and spoke with a heavy accent that was difficult to understand, so Eliza was thankful that she didn't get asked anything when she was presented, just received a smile and a nod. She seemed, Eliza concluded, dull but quite pleasant. Indeed she felt sorry for the woman; imagine having a husband who laid with anyone he had a mind to.

A group of musicians was playing on a raised stage at the far end of the room and people perambulated gently up and down, joining one group or another and telling jokes, whispering gossip, laughing extravagantly and looking at each other critically to judge how finely dressed they were. Out of the corner of her eye Eliza was very aware of the presence of Valentine Howard. She saw him kissing the hand of one of the ladies-in-waiting, flirting with Barbara Castlemaine, bowing and engaging in a brief conversation with an older man, throwing one arm around the ghastly Henry Monteagle as they shared a joke. If only he was an ordinary person and not a sir, she thought; if only he was a manservant or a merchant. Or failing that, if only *she* weren't quite so ordinary. She glanced at the king again. *Might* it be possible that he and her mother had been lovers?

She thought of her mother: her sweet, homely, rounded mother, and then tried to imagine her with the sophisticated, aristocratic and educated Charles. She inwardly shook her head. No, as wonderful as it would be, it was just not possible ...

A soloist was singing from an opera on the stage when Nell suddenly appeared and gripped Eliza's arm.

'Look, there she is!' she said.

'Who?' Eliza asked.

'The new lady-in-waiting – Louise de ... de something or other I can't pronounce.' Nell lifted her nose in the air. 'Just look! Now, why would the king want *her*?'

Eliza looked. The girl was maybe a year or two older than herself, with fluffy blonde hair which stood out in a halo around her head. She wore white muslin and was rather plump. Eliza thought she was extremely pretty, but wasn't tactless enough to say so to Nell.

'She is disgustingly upper class *and* a French Catholic,' Nell said, 'so the people won't like her.' She giggled a little. 'She also has a squint in her eye.'

'*Has* she?' Eliza asked. 'How do you know?'

'One of my spies told me.' Nell looked at Eliza and went cross-eyed, making her laugh. 'The king calls her Chubbs, but I shall call her Squintabella.'

Towards the end of the evening, when the queen and some of her ladies-in-waiting had retired, the king called for 'his Nelly' to dance. She demurred at first, saying that she was too grandly dressed and that her hair would tumble down and make her look a fright, but the king insisted – and of course Eliza knew that Nell relished the idea of performing in front of Barbara Castlemaine and Louise.

The musicians struck up a jig and Nell began to dance lightly, daintily, lifting her gown, pointing her feet and hardly moving from the one spot, and Eliza was reminded of the first time she'd seen her dance in Old Ma Gwyn's downstairs room. How different the circumstances were now ...

Nell danced until she was breathless, then twirled around for a final time and gave a low, deep curtsy to the king, making him and the audience break into spontaneous clapping and cheering.

Following Nell's performance, Eliza was rather hoping that the king might notice her and ask her to sing, but he didn't. Instead, wishing the company a good night, he got up and went out, surrounded by a sea of little dogs.

People began to disperse, carriages were sent for, last-minute assignations were made. Just as Eliza and Nell were about to leave the room, Chiffinch appeared.

'Madam,' he said to Nell in a low voice, 'the king requests your company in his chamber tonight.'

Nell's eyes gleamed and she raised her eyebrows at Eliza. 'You must take the carriage home on your own, Eliza, and then send it back to me here after,' she whispered.

Eliza thanked her excitedly. To travel on her own in the carriage! That almost made up for not being asked to sing.

As Nell followed Chiffinch out of the room, Eliza was disconcerted to be approached by Valentine Howard, who asked if she required transport home. Their paths hadn't crossed all evening and she was about to reply graciously that she didn't, thank-you-kindly, when Henry Monteagle lurched towards them.

He looked at Eliza disparagingly. 'I do believe that's one of the orange girls!' he said. 'Good God, Val, don't you care who you lay with? 'Tis certain she'll have the pox.'

Valentine Howard glanced at his friend, looking as if he was about to say something in reply, but Eliza gave him no chance. Sweeping by, she inclined the merest nod in his direction and gave him an aloof, 'Goodnight to you, sires.'

A swell of laughter broke out in her wake. 'Snubbed by an orange girl, eh, Val?' Henry Monteagle jeered. 'She ought to pay for that.'

But Eliza didn't wait to hear if there was any response.

Chapter Eighteen

As they sat together in the tiring room of the theatre, Eliza glanced at Jemima's slim white hands: dainty hands which had never washed a dish, peeled a vegetable or cleared ashes from a fire. A narrow gold band on the left hand said that she was a married woman but, Eliza thought, for the amount of times she had seen William Wilkes since the marriage ceremony, she might just as well have not been.

Eliza looked around them. ''Tis dreadful tedious without Nell,' she said, sighing, and Jemima nodded and added a sigh of her own.

The theatre was quiet apart from cleaners and a handful of women seamstresses working in the costume department, for there was no play running at present. *Secret Love* had been a week-long success, but now most of the theatre company had gone off to provide entertainment for the king and his court whilst they took the waters in Tunbridge Wells. The queen, apparently, had been behind this excursion, for the waters were said to be beneficial in the conceiving of a child.

'Shall we take a stroll?' Eliza asked, looking now at Jemima's pale, drawn face. 'I am sure some air would do you good.'

Jemima's hand went to her stomach, embracing the swelling there.

'Do you feel … all right?' Eliza asked tentatively.

The hand was quickly removed. 'Of course!' Jemima said with a semblance of brightness. 'I'm perfectly well.'

'Then shall we walk?'

'But where?'

Eliza shrugged. 'To see the wild animals in the Tower? Or to see the lunatics at Bedlam?'

Jemima shuddered.

'Shall we shop, then?' she asked, and then, remembering that she only had a few coins for food and they had to last until Nell came back, added, 'Or at least look in the windows? Shall we go to the Bridge and see the new shops?'

Jemima shook her head. ''Tis too far off. I don't wish to walk that far and I have no money for a sedan.'

'Then let's go to Covent Garden and see the shows. There's Punch and Judy and some clowns and a performing bear – and I did hear there's a curious tin dog that can bark at you.'

Jemima nodded and, managing a smile, went to get her cloak. Eliza glanced at her as she moved across the room: her bulge had dropped considerably now, which meant, Eliza knew, that the child's head must have engaged. Was Jemima aware that the birth was quite close? And where was darling William, anyway? Had he gone to Tunbridge Wells with the rest of the court? Suppose she had to send for him in an emergency – how would anyone find him?

'Has Mrs Trott spoken to you about … about

anything?' Eliza asked when they were walking through Covent Garden, for Nell, before she'd gone away, had asked the seamstress with whom Jemima lodged to speak to her in the hopes that Jemima might own her condition.

Jemima shook her head, seeming to be interested in some act they were passing with clowns and a bear on a rope.

'Are you sure?' Eliza persisted.

'Indeed I am.' Jemima pursed her lips. 'I don't like Mrs Trott,' she said. 'She's always asking questions and is too interested in one's business.'

'She's only trying to help,' Eliza began, but Jemima had moved off again and now stood before a wooden stall and was reading of a number of troublesome ailments which a quack's medicines purported to cure.

She stood looking at these for some time, and then took Eliza's arm and, leading her a short distance away, spoke to her in a low voice. 'It says ... says that there is an elixir which cures female troubles and brings down a woman's monthly courses,' she said, her face flushed with embarrassment.

Eliza nodded, puzzled as to what the other girl was getting at.

'Do you think you could purchase some of it for me?'

'To ... to bring down your courses?' Eliza asked.

Jemima gave a slight nod.

Eliza stared at her, startled. 'But Jemima, this is for ... where ...' She paused and started again. 'This is to be used where your courses are merely late, when you haven't seen them for a month or two. Not ... not ...' She motioned to Jemima's belly with her hand. 'Not when you are so far with child.'

'Don't say that!' Jemima said, and she gave a little cry of distress and began walking away, her cheeks pink.

They continued through Covent Garden and down past the maypole in the Strand in silence, with Eliza now seriously worried at Jemima's inability to comprehend what was happening to her. Could she really not know she was about to have a child?

Further down the Strand, towards Whitehall, were the houses of several notable astrologers, and on these were displayed posters and hangings depicting signs of the zodiac, pentangles and various other magical symbols. The largest of these houses bore a bill saying that the practitioner was the seventh son of a seventh son and could tell the questor which part of the country was best suited for him to live in, if he or she would be happily married or whether their spouse was unfaithful.

Eliza's attention was caught by a sign at another door saying that Doctor Cornelius, the necromancer within, could raise the wind, call the spirits down and cause the face of one who was missing to be seen in a glass sphere.

'Cause the face of one who is missing to be seen in a glass sphere ...' she repeated to Jemima. 'Do you think these things are true? Can magicians really do these things?'

Jemima shrugged that she didn't know.

Just imagine, Eliza pondered, if the face of her real father could be seen. If she could know who he was, how happy she'd be! Maybe it was also possible that such a powerful necromancer would be able to divine his name ...

As she read the words over, a serving woman came out of the house and curtsied to the two girls.

'Good day, ladies,' she said. 'Do you seek an interview with Doctor Cornelius?'

Eliza took a step backwards, stammering that she didn't know.

'He's my master and is both wise and skilled,' said the woman. She lowered her voice. 'He has divined many curious things by looking in his glass.' Eliza didn't speak and she continued, 'He can find out if your lover is faithful, ladies, or tell you the best way to seek riches, or divine the meaning of dreams.'

Eliza bit her lip. 'It says ... says that he can see someone's face in a glass sphere.'

'Oh, he's most skilled at that!' the woman cried. 'He can show you the face of your true love, or that of a friend far away, and tell you if they're dead or alive. Doctor Cornelius is a true seer!' She glanced at Jemima. 'He can tell you of the sex of your forthcoming child.'

Jemima gave a little cry and pulled her cloak around her.

'I don't have much money,' Eliza said, feeling the few coins in her pocket.

'You can give what you have now, and pay the rest when what the doctor predicts has come true,' the woman said. 'That's how sure he is of his skills!'

As Eliza, yearning to go inside, hesitated, Jemima touched her lightly on the arm. 'I'm going to walk back now,' she said, 'but you stay if you wish and see the magician.'

The woman nodded. 'Speak to him now!' she said,

taking Eliza's arm. 'Just walk up the stairs and take a seat outside his consulting room.'

Eliza was won over. 'Will you be all right walking back on your own?' she asked Jemima.

'Of course.' She gave Eliza a reproachful look. 'I am perfectly well, you know.'

She went off and Eliza, forgetting for the moment about Jemima and nervous and excited on her own account, climbed the stairs to Doctor Cornelius's consulting room.

There was a young woman already waiting on a bench at the top of the stairs and she smiled at Eliza. 'It won't be long to wait,' she said. 'I'm next, but I've just one question and shall be in and out again in a moment.'

Eliza sat down. 'You've been here before?'

'Oh yes!' The girl nodded vigorously. 'If ever I'm in doubt about anything I always come to Doctor Cornelius.'

'And he serves you well?' Eliza asked, glancing at the girl's gown and shoes as she spoke and guessing her to be of the middling sort.

'He's most skilled!' the girl said earnestly. 'I hardly need to ask a question before he has divined the answer.'

'And – if you will excuse my being curious – what sort of things have you asked him?'

'Oh, if I should choose one beau over another, or if I should obey my father as to certain things or how soon I should recover from an illness.'

'And have you ever asked him to look in his glass to see the face and form of someone?'

'I have!' the girl said. 'I had a sweetheart who was a

sailor, and as I hadn't heard from him for months, I thought him dead. I had Doctor Cornelius look into his glass and he saw him, clear as anything, on an island in the South Seas!'

Eliza gasped.

''Tis true! And six months later he was home again. Though our romance didn't last long, for he'd met a native woman there and later went back to her.'

'Oh, I'm sorry,' Eliza said.

''Twas no matter!' the girl said. 'I soon forgot him and found a better. But tell me, are you here to see your sweetheart in the glass?'

Eliza shook her head. 'No. I hope to have news of my father.'

'Why is that, then?'

'Because the man I thought was my father is not,' Eliza said somewhat sadly. 'And now I long to know who my real father is.'

'Can't you ask your mother?'

Eliza shook her head. 'She's been dead this long while. And I've written to my aunt to ask, but she hasn't replied.'

'Well, it's a pity if you have no father,' the girl said, 'for they're a great asset to a girl, especially if they're wealthy and can give her a large marriage settlement.'

'I don't mind so much about the settlement,' Eliza said, 'I just want to know who he is.'

'Come in!' a strong voice called from behind a curtained door, and the woman got up. 'I really won't be long,' she said, smiling at Eliza.

She reappeared just a few moments after. 'I hope you find what you seek,' she said before clattering down the stairs.

Eliza was summoned a moment later and nervously opened the door to see an elderly man with grey, frizzled hair sitting at a small card table. There were some strange objects in front of him: half a large rock containing purple crystals within, a dried lizard-like creature, some ancient papers bearing magical symbols, a skull and a bundle of herbs tied with red ribbon. Eliza, following a gesture from him, sat down in the chair opposite and surveyed all these things nervously, then got out the three coins from her pocket and placed them on the table.

'I'm afraid this is all the money I have at present.'

Doctor Cornelius didn't reply to this, just studied her face carefully for some time. After withstanding this scrutiny for several moments and nervously seeking to break the silence she blurted out, 'My name is Eliza and –'

The doctor raised his hand. 'I know this,' he said. 'I am all-seeing.'

Eliza lapsed into an embarrassed silence, and another few moments passed before the doctor said in a ponderous voice, 'Your name is Eliza and you seek your father.'

Eliza felt a shiver of excitement and fear run through her. 'That's right.'

'You seek your father to determine who he is,' he continued and, on Eliza nodding agreement to this, turned and took a large glass globe from the shelf behind him. 'I will now command his image to appear.'

Placing the globe on the table, he hunched over and peered into it. Eliza moved to the edge of her seat, her body taut, straining to see whatever *he* was going to see.

'I see your mother here in the glass,' he said after a moment. 'She has you, a babe wrapped in a shawl, with her.'

Eliza couldn't speak for a moment because of the lump in her throat. 'Is it really my mother?' she asked. 'Is she small and plump?'

Doctor Cornelius nodded. 'Although I cannot see her features clearly because she wears a shroud and has a veil across her face. She's not of this world.'

'No, she isn't,' Eliza confirmed sadly.

'And the man you once thought was your father is not!' He held up his hand again to prevent Eliza speaking, and another moment went by. 'I now see your real father,' he said. 'He is come to stand behind your mother.'

'Oh!' Eliza's eyes filled with sudden tears. 'Who is he? What does he look like? Is he dead too?'

The doctor lifted a candle over the globe. 'He doesn't wear a shroud, so he is still in this world,' he intoned. 'He's tall and black-haired. He speaks his name. It is …'

He paused again for a long, long moment, and Eliza became quite tense with anxiety and apprehension, fearing that she might faint or scream or gibber like a madwoman if the strain went on for much longer.

'His name …' he said, then, 'but ah … he's disappeared! Clouds have crossed his image and he's gone.'

Eliza gave a sob of disappointment. 'But where's he gone? Won't he come back?'

Doctor Cornelius shook his head with an air of finality. 'Not this day. But if you wish, come tomorrow and I'll seek him again.' He lifted the globe and placed it back on the shelf. 'It's most fatiguing seeking images in a glass,' he said, glancing at the three coins Eliza had placed on the table. '*Most* fatiguing.'

'I'll try and get more money,' Eliza said immediately. 'I'll get more and return another day.'

The doctor nodded sagely. 'A gold coin is good,' he said, 'for the brightness of it attracts the spirits.'

'Then that's what I'll bring!' Eliza said, promising herself that – even though a gold coin might be as hard to come by as a unicorn's horn – she'd obtain one and discover her father's name.

My father! Eliza thought all the way home. My father, there in the glass. He was *seen*. I can find out his name. She smiled to herself: it didn't appear that he was the king, then, for Doctor Cornelius would surely have recognised him straight away.

But what should I do when I know his name, she wondered. Go to him and declare myself, send a letter telling him I am my mother's daughter, or get someone to speak to him on my behalf? What would be best? And how will I know where in the country to find him?

Pondering on these things, she arrived in Lewkenor's Lane to find a letter waiting for her and, eagerly turning it over, immediately recognised her uncle's seal on the back of the folded paper.

At *last*, she thought ... but how strange that the reply from her aunt had come on the very day that she'd consulted Doctor Cornelius. There was some link here, surely; some miraculous connection between the two incidents.

Anxiously she broke the seal, unfolded the paper and read the following:

My dear child,

I am sorry to be the bearer of bad news, and indeed I've pondered for some time as to whether it would do good for you to know that which I am about to impart.

Finally, though, I decided that you should know the truth so that you can fully understand that you have no claim to either your father's estate, nor your mother's. To this end I must tell you that – as you have discovered – you are not your father Jacob's child. But neither are you your mother's.

Eliza stopped reading at this point and, not understanding what her aunt could possibly mean, went back to the beginning of the letter and started again. Finally, still bewildered, she read on.

I understand little of the matter myself, and only became aware of it on your mother's deathbed, when my dear sister confessed to me that Jacob wasn't your father, nor had she given birth to you. I questioned her words, thinking she was delirious and asking, to humour her, if you were a faerie child, but she repeated the above assertion, telling me that she didn't wish to die without telling the truth. She lapsed into unconsciousness shortly after this and didn't speak another lucid word.

Tragically, she died the following day, and with all the funeral preparations to be attended to, I never queried things nor thought it would be useful to raise the question of your provenance. By my observation of your looks, colouring and demeanour, however, so different from that of your brothers, I came to the conclusion that my sister was speaking the truth. I did try once to ask Jacob about the matter but found him completely uncommunicative on the subject, and since his remarriage have not sought to ask further, nor hardly had contact with him.

My prayers go with you and I sincerely hope that you may overcome this sad accident of birth, find the strength to put it behind you and make your own way in the world. I can, however, throw no more light upon this subject.
Thomasina Walker

Eliza read this letter through twice more, then ran upstairs and threw herself on to the bed in despair. She belonged to no one! She had neither father nor mother, brothers nor sisters, but had probably been left, unwanted, on a doorstep or in a church porch – a bastard child, for sure. She had no family, no status, no birthright, no name. She was no one!

With this knowledge came a sudden awareness of the truth about what Doctor Cornelius had said. How could she have been so witless as to just sit there believing everything he'd told her? Of course he hadn't seen any figures in the glass – nor had he imparted anything which she herself hadn't already told that so-friendly woman waiting outside his door.

The whole thing had been a charade designed to get money from her. Hadn't she lived in London long enough to see through something like that? What a booby fool she'd been!

Chapter Nineteen

Another week passed. News came back to the theatre that the king and certain of his entourage had moved on to Newmarket to attend the races, and as Nell didn't return to London, Eliza presumed she'd gone with them.

She kept herself busy as best she could: walking with Jemima or practising her writing, darning her stockings, washing her linen, cleaning. Sometimes she'd go to the theatre and find herself small jobs to do, just to keep occupied. She was scared that if she didn't fill every moment then one day she'd find herself walking into the City again, seeking out the man she'd always thought of as her father and demanding to know where she'd come from. Reflecting on this, however, she realised that each time she discovered something about her background, the worse it got: it might have been better to have left things as they'd appeared to be when she'd left home. At least she'd had a name and a father then, and brothers and half-sisters. At least she *thought* she'd known who her mother was. Now she had no one.

Coming back from the theatre one evening she was dismayed to find the door of her room padlocked and barred across with four sturdy planks of wood. The landlord, she knew, lived at the other end of the street in his own large house, and she went straight there to find out what had happened.

Angrily he told her that he'd done this because Nell had omitted to pay her rent.

'I've given her weeks and weeks of credit and I've sent her bills,' he said. 'Now she's out of the place – and you are, too.'

'But Mistress Gwyn can't read bills,' Eliza said, staring at the fellow – a grubby, niggardly-looking man – with dislike. 'I'm sure if she knew about it she'd have paid you.'

'She doesn't have to read to know she ain't paid the rent for six months!'

'She's away at the moment with someone very important –'

'I don't care if she's away with the king himself!' the fellow said, his words making Eliza start and almost smile. 'I don't run a poor house. I don't house folk for nothing!'

'She'll be back soon! Next week for sure. But in the meantime,' Eliza put on her most appealing look, 'I've nowhere to go.'

'That's your look-out!' With that, he went to shut the door.

Eliza pushed at it desperately. 'I'll see you get double the rent!'

'I'll see you in the debtors' prison!' came the reply.

Eliza went back to examine her door again and found that the padlock was weighty and the planks had been hammered home with heavy nails. Even if she'd had the right tools she'd never have had the strength to prise them out.

Despairing, she sank to the floor in the hall. She couldn't lodge with Jemima, for Mrs Trott's house was tiny and Jemima already shared a bed with young Matilda Trott, and neither could she sleep overnight at the theatre, for there were nightwatchmen who patrolled it. She had no money – absolutely none at all – so couldn't take even the meanest room in an inn. She was hungry, too. Inside Nell's room was milk, bread, cheese and some hard sausage, but she had no hopes of getting to these. Nor could she reach her best gown or any of her other trinkets, which might be pawned in order to raise a little money.

How fragile her existence was, she realised. How easily she might find herself in the gutter. Even her friendship with Nell was based on her being able to arrange hair – what sort of foundation was that for someone's life? As if she'd not suffered hardships enough, she thought: no family, no real friends, no money – and now no home …

She gave way to a few tears, then forced herself to dry her face on her petticoat and go through everyone she knew in London from whom she might borrow money. After some considerable thought, however, the only name which came to mind was Old Ma Gwyn's. But what would the old trugmouldy expect her to do in return?

Eliza sat there pondering the matter for some time, then quickly resolved that she'd go over to Coal Yard Alley at once, before she ended up having to sleep in a shop doorway. Ma Gwyn surely couldn't turn her away – and if she expected her to do something disagreeable in return for her accommodation, then she'd just walk out.

Hurrying along Henrietta Street, Eliza happened to glance over to the royal bootmaker's shop and noticed that, as before, a small crowd was standing outside. Crossing over, she peered through the window and wasn't too surprised to see Claude Duval, dressed in an elegant dove-grey velvet riding coat, deep in conversation with the shopkeeper.

Immediately it came to her. Of course! He'd lend her some money. He knew Nell very well, and Nell would ensure that he was recompensed as soon as she returned.

Boldly Eliza stepped past the gaggle of onlookers and into the shop, where she was charmed to be bowed over and have her hand kissed by Monsieur Duval, there to collect the boots he'd ordered the month before. After he'd settled matters with the shopkeeper, Eliza asked if they might have a word in private before going outside.

'For I've a particular favour to ask of you,' she added.

'Of course,' Claude Duval replied gravely. 'Any matter which distresses a lady – and I see by your so-beautiful green eyes that you are troubled – distresses me.'

Eliza, blushing at his words, told him how Nell had gone away with the king but had forgotten to pay her rent beforehand.

'Ah – of course, I remember now,' he said. 'You are the friend of Mistress Nelly. I met you in this very shop.'

Eliza nodded. 'That's right. And, you see, Nell's landlord has boarded up the room and I've no way of getting my food and clothing – and nowhere to sleep.'

Claude Duval smiled playfully. 'So you wish to sleep with me?'

'Oh no!' Eliza cried, embarrassed. 'Not that!'

'Would that be so bad?'

'I assure you, sire, I didn't mean –'

He smiled. 'I'm teasing you, but now I take pity on your blushes and your maidenly ways ... you want to borrow some money, is that it?'

Eliza nodded. 'Please. Just until Nell returns.'

He looked at her consideringly for a moment, then said, 'I'm not a moneylender. I don't believe in lending or borrowing money.'

Eliza bit her lip. She hadn't thought that he would actually refuse, or she wouldn't have dared ask in the first place.

'I see,' she said, swallowing hard. It was back to Old Ma Gwyn, then.

'I will *give* you some money. But you will have to do something to earn it.'

Eliza looked up at him, aware of the crowd in the doorway nudging and murmuring to each other as they stared at the tall highwayman.

'What ... what would I have to do?'

'Carry out a small job with me.'

'A *robbery*?' Eliza gasped.

He shook his head. 'Not exactly a robbery. Look, I'll buy you something to eat in a coffee house – we can call it an advance of your fee – and explain.'

And to Eliza's intense pleasure he bowed, offered her his arm and they walked out of the shop together, the gaggle outside the shop melting away before them.

Eliza had never been into a coffee house before and

found it fascinating: the smoky air, the rich, enticing smell of the roasting beans, the glint of the brass on the coffee-making equipment, the velvet banquettes and the proliferation of interesting pamphlets and even more interesting clientele.

The men within – they were all men, Eliza noticed – glanced up as the couple arrived and then went back to their gossip and their intrigues. Claude Duval ordered two dishes of coffee and Eliza gingerly began to sip from hers. It was very hot, strong and rather bitter and she wasn't sure that she liked it, but she persisted with it, thinking it all part of the experience. Food was ordered – a thick grouse soup, followed by crimped cod and oyster sauce – and whilst they were eating, Claude Duval explained that he'd been involved in a card game the previous evening and lost a deal of money.

'Four hundred and twenty guineas, to be precise,' he concluded.

Eliza's eyes and mouth both opened in shock. 'Four hundred ...' she gasped.

Duval smiled. 'This is nothing,' he said. 'I've lost one thousand guineas and my horse at a game before now. I didn't have my wits about me last night, however – mostly because I was constantly plied with strong spirits – and I was finally hoodwinked by a cheating young rascal who used marked cards.'

'Who was it?' Eliza asked. 'Did you know him well?'

'Passing well,' Duval said. 'But I shall not tell you his name – that might be dangerous for you.' He smiled. 'Instead, as he is a sitting target, we shall call him the duck.'

Eliza nodded.

'I didn't find out about the marked cards until he'd gone. But now I want my money back.'

'So ... so will you hold him up on the road?' she asked, rather thrilled at the idea.

'Possibly. But it's like this: the carriages of the aristo-ducks don't always stop at pistol point now, instead they drive straight on in the hopes that the highwayman won't fire indiscriminately.' He shrugged. 'Either that or they have an armed outrider with them.'

Eliza nodded, nervously wondering what he was going to ask of her.

'But,' he continued, 'if a beautiful young lady was standing crying at the side of the road, *then* a carriage would stop.'

'Oh,' said Eliza.

'And that, my dear, is where you come in ...'

At nine o'clock, shaking with cold and nerves, Eliza stood on one of the turnpike highways out of London. To one side of the road, idly nibbling at the grass verge, was Master, Claude Duval's horse, a tall and powerful beast with heavy leather panniers but no marking or colours on its blanket. The highwayman had got intelligence from someone in 'the duck's' household that he was leaving London that evening to join the king and court in Newmarket and had also worked out, by learning at what time the man had ordered his carriage to be ready, at approximately what time he'd be passing this particular spot.

There was a flaming torch on a wall at the side of the road and Eliza stood just outside its light, being coached by Claude as to what she should do. Some adjustments were made to her appearance (a smear of mud on her face, a torn bodice and her cap dislodged) and she was ready.

'Now stand back from the light and wait until you hear my whistle,' Claude said. He lowered his black mask into place across his eyes and settled his hat on his head. 'I shall be further up the road on Master and won't make a sound until I recognise the duck's coat of arms on the side of his coach.'

Eliza nodded, shivering, hardly believing she was doing such a thing. To aid and abet a highwayman! He made it sound all so easy, but if she was caught she knew full well that she could be hanged. And a plea that she'd just been assisting a friend who'd been cheated wouldn't help at all.

She breathed deeply. It was just like acting, she told herself. Another acting job. Only, of course, much more dangerous.

'Remember, you just have to make his carriage halt, then you can go. Run off as fast as you can and I'll meet you back at the coffee house at ten o'clock.' Swiftly, Claude raised Eliza's hand to his lips. 'Here's to our success at netting the duck,' he said before melting into the shadows.

It was ten minutes later when Eliza heard a low whistle, like that of a night-jar, and just a few seconds after that a carriage trundled into view. It wasn't a large carriage, but one built for speed rather than comfort, and because of this Eliza was pleased to see that there was just a single driver in the front seat.

She ran out to where she could be seen and stood by the roadside with her arms wrapped around herself, bent over, crying.

'Help!' she cried as it drew near. 'Oh, help me, please!'

The driver glanced sideways at her, but didn't rein in the horses. As the carriage drew level she saw, though, that the carriage window was open slightly and its curtain only partially pulled across.

'Oh, please help a poor maiden!' she cried just at the opportune moment. 'I've been attacked!'

For a split second she didn't think it was going to work, but then she saw a movement within the carriage as it passed. A head appeared at the window and a youth shouted, 'Hold up there, driver! Whoa!'

The reins were jerked back and there was a neigh from the horses. The carriage skewed a little on the dusty road, then came to a halt. Before it had fully stopped Claude Duval came thundering up on Master and brandished his pistol through the open window.

'Your money, or your life,' he said curtly. 'I would like, if you please, to take exactly four hundred and twenty guineas from you.'

There came a series of oaths from within the carriage. 'Damn you, Duval!' a voice said. 'Damn your bones. It *is* you, I know it!'

Eliza heard these words in terror and agitation, then turned and began running as fast as she could through the trees and bushes at the side of the road. Reaching the City gates she slowed to a walk and tried to compose herself. Tucking her hair behind her ears she retied her cap, then made her way to the coffee house. She knew it would not have been seemly for her to have gone in on her own, so she stayed in the shadows outside, waiting for Claude Duval, her heart still thumping fit to burst.

Had she been seen? Had she been recognised? Closing her eyes, leaning against the wall, she tried to calm herself and force her heart to stop its pounding. How strange, how frightening, that she'd actually known the youth in the coach – for it had been none other than the king's son: James, the Duke of Monmouth.

Chapter Twenty

Eliza found herself in possession of twenty guineas, more than she'd ever had – more than she'd ever *seen* – in her life. After leaving Claude Duval, she was first of a mind to go to Lewkenor's Lane and settle with the landlord, but then, passing the Star, a large and notable tavern on the Strand, decided on a whim that she'd book herself in, for it was growing late and she thought Nell's landlord might not be willing to get his tools and reopen the room at such an hour.

Feeling very grand, for the Star was a tavern which attracted a fashionable trade, she went in and asked to take a room. 'A good-sized single room, mind, with clean linen, feather bed and some candles,' she requested of the innkeeper's wife, trying to sound as if she stayed in taverns every day of her life. Noticing that in the huge fireplace a hound was walking a treadwheel which turned a fine suckling pig on a spit, she also asked that some hot sliced pork be sent up. This didn't get eaten, however, for after taking a glass of wine and lying back on the bed, Eliza was filled with such a weary relief that all had gone well that she did no more than close her eyes and begin to drift towards sleep. Monmouth, she thought, surely couldn't have recognised her. She'd been well back from the light – and besides, he'd only seen her a couple of times before that, and always in a crowd.

The next morning she was still undecided about what to do. If she'd known that Nell was coming back to London soon, then a decision might have been easier, but there was every chance that the king and court might go on to York after Newmarket, or decide to pass some time in Windsor, and the idea of staying at the Star was a lot more appealing than being on her own in Nell's dingy room.

Putting off the decision for the moment, Eliza decided to go to Jemima's lodgings, see how she was faring and if she'd yet had word from William about their intended passage. She also badly wanted to confide in someone about her situation – about the fact that not only was her father *not* her father, but that her mother wasn't her mother either. It didn't seem likely that Jemima would be able to offer any advice on the subject, but Eliza felt an overwhelming need to speak about it.

Jemima was not at Mrs Trott's, however, so from here Eliza went to the theatre, thinking this the only other place she was likely to be. As expected, she found Jemima in the tiring room, staring listlessly at nothing, her capacious cloak swept both around her and the chair she was seated upon so that almost no part of her body could be seen.

'Are you well?' Eliza asked her.

Jemima nodded, rocking backwards and forwards aimlessly in her seat. 'I'm just waiting for something to happen. For William to come for me, or to hear that we have passage on a ship. I'm endlessly waiting,' she said bleakly.

'I'm sure it won't be long,' Eliza said, thinking the very opposite. 'For surely he must see that you're ... you have ...' Her voice faltered, then faded away, and she wished she hadn't started the sentence, for she knew Jemima would clam up if a certain subject was mentioned. 'I wonder how Nell fares in Newmarket?' she said instead. 'I wonder if the king has other mistresses there with him?'

'He has a *wife* there with him.'

'He has,' Eliza agreed. 'And that would be enough for some men.'

A moment went by without either of them speaking, and the only sound was Jemima's chair creaking as she rocked. Suddenly, though, she gave a strange, strangled cry and Eliza looked over to see her face screwed up with pain.

'What is it? What ails you?' she asked urgently.

Jemima shook her head, her face still contorted. 'It's ... nothing. A cramp.' She panted a little as she spoke. 'I hurried here this morning and twisted something ... something inside me.'

'But Jemima ...'

The girl turned her face away suddenly. 'I'm looking forward to the next production here,' she said, her voice high and strained. 'It's going to be another play by Wycherley, did you hear?'

Eliza shook her head. 'I didn't know that.' As she spoke she looked at Jemima anxiously, wondering if it was her time, trying to think of some ordinary subject on which to speak. 'Nell will be sure to take the lead in it, don't you think?'

'If she has enough time what with attending to the king,' Jemima said, and then gave another cry, louder than before, and bent over double in the chair.

'Jemima!' Eliza cried. As she ran to help her, Jemima slid sideways off the chair and fell to her knees. Reaching her and putting her arms around her Eliza asked urgently, 'How often are you getting these pains?'

Jemima shook her head.

'How often?' Eliza demanded.

There was no reply.

The spasm passed and, trembling all over, Jemima tried to hoist herself back on to the chair. She failed, ending up on the floor again.

'It's all right. It's nothing …' she said weakly.

'It *is* something,' Eliza said, determined that she wouldn't be put off. 'You're in labour with your child, Jemima.' She waited for this to sink in and added, 'I was present at my stepmother's birthings and I know the signs.'

'No! It's not that. It's –'

'Don't be so stubborn!' Eliza said, feeling very frightened – and cross enough with Jemima to defy her. 'You're about to have your child, and if we don't act quickly it's like to end up on the tiring room floor.'

As she spoke, she held Jemima under her arms and braced her gradually upwards until she regained the chair. Once seated, Jemima burst into frightened tears.

'Get William,' she said. 'Oh, please get William! He should be here with me.'

'William can do no good here,' Eliza said. 'This is women's work.'

'But he must be told!'

'He'll be told,' Eliza said briefly, casting her mind back to when her stepmother had last been in labour and trying to remember the different stages to be passed through. She'd hardly noticed these at the time, however, for Louise's birth had been attended, as was the custom, by a bevy of local women: gossips, neighbours and Lady Acland from the big house – as well as an experienced midwife. Eliza's duties had merely been to dab her stepmother's forehead with lavender water and make an endless supply of chicken broth to sustain her.

'Have you consulted anyone?' she asked her friend and, as the girl shook her head, felt annoyed with herself for not anticipating the inevitable. Jemima was still in denial, but *she* should have found out the name of a midwife from a quack or one of the theatre women in readiness. Oh, why hadn't she done so? 'Do you think Mrs Trott will know of a midwife?' she asked now.

'Oh, please!' Jemima curled into another spasm and, when it had passed, said, 'Let's deal with it ourselves. You can help me, I'm sure. There's no need for anyone else. You know what to do!'

'I do not!' Eliza said in dismay. 'And indeed I can't have a child's life – or *your* life – on my hands. We must have proper help.'

Jemima burst into fresh tears but Eliza didn't allow them to sway her. 'First we must take you back to Mrs Trott's and then –'

'Not there! Let's go to your lodgings, where no one knows me.'

Eliza shook her head. 'We can't,' she said briefly. She thought of her room in the Star; the innkeeper's wife would be sure to know of a midwife nearby. 'We are best to go to a nearby inn,' she began, but Jemima burst into such a torrent of tears that she feared hysteria might set in if she didn't give way. 'Very well,' she said, troubled almost to tears herself, 'if you refuse to move you'll have to lie-in here. But we must send out for help.'

Jemima didn't reply, for another pain had seized her, and when it had retreated Eliza half-pulled and half-carried her across the tiring room, along a corridor and into a small dressing room which Nell sometimes used. It had no bed nor settle, but contained several chairs and a quantity of cushions, and was very light, with three casement windows open to the sky.

'This will be more private,' Eliza said, and she gathered together some of the cushions and laid a sheet over them on the floor, then encouraged Jemima to get on to this makeshift bed while she went to seek out a midwife. She also promised her that she'd send word to William, and accordingly gave a shilling to an errand boy and instructed him to go to the Wilkes' household in Whitehall, request to see the master in person and tell him his presence was sought urgently.

The cost of Mistress Reynolds, the midwife, was two pounds, which she said crisply was for a live or dead birth. She lived close to the theatre and had come recommended by a nearby apothecary, although the matter was urgent enough for Eliza to have taken more or less anyone she could find.

She was a short, wiry woman and hard-faced, but clean-looking and decent.

'This is a strange place to give birth,' she said, looking around the room. 'Hasn't the girl got any mother to help her? No sisters or cousins to attend the occasion?'

Eliza shook her head. 'She wants to be very private,' she said, dabbing Jemima's forehead with a damp cloth.

'Is it a natural child?' the midwife asked in a low voice.

'No!' Jemima cried. 'I have a husband and we are legally wed!'

Mrs Reynolds and Eliza exchanged glances over Jemima's head.

'Of course you are, my sweeting,' Mrs Reynolds said soothingly, opening her bag. As well as clean rags, bowls and scissors, she'd brought with her a piece of jasper with a hole in it, and she tied this round Jemima's thigh, saying it would help hasten the birth. She'd also brought a birthing stool made of sturdy oak, its seat cut away to leave a new-moon shape, which Jemima would be required to sit upon in the final stage of labour.

She told Jemima that until then she should keep moving as much as possible, so Eliza was engaged to walk the room with Jemima leaning on her heavily and digging her fingernails into her forearms whenever the pains came. Periodically she'd lie down on the cushions and writhe around, or sometimes take a little cordial. Every once in a while she'd beg Eliza to go to the front of the theatre and see if word had come from William, and Eliza would agree, only too pleased to have an excuse to leave the overheated room where the perilous process of childbirth was being enacted.

The boy whom Eliza had sent to seek out William

Wilkes eventually returned to report that the master of the house was away with the king and court, but whether in Newmarket or elsewhere Wilkes's servant didn't know. This news, however, Eliza kept from Jemima, thinking that she should have some hope that William might appear.

Mrs Reynolds had been there perhaps three hours when she sent Eliza to the apothecary to obtain feverfew boiled in white wine to aid the birth, and after five hours with the child still not coming forth she dictated a list of ingredients: cinnamon, saffron, betony and maidenhair which Eliza was instructed to purchase, mix with a raw egg and feed to Jemima by the spoonful.

The concoction being consumed, the birth was still not progressing as fast as it should have done, and Jemima was as white as the sheet on which she lay and dotted all over with sweat. She writhed backwards and forwards, moaning softly to herself. Observing her pains, Eliza remarked to Mrs Reynolds in a low voice that under no circumstances would she be having children herself, but that lady just smiled grimly and said that she'd oft heard that in the last thirty years, but had not yet heard of how to prevent them.

Eliza began singing to Jemima, soothing country ballads that she'd learned in childhood, and these did seem to calm her somewhat. Another hour went by and, in the hopes of speeding things along, Mrs Reynolds seated Jemima on the birthing stool with Eliza kneeling behind her and supporting her upper body.

Jemima was keeping up a constant moan now, as if

one great continual pain was racking her body without pause.

'Is she all right?' Eliza kept asking in a whisper, between ballads, and each time was only partially reassured by a brief nod or a shrug from Mrs Reynolds. Oh, how long it all took, Eliza fretted. So painful. So dangerous. Suppose Jemima died?

At last the midwife examined Jemima once more, then sighed greatly and beckoned Eliza outside.

'I fear that the child is in the breech position,' she said.

'What's that?'

''Tis upside down.'

'Is that bad?' Eliza asked fearfully.

Mrs Reynolds nodded. 'Bad for a first birth particularly, for no babe's head has been down the birth canal to stretch it beforehand.'

Eliza's eyes filled with frightened tears. 'But what will happen?'

'If the babe is not born soon it will die,' Mrs Reynolds said, shaking her head. 'Or your friend may die before she can give birth to it.'

'But is there nothing that will help her?' Eliza implored Mrs Reynolds. 'Surely with all your knowledge you can do *something*?'

Mrs Reynolds shook her head, wiping her hands on the bloodied apron she wore. 'The only hope is a doctor wielding an instrument to pull the child from the womb. Doctor Chamberlen is one such, but he is not for the likes of us, for he attends only moneyed people.'

'I have money!' Eliza said. 'I have near twenty guineas.'

'That *may* be enough,' Mrs Reynolds said doubtfully, 'but he lives in Greenwich and may not travel this far.'

'Oh, but he must!' Eliza said desperately. 'He must be made to come!'

There was a sudden, horrific and long-drawn-out scream from Jemima, and Eliza and Mrs Reynolds rushed back into the room to find the birthing stool upturned and Jemima sprawled backwards, a bloodied, glistening baby between her legs.

Eliza gave a scream of her own on seeing this, terrified in case mother and child were dead, but Mrs Reynolds ran to the baby and picked it up, and it immediately let out a thin wail.

'Bless me, she did it on her own after all!' Mrs Reynolds said. 'You have saved your money.'

'It's all right?' Eliza asked fearfully. 'It will live?'

'It seems so.' Mrs Reynolds held the child – a boy – a little distance from Jemima's body and, asking Eliza to pass the scissors, cut the cord that joined mother and child. 'He seems well and healthy enough,' she said.

The child was named William by a near-fainting Jemima, and Mrs Reynolds wrapped him carefully in strips of linen, placed him in an egg basket that Eliza had previously found in the props department, then concentrated on the next stage of labour: ensuring that the afterbirth was delivered. While this was going on, Eliza threw away the soiled linen and cleaned the room, then swept the floor and sent out for some strewing herbs from the market to freshen the atmosphere.

Feeling more confident now about the child's

survival, she also sent for some lengths of soft swaddling cotton for him, and a gown and bonnet. He was not a pretty child, she thought, gazing at him in the egg basket, for his face was squashed and scarlet and he had no hair. Her little sisters had looked much the same, however, and by and by they'd improved.

As to Jemima, she thought, well, as soon as she was strong enough, she'd order a sedan chair to take her back to Mrs Trott's. For the time being, though, she dragged in an easy chair from the tiring room which would serve as a lying-in bed, and found an old velvet drape to act as a counterpane.

All this being achieved and Jemima being tucked up and near-prone in the chair, Mrs Reynolds spoke to her gently to ask what she intended to do next.

'Will you go home, dear?' she asked. 'For I suspect you have no facilities here for caring for a child. Nor much idea about it,' she added, for Jemima didn't even appear to know that the child should be put to the breast to feed.

Jemima looked up at them both. 'William,' she said in a pathetic tone. 'Does William know that he has a son?'

'I couldn't reach him, for he's away with the king,' Eliza confessed. 'But I'll find out where he is and send a message by rider.'

Jemima sighed and closed her eyes wearily.

'But let us think to your babe ... have you a wet nurse in mind?' Mrs Reynolds asked gently and, on Jemima just turning an exhausted eye on her, added, 'It would be for the best, perhaps.'

'Mrs Reynolds, do *you* know of a wet nurse?' Eliza asked, no reply being forthcoming from Jemima.

She nodded. 'I know a good matron in the country – in Barnes, where the air is said to be good. She would care for him until such time as he could be taken into the family again.'

Eliza thought that Jemima might object to her child going out of town, but she didn't seem to have any strength to do so.

'This matron has an infant of her own and a good supply of milk,' said Mrs Reynolds. 'She'd tend your babe and love it as her own.'

Jemima merely blinked at them.

'Do you want that, Jemima?' Eliza asked, wondering if she knew what she was agreeing to. 'For the babe to go to a wet nurse?'

Jemima gave a slight nod. 'But we'll send for him soon. His father and I will send for him,' she said in a whisper, and after saying this fell into a deep sleep.

Chapter Twenty-One

The baby, young William, had already been in the country for over a week when Nell, the king and the rest of the court came back to London, having travelled from the races in Newmarket to those of Windsor, where they'd occupied some of the castle. By this time Eliza had settled matters with Nell's landlord and was living back in Lewkenor's Lane, and Jemima was back with Mrs Trott. Eliza had visited her three times but each time found her still in bed, listless and melancholy, her face to the wall. She only stirred once – when Eliza mentioned William's name – but on ascertaining that Eliza had no news of him, had turned away once more. Mrs Trott not being particularly interested in the welfare of her lodger, Eliza had no idea of what to do. She decided, therefore, that she could only wait until Nell returned and see what she advised.

After Eliza had listened with excitement to Nell's tales concerning the courtiers' taking of the waters at Tunbridge Wells, and the masques, dances, musical entertainments and bedroom parties at Newmarket and Windsor, she then began to tell Nell all that had happened in her absence. Nell listened sympathetically to the tale of her visit to the magician and subsequent letter from her aunt, and was highly amused by the tale of Eliza and Claude Duval, especially when she heard that it was the Duke of Monmouth who'd been robbed.

'He told us that Duval held him up, and he was mighty cross about it!' Nell said, bursting into delighted laughter. 'He didn't say that Duval was merely taking back what he'd been cheated out of at cards, though.'

'And did he mention an accomplice being involved in the crime?' Eliza asked nervously.

'He said that Duval had used a lure, a girl partner, but I don't think he said anything more.' Nell hesitated, 'Just a minute, though ...'

Eliza looked at her in alarm. '*What?* Did he mention me?'

Nell looked at her wide-eyed for a moment, and then gave a screech of laughter. 'Of course not! I was merely teasing you!'

Eliza breathed out again. Nell did love her jokes ...

As they chattered, they were threading their way through the crowded streets of Covent Garden, for Nell had told Eliza that she'd something particular to show her and wished them to see it on foot.

'But what of William Wilkes?' Eliza asked when she'd told Nell the news about the birth of young William. 'Did he get my message? For I spent two pounds on sending a rider to Newmarket to tell him that Jemima had been confined.'

'He got the message all right,' Nell said. 'He told me of it.'

'And was he happy to hear he had a son? What did he say?'

'He was happy all right. The scurvy wretch celebrated by taking a whore to a gaming club and losing three hundred guineas!'

As Eliza sighed, appalled, Nell continued, 'He's a scoundrel and good for nothing at all! Why, you should see how he, Monteagle and Monmouth behaved in Newmarket with their drunkenness and their gambling and their rampaging through bawdy houses! I don't know how the king tolerates them, indeed I don't. And as for Rochester – he engages in activities which even I have never heard of!'

Eliza noted to herself that Nell had not mentioned Valentine Howard as being in this little group of ne'er-do-wells, but decided not to mention his name in case she was teased.

'But how will Jemima manage?' she asked instead. 'Is William Wilkes ever going to take her away to the Americas to start a new life?'

Nell left Eliza's side to dart across the cobbles to a shop window and admire a purple hat bedecked with a froth of ostrich plumes, then returned to take her arm.

'No, he's not, is the plain answer,' she said. 'For I questioned him on the subject when he was fairly sober, and he said there's no point now, for Jemima's father has seized her fortune and tied it up in law.'

'How has he done that?'

'He's had her grandfather's money put in a trust so that Jemima can't touch it until she's thirty-five. He placed a notice in the *London Newes* to advertise this, and that's how Wilkes discovered it.'

'But what will happen to her?' Eliza asked anxiously.

They paused, waiting for a gap in the traffic, then proceeded across the Strand, past the maypole and towards St James's, where the nobility had built many fine homes.

'As far as that rogue is concerned – nothing,' Nell said. 'He doesn't want her without her fortune, that's certain.'

'Poor Jemima!' Eliza said, her eyes filling with sympathetic tears. 'But what of their marriage? Will he have it annulled?'

Nell shook her head. 'No need, for 'twas not a marriage. The reverend gentleman was but a trickster, and 'twas all done in the hopes of fooling Jemima's family into giving her up. Just as William was about to inform her father of the deed, however, he read in the *Newes* that she was not to receive the money and realised that the whole charade had been for nothing.'

'Oh!' Eliza shook her head, horrified, 'and what of the babe ...'

Nell sighed and pulled a dismal little face which said she had no idea, but then seemed to dismiss all from her mind as she came to a halt in Pall Mall.

'Look,' she said to Eliza. 'This is why we didn't take the carriage this morning, for I wished to look upon something from a distance and observe every detail as I came closer.'

Eliza, still thinking of Jemima and wondering if she could tell her of William's true nature, looked at her in some confusion. 'What do you mean? What do you wish to look upon?'

'That house,' Nell pointed further down the street. 'The redbrick house with the sign of the Flying Swan over its door. Is it not a fine place?'

Eliza looked and nodded. 'It's *very* grand.'

'Who do you think lives there?'

Eliza said that she hadn't the least idea.

'Then I'll tell you!' Nell said with a squeal of joy. 'Mistress Eleanor Gwyn lives there, for the king has taken a lease on that house and given it to me!'

Eliza, gasping, followed her to stand on the other side of the road from the house in question, which was five storeys high and very wide, with large windows and two front doors.

'It has many rooms – about forty, I believe,' Nell went on excitedly, 'and a courtyard for the carriage and horses, and a large garden which backs on to St James's Park so that His Majesty and I may talk to each other over the wall when he takes his morning constitutional!' She squeezed Eliza's arm. 'I'll have servants in livery and everything very fine, and *you* living with me if you wish.'

'Oh!' Eliza said, quite overcome.

'And one more most excellent thing,' Nell said, her face wreathed in smiles. 'What do you think it is?'

Eliza shook her head, staring at her wide-eyed. As if going on a tour with the king as his principal mistress, receiving all the fine clothes and jewels you could wear *and* being given such a well-situated and extensive house wasn't enough ...

'Why,' Nell said, 'I'm expecting a baby.'

Eliza gave a little scream.

''Tis true. I'm to have the king's child! *Now* let Squintabella try and take my place.'

Within a week, redecoration of the house was well under way, furniture, tapestries and paintings had been ordered and Nell, Eliza and a small retinue of staff were almost ready to move into the house at the sign of the Flying Swan. Eliza had been given two new gowns and caps in pale blue – Nell's livery colour – and several long starched aprons. She'd also been assured that her presence would still be needed as a maid/companion, and that she'd now be paid a proper living.

'For you know how I like my things, and how to dress my hair so well, and what colours suit my complexion,' Nell said on one of their last nights in Lewkenor's Lane. 'And now that I bear the king's child there'll be *endless* money to spend on gowns and shoes and fripperies, and I'll need someone who's willing to go to the shops on any whim.'

Eliza laughed and agreed that she'd love nothing more than to live with Nell and provide these services whenever and wherever they were needed.

'I can well do this for you,' she said, 'for I have no other ties on my time, no family and no one else to consider at all.'

'We'll soon find you someone to consider,' Nell said. 'There are many rich young men who'd love to bed a girl as pretty as you.'

Eliza nodded and smiled, but did not say what she usually did on these occasions: that she yearned to be loved for herself, not for her looks, and nor did she want to become someone's mistress and be cast aside when her lover married. She'd be regarded as no more than a whore, then, and no decent man would ever wish to take her.

'And maybe,' Nell said, 'you'll be able to find your family, for at Tunbridge Wells I spoke to the king's astrologer and he's the cleverest man imaginable and can find out anything in the world!'

Eliza shrugged. 'After attending on the charlatan necromancer who claimed to see my father I don't know if I can believe that.'

'Astrologers are different – even the king believes in Doctor Deane. Why, he forecast that I was with child fully a week before I found out myself.'

'But that's not difficult,' Eliza said, 'for surely anyone who sleeps regularly with a man soon finds herself with child?'

'But he told me many other things – about my sister and my mother, and how it was forecast in the stars that I should be the king's mistress, and that the king might find other mistresses but would never forsake me as long as he lived.'

Eliza struggled for a while, but the notion was irresistible. 'Do you really think, then, that he might be able to tell me of my family and where they might be found?'

'Of course,' Nell said. 'Or at least he can point you in the right direction.' She squeezed Eliza's hand. 'Write down your birth date and the place where you were born, and then write my own details along with these and we'll have him cast a proper birth chart for each of us.'

'I'm not sure of my birth date any more,' Eliza faltered. 'Nor where I was born, for if I'm not the child of the parents I thought were mine …'

'You're sure to have been born on the same date. And at least must be from the same area, or very close.'

'I've always believed my birth day to be the third of

November. My mother used to tell me that she went into labour on Saturday night and gave birth to me on Sunday morning in time for church.' Eliza smiled at the childish tale, but then the smile faded. Why go on believing that? It had all been lies …

'Put what you know down on paper,' Nell said, 'and we'll see what transpires.'

A few days later they received a message from the astrologer to ask that the two young ladies whose charts he had cast should go along to his consulting room, to be found on London Bridge at the sign of the Pen and Star. Eliza took the opportunity of this carriage ride to ask Nell about the new French lady-in-waiting, Louise de Keroualle, and whether she'd also been travelling with the court.

Nell nodded, pulling a sour face. 'Squintabella?' she said. 'Yes, she was there, as was Barbara Castlemaine and her brood – and Queen Catherine too!'

'And does the queen honestly not mind all these mistresses?' Eliza asked.

'She does not!' Nell said. 'She seems to tolerate us all. I believe she thinks that as long as the king is kept happy in the bedchamber, then he won't bother her too much.'

At the astrologer's house they were shown into a room with a dismal aspect. There were two tables covered in a confusion of dusty, yellowing papers, charts and scrolls, and above these were pinned parchments showing different conjunctions of the planets and their positions in the heavens. The room was lit by two miserable tapers and the stinking miasma from the river outside seeped through its closed windows and set Eliza to coughing.

Doctor Deane was wearing the same faded black scholar's gown that he'd been wearing when Eliza had seen him at the palace. He rose to his feet as they entered the room and, looking from one to the other, gave Eliza a deep bow whilst holding on to his wig. To Nell he gave a more cursory acknowledgement.

The girls exchanged glances and raised eyebrows; Eliza felt she wanted to laugh. He hadn't even got *that* right.

'Good day, Doctor Deane,' Nell said in a forthright tone. ''Tis me, you may remember, who's mistress to the king. This is Eliza, my companion and maid.'

'Quite so, madam,' Doctor Deane said, not looking in the least bit put-out. 'You must forgive my greeting your companion first, but she's high-born and so convention demands it.'

Eliza bobbed a curtsy, trying not to laugh. 'Thank you, sire – but I'm not high-born!'

'And how do you know that, madam?' he asked sternly.

Eliza looked at him, somewhat confused. 'Because ... I was born in a poor village in Somersetshire, and my parents – at least, my foster parents – were in reduced circumstances and perhaps took me in to earn a little money.'

Doctor Deane smiled slightly. 'But from where do you think they acquired you?' he asked and, turning, he reached for a rolled parchment and spread it out across his desk. Eliza looked at Nell, startled, and they both drew closer to stare at it.

On the parchment had been inscribed a large circle and this was divided into twelve segments. Over these had been drawn geometric shapes, with crosses and astrological signs. Eliza thought it looked very pleasing and interesting, but didn't have the least idea what it meant.

'This is your birth chart, milady,' he said to Eliza, 'showing where the planets were in the sky at the time of your birth.' He traced with his finger. 'See the second house – the house of money – has the Sun and Jupiter conjoined, and the tenth house – the house of fame and fortune – has Jupiter rising. The Sun is in the seventh house, and all the major planets are in the ascendant, which leads me to the conclusion that you're very high-born.' He paused and declared solemnly, 'What happened to you *after* your birth is another matter.'

Eliza was stunned into silence.

'Perhaps, indeed, you're a member of the nobility and only posing as maid to Mistress Gwyn to try and fool me?' Doctor Deane asked, frowning a little.

'No,' Eliza said. 'Not at all. But I can't really believe –'

'She may not have got the timing exactly right,' Nell interrupted. 'What difference would it make if she was born, say, a few hours before or after this time?'

'According to the chart I've prepared,' Doctor Deane said solemnly, 'milady here was born with almost every planet in a favourable position. Her birth a few hours before or after would only alter things very slightly.' He turned to Eliza and looked at her steadily for some moments. 'You have a noble forehead, clear eyes and are tall for a woman, and none of these traits are seen in peasant stock. I stand by my belief that you're of the nobility.'

Nell gave a peal of laughter. 'That shows me my place, Doctor, for I'm short enough to be knee-high to a bear!'

Eliza smiled, but hardly heard Nell's joke. Could her earlier fantasy really be true? She thought about this while Doctor Deane was going through Nell's chart with her, explaining how the different planets acted and reacted, and only spoke again when he'd finished.

'Could it be,' she asked then, 'that I'm related to the king?'

He smiled slightly as he shook his head. 'I said *high*, I didn't say the highest in the land.'

'But if I *am* high-born, when will I find out about it?'

Doctor Deane spread his hands. 'Who knows? Astrology is not an exact science, and your future is also subject to your own will. You may never discover who you are – or you may, perhaps, come into your birthright and take your rightful place in the world.'

Eliza struggled to make sense of this. 'So I may not ever find out my origins. But are you able to tell me where I might discover my real family?'

'I'm an astrologer, madam,' he remarked dryly. 'Not a fortune-teller.'

Eliza shrugged. Everything was too vague, too fantastical. And even if it was true that she was high-born, if she wasn't going to find her family, then what was the point of knowing such a thing?

Chapter Twenty-Two

When Eliza moved with her few trifles over to Nell's new house she discovered, to her great delight, that she'd been given a room of her own. It was only a very small one with a high window, but it overlooked part of the garden and also the ancient brick wall that ran around Whitehall Palace, some of the roofs of which could be seen in the distance. In the room was a fireplace, an iron bedstead with real feather mattress, a nest of drawers and a low rocking chair, and to this Eliza added a mirror which she'd bought with the remains of the money given to her by Claude Duval, and a wooden stand on which to hang her undersmocks and gowns.

Lying on her bed and surveying all this one afternoon, she felt content. Or, she thought to herself, *almost* content. She searched her mind for what it was that eluded her: a sense of permanency, perhaps, for the king seemed fickle and she feared Nell could lose her position and thus her house at any time. And if Nell lost all, then *she* would lose all too. There was also no sense of stability, no family, no feeling that she belonged to someone irrevocably and someone belonged to her. As for what Doctor Deane had told her – well, it was a wonderful story. A wonderful, fantastical story – like a fairy tale, she thought, and that was the only way she could allow herself to think of it.

There was a sudden high call of 'E-liiii-za!' from downstairs and she jumped to her feet and ran down.

'I should have asked the maid to call you but I forgot,' Nell said, meeting her on the polished wooden staircase. 'It's so difficult to get used to having servants!' She took Eliza's arm and turned her round. 'Now, tell me what you think of my new drawing room,' she said and, opening the double doors before them, gave Eliza a gentle push inside.

Eliza gazed around the fine room with its gleaming wood panelling, colourful tapestries and carved mantelpiece with wooden garland of intricately worked fruit and flowers.

''Tis beautiful – and all most excellently done,' she said, looking around and gasping with delight.

'But we must go to the shops, Eliza,' Nell said. 'I need more damask and velvet drapes and you must help me with the colours. I also need some oil paintings, a quantity of blue and white Delft china and all manner of little treasures to place on the shelves.'

Eliza looked at her questioningly. 'What sort of little treasures?'

'Boxes inlaid with pearl, some framed miniatures, marble statues, Chinese vases and lots of costly silver items so that the king feels quite at home when he comes to visit. Oh, and I want some clocks – the king loves clocks!' Nell paused for breath and then went on, 'You should see the bed I've ordered. It has four posts which reach the ceiling and draperies of cloth-of-gold, and is inlaid at the back with the king's royal coat of arms in appliqué and precious stones. I've also ordered a comfortable close-stool to match it, with a padded velvet seat.'

Eliza raised her eyebrows, smiling.

'I wish the king to be at ease whatever throne he's sitting on!' Nell continued with a giggle. Stopping suddenly, she ran her hands over her stomach. 'Does it show yet that I'm with child, Eliza?'

Eliza scrutinised her figure carefully. 'A little, but your gown is so stiff with embroidery and you're wearing so many petticoats that I can't tell which is your finery and which is you. But how many months are you?'

'About four or five, I think.'

'And are you ...' Eliza hesitated; she didn't wish to cause offence but was desperately curious to know, '... are you completely sure that it's the king's child you're carrying?'

'Eliza!' Nell said, affecting to be shocked. Then she laughed. 'I haven't lain with another man since my first time with the king. And I won't do so again.'

'Not ever?'

Nell shook her head. 'There would be too much to lose and I'd be stupid to trifle with his affections. Not like some I could mention.'

'Barbara Castlemaine?'

Nell's eyes gleamed. 'Her latest lover is Jacob Hall, the fairground tightrope walker!'

'No!'

'She's just *insatiable* in her longings,' Nell said, wrinkling her nose in disgust. She pulled Eliza over towards the settle in the window. 'But I want you to start reading me the new play. Do you have it there with you?'

Eliza nodded and held up the inked sheets. The play had been written by Charles Hart, who had forgiven Nell for passing him over for the king and was anxious now to use this connection as a means of rising in the world.

'The king was most intrigued to hear news of it,' Nell went on. 'A comedy by Hart called *The Prince and the Courtesan*, with *me* playing the courtesan – well, of course he was!'

Eliza laughed. 'He'll be wanting a part in it next.'

'As a matter of fact he's been saying that for some time.'

'Not *really*?' Eliza thought of the difficulty of it all: of His Royal Highness lolling around backstage with the rest of the players, of him dressing in the shabby room where Jemima had given birth and holding court in the tiring room to receive the fops and gallants after his performance – for everyone would want to come along and tell His Majesty how wonderful he'd been. And what if he wanted to bring all his dogs with him? 'He couldn't really do such a thing, surely …'

Nell shrugged. 'He's the king and can do anything he likes! He loves the theatre and masquerading, and we could arrange it.' Nell frowned a little. 'The only thing is, those of the high church might say that it was unseemly for the head of the Church of England to appear on stage with *actresses*.'

Eliza thought for a moment. 'What, then, if he were disguised?'

'At a foot and a half taller than most men that could be difficult.'

'Not so,' Eliza said, picking up the script, 'for I

began reading this last night, and there's an ideal part for him.'

'Really?'

Eliza nodded. 'In the play, the courtesan –'

'Who's very beautiful and talented, I'm sure!'

'Of course,' Eliza confirmed, and continued, 'the courtesan is loved by a prince, but he's just one of many men who seek her favours. She has promised to be true, however, and so he follows her around the country to make sure she stays faithful.'

'Yes, but how –'

'Well, he disguises himself as a dancing bear to do this, so that the courtesan won't know he's spying on her!'

Nell began laughing. 'A prince disguised as a dancing bear – an excellent part for the king to play. But 'tis a pity that a bear can't speak, for the king will have no lines to say.'

Eliza smiled. 'He will, for the bear speaks to the audience when there's no one else about. He tells the audience, in rhyme, that he intends to follow the courtesan and see if she's faithful.'

'And then what happens?'

'One of his rivals in love, finding out that Brown Bear's costume conceals his enemy, takes a gun and pretends to shoot him. The play continues with the bear limping around wounded, and goes through plots and counter-plots until at the final curtain the bear reveals himself as the prince. 'Tis very funny.'

Nell clapped her hands. 'Perfect!' she said. 'I'll tell the king about it tonight.'

The next morning, Eliza, arriving at the theatre early,

was surprised to find Jemima already there. Looking at her drooping shoulders, drawn face and lank hair, Eliza wondered guiltily if she should have tried harder to visit her or engaged her on an excursion to take the air, for in the three weeks since William's birth she'd hardly seen the girl. She'd been so busy since Nell's return to London that her concerns about Jemima, her wish to tell her of William's real character, had been pushed to one side.

'How are you, sweeting?' she asked now, squeezing her friend's hand.

A listless eye was turned on her. 'Is there any news of William? How is my husband?'

Eliza, unprepared for this question or indeed for seeing Jemima at all, couldn't think of what to say in reply and just bit her lip.

'Is he back in London?' Jemima asked, her voice rising. 'Why hasn't he visited me? Does he know of our child?'

Eliza patted her hand, trying to compose the words she knew would have to be said.

'I must see him!' Jemima said plaintively. 'I must see him or die of heartbreak!'

Eliza would have deemed this an exaggeration with anyone else, but looking at Jemima's sorry condition decided that this might be a distinct possibility. She searched her mind for ways to sound positive.

'Are you eating well?' she asked Jemima. 'And have you planned when you'll visit little William? Have you heard from Mrs Reynolds as to his welfare?'

Jemima shook her head miserably. 'I haven't seen my Williams. They are both lost to me! How can I care whether I eat or no?' Her hand clutched at

246

Eliza's. 'But tell me truthfully, have *you* seen William? Does he know I've been confined?'

Eliza swallowed. 'I haven't seen him,' she said, 'but he does know of the child.'

'Then why doesn't he come to me?' Tears began to drip down her cheeks. 'Oh, I'm truly lost!'

'He … he …' Eliza stammered, then pulled Jemima on to a settle and sat down next to her. 'Jemima,' she said slowly, ''tis a sad and difficult thing I have to tell you, but you must be very brave and think of all you've gained from having known William. Your child, for instance. If you hadn't known William then he wouldn't have been born.'

Jemima looked at her with her brimming eyes. 'What are you trying to say?'

'I'm trying to say that William, the man you think of as your husband –'

'The man I *think* of!' Jemima said. 'How dare you say such a thing? He's truly my husband and you were there to sign as witness to it.'

Eliza took a deep breath. 'The thing is,' she began, taking her hand again and squeezing it, 'Nell told me – and it was William himself who told her – that the marriage ceremony you went through was a sham. The minister who married you was but a false one.'

Jemima stared at her, but her expression showed little acknowledgement that she'd understood.

'William went through the ceremony to try and persuade your father that he was in earnest, so your family would give up the fight for you. The reverend gentleman being false, however, the marriage vows you took have no veracity. They are meaningless. And then William found out that your father had virtually disinherited you,' Eliza went on gently, 'and so all his efforts had been for nothing.' Jemima did not react to any of this and it seemed to Eliza that she'd almost gone into a trance. 'I'm sure he cared for you once, very deeply,' she went on, 'but he and those gentlemen who surround the king have a certain attitude towards women. They live for pleasure and to satisfy their needs and nothing else.'

'No!' Jemima said in a high, frightened voice. 'William is not like that.'

Eliza knew that William was very much like that, but thought it best not to insist upon it. 'All is not lost, Jemima,' she said gently. 'You must think to your child, now. Think of what is best for him. Perhaps ... perhaps you could take him home to your family.'

'My father would kill me!' Jemima said. She stood up abruptly, pulling her hand away from Eliza's. 'Besides, you're wrong. William *will* come for me. He's promised to do so.'

'But, Jemima –'

'And then we'll collect our child and go to the Americas together and live out the rest of our days! He promised me this and he won't let me down. No one could be so cruel!' Saying this she ran to the door of the tiring room and looked down the passage, as if she was expecting him to appear at any moment.

'Jemima, please –'

'If all you have to tell me are lies about William then I don't wish to speak to you!'

'Let us speak of other things, then.'

'I don't wish to speak to you at all!' Jemima's pallid face became so rigid and threatening that Eliza immediately took two steps backwards.

Perhaps Nell would know what to do, she thought. Perhaps Nell could persuade William to speak to Jemima – or at least urge him to acknowledge his son and pay for his future upkeep. It was, Eliza thought, a wretched and pitiful affair, with a girl driven half-mad and an unwanted child who might end up in the workhouse. Oh, pray God that such a thing should never happen to her!

Eliza sought Nell's advice, and she managed to speak to William the following evening. He, though, as expected, showed a complete lack of concern for both Jemima and young William. Ascertaining Jemima's real name and address from him, however, Nell gave these to Eliza who sent out for parchment and ink and, after several trial attempts, eventually wrote the following:

From the King's Theatre, Drury Lane.

To Sir Horace and Lady Rotherfield,
My first wish is to apologise for my writing skill. Your daughter, who has been my dear friend these past months, has done much to improve my abilities, but I fear these are still somewhat lacking.
However, I will come to the point. Your daughter, called Jemima by us, has been estranged from you for some time and was, I fear, seduced by a man who, although gentle-born, was no gentleman. He wickedly deceived Jemima and even went through a form of marriage ceremony with her, to which I was witness.

Over three weeks ago, Jemima gave birth to a child, a healthy boy whom she named William. He is living with a wet nurse at some distance, which means that Jemima has little contact with him. She has also been completely abandoned by the man she thought loved her, for the marriage ceremony was just a fake.

Sir and madam, Jemima does not know that I am appealing to you, but I beg you, if you can find it in your heart to forgive her, then take her back into your family. I fear for her very much if you do not, for she has neither the means nor the ability to survive in London, being a gentle creature who may be usurped by others. She is very frail in body and spirit and needs the stability of your household about her and, because she has been extremely ill-used, a mother's tender care.

Please forgive my boldness in writing to you. I can assure you that I do so only with Jemima's best interests at heart, and remain, dear sir and madam, your faithful servant,
Eliza Rose

Eliza read through her letter once more and then sealed it using Nell's new brass seal and a stick of red wax. A mother's tender care, she thought to herself ... and tears of self-pity came into her eyes. She reproved herself, however, hurriedly threw a cloak around her shoulders and made her way towards the post agent without more ado. The sooner Jemima's family received the letter, the better.

Chapter Twenty-Three

'The king won't come to the theatre to rehearse,' Nell said to Eliza. 'We must go there instead and put him through his lines.'

'Go to the palace to rehearse?' Eliza asked in awe.

'Of course!' Nell replied in a matter-of-fact tone.

They were in Nell's little dressing room where she'd just had some costume fittings for the new play. Because, naturally, her size was going to increase due to her pregnancy, the wardrobe mistress had designed her outfits with a series of ingenious tucks and seams which could be let out. Now Nell slipped her arms into a white satin robe with ruffles down the front, wrapped it around herself and tied the belt.

Outside, a handbell rang six times. 'Six of the clock and a fire in Eastcheap!' a bellman cried, and both girls went silent for a moment, listening for more news, for everyone remained anxious about fire. 'But flames all contained!' he went on, and they both relaxed a little.

'Could ... could Jemima come once to the palace with us, do you think?' Eliza asked.

Nell sighed.

'I know,' Eliza said. 'I know she's –'

'Tiresome! And miserable and slovenly. I'm sure she

doesn't wash from one week to the next.' Nell patted her own immaculate ringlets. 'Why, her hair looks like a squirrel's lair.'

'But she suffers from a melancholy and so has no interest in herself,' Eliza said. ''Tis not her fault. It sometimes happens to a woman after she's been brought to bed. And she has been *so* let down.'

'She is such dismal company, though. The king loves me for my wit and my gaiety, Eliza! I couldn't think of inflicting such a sad creature on him.'

Eliza shrugged. 'I was just trying to think of something that might cheer her. Some excursion to give her more to think on.'

'She certainly needs it,' Nell said, 'for she's so thin and pale she puts one in mind of a spirit creature.'

'I almost fear for her sanity,' Eliza said. 'I wrote to her father and mother five days ago. Surely they must have had the letter by now?'

'Had the letter and torn it up, I shouldn't wonder – for didn't she say that her father was an ogre? But I have just thought of the very thing! Why don't you take her out to Barnes to see little William?'

'Oh, could we?' said Eliza, delighted.

'You may take the carriage and ride there and back in style. Surely *that* will improve her spirits.'

The excursion was planned for the end of the week, although Eliza, thinking about it later, had her doubts that even *that* would work: Jemima had been so dreadfully miserable lately that even talking about the baby brought on more tears. What else could they do for her, though?

The following day Nell and Eliza had an appointment

at the palace in order to acquaint the king with his new role in *The Prince and the Courtesan*. As few people as possible were going to be let into the secret beforehand, for the king wanted to invite the queen and the court to the theatre and only reveal at the final curtain who was playing the role of Brown Bear.

'The king thinks it the most excellent charade ever devised,' Nell said. 'Everyone will be thrilled when they discover it's he.'

Eliza wore an old outfit of Nell's for the occasion of the visit: a gown of heavy scarlet brocade with a very full skirt and tiny glass buttons all down the bodice. Being taller than Nell, she'd attached a border of dark blue to the skirt hem in order to lengthen it and, her hair having now grown to below ear-length, Nell lent her some pretty red-enamelled hair combs to wear in it.

The new house being just a short distance from Whitehall, Nell said it was hardly worth getting the carriage out and they would go on foot. On leaving the house she regretted this, however, for the moment they closed the front door they were besieged by a great number of street vendors – news of Nell's new fortune and address having moved through London's underclass very quickly.

'What d'ye lack, ladies? What d'ye lack?' came from all round them, and then Eliza heard the shouted merits of merchandise of every description: shellfish, poultry, hot eels, rat poison, ballad sheets, flowers, pickled whelks, shirt buttons and matches. The delights of these goods being loudly and continuously shouted contributed to so great a hubbub that both girls had to put their hands over their ears. Their way to the palace now being seriously impeded, Nell finally turned on the crowd and, putting her hands on her hips, gave vent to such foul language that it stopped the sellers in their tracks. Then, her lips twitching with the effort not to laugh, she took a handful of coins out of her pocket and threw them into the air.

As the crowd scrambled for the money, she took Eliza's hand and together they ran across the cobbles for the safety of the palace.

'Next time,' she shouted to Eliza, 'we'll take the carriage!'

They were admitted into Whitehall Palace by an aide. As they were led along a seemingly endless corridor and travelled up and down stairs, Eliza's eyes, as before, were everywhere: marvelling at the rooms, admiring the furnishings and flowers, seeing how the servants worked, observing the clothes of anyone they saw and continually gasping with amazement at the sheer scale of the place.

Eventually they were shown by an equerry into a salon where the king and queen were seated, the queen surrounded by her ladies and the king by his brown and white spaniels. It looked, Eliza thought, almost like a normal domestic scene – but one vastly scaled up and situated in a palace instead of a cottage.

Nell and Eliza sat down with others already seated on benches waiting to see either His or Her Majesty. There was a milliner, Eliza noted – or at least a woman carrying several hats – and what could have been a seamstress and a haberdasher waiting for the queen, and several dark-suited men of business to see the king. One of these came up to Nell and kissed her hand effusively several times; Nell told Eliza it was Mr Samuel Pepys from the Admiralty, who was famous for having been first to inform the king of the Great Fire.

The girls waited their turn, Eliza thinking it all so fascinating that she wouldn't have minded sitting there all day. At one point, the queen, her visitors having spoken and departed, rose to look out of the window to the garden beyond. As she got to her feet her six waiting women, as one, also rose to look out of the same window. When she sat down again and, drawing out her embroidery frame, began to sew, they did likewise. Her every glance was noted by them, her every whim satisfied and, watching her leading such a charmed life, Eliza began to see how a queen might be reluctant to relinquish her position.

At last, the others having departed, it was Nell's turn to be presented. Smiling broadly, the king indicated that Nell should approach and kiss his hand.

'Well, have you brought my outfit, Nelly?' Eliza heard him ask.

Nell shook her head. 'No, sire. You must be measured and have some fittings first.'

'And will I look very fearsome when I'm costumed?'

'You will look very fearsome and be very hot, for the material is thick wool and all over ragged, like the coat of a real ...' her voice dropped to a whisper, '... brown bear!'

They conversed some more, but Eliza kept her head low, knowing it was not decorous to look the king in the eye before she'd been acknowledged by him. His attention was exclusively centred on Nell, however, and it wasn't until the three of them, together with the dogs, moved into a small and lavishly furnished privy chamber to go over the play script that the king addressed Eliza. She'd been hoping that he might have remembered exactly who she was and mention the promised singing lessons, but although he was polite and charming he didn't give any indication of ever having seen her before. He spent some time reading the script, and gave some pages to a clerk so that his own speeches could be copied for him, but to Eliza's embarrassment a lot of the time there was spent in play, with the king tickling Nell or pretending to listen to the baby by putting his ear to her belly. There were several times during this tomfoolery when Eliza could hardly believe what she was hearing: Nell calling the King of England her naughty boy, her Charlie, and the king speaking to his 'pretty little Nelly' in a soft and silly voice.

When these interruptions to the reading happened Eliza would busy herself talking to the puppies, or walk around the room and pretend interest in one of the many clocks which were all ticking and chiming in different tones and at different times. She often felt herself going pink with embarrassment, however, and it came as a considerable relief when the king and Nell, after sharing several intimate kisses, said they would retire to another chamber and Eliza was free to go.

Eliza curtsied her way out of the room and, so anxious to be away that she did not wait for an equerry to escort her, found herself she knew not where. She walked for what seemed like a mile along one corridor and down a staircase at the end, but this led to a blank wall. Retracing her steps, she came back to where she thought she'd started from, but found herself in a completely different part of the palace. There were no servants around to ask directions from and, although several well-dressed people passed, Eliza feared to approach them in case they were of the nobility and she made some ghastly mistake in addressing them.

Up and down stairs she went, along corridors and back again, eventually becoming desperate and almost tearful. How embarrassing, she thought, how shameful, to be discovered there in the morning still wandering about. Resolving then to go down to the kitchens, locate the servants' quarters and ask them the way, Eliza came towards a double door with a small curtained-off staircase beside it. Her hand was on the curtain to pull it to one side when the double doors suddenly opened and a gaming scene was presented to her: a smoky room, two round tables and several elegantly dressed men and women sitting with neat piles of money in front of them.

Eliza, startled, pulled aside the curtain and began to go down the staircase as quickly as she could, but a person who'd come out of the room gave a shout, then ran down several steps and caught hold of her arm. She turned in alarm to see who it was – and stared straight into the leering face of Henry Monteagle.

Chapter Twenty-Four

'Hold!' Henry Monteagle came closer so that he was breathing into her face. 'Where are you going, my pretty one?' He gave a sudden, harsh laugh. 'Or more to the point, where have you *been*?'

Eliza did not reply, for her heart had started to hammer with fright and she needed to calm herself before she spoke.

'Answer me! You've been bedroom-visiting, I'll be bound. Have you been attending on the Duke of Monmouth, perhaps?'

'I have not,' Eliza replied after a moment, in as haughty a voice as she could muster.

'Then why are you wandering around here? You've had an assignation with someone, haven't you?'

He was, Eliza thought, such an objectionable oaf that she saw no reason to explain her movements. She tried to prise his fingers from her arm.

'Where I've been is nothing to do with you, sire,' she said, her voice trembling. 'Kindly let me go.'

He gave a drunken oath. 'You're mighty high for a street wench! Because that's what you are, isn't it?'

'I am not, sire.'

'I've seen you before, though.' Monteagle screwed up his face, trying to remember. 'In some bawdy house or other, I'll be bound. Or ... or at the theatre.' He looked at her through narrowed eyes, swaying slightly on his feet. 'Yes, you're an orange girl, aren't you?'

Eliza didn't reply.

'Nothing but a pox-ridden orange girl tricked up to look half-decent!'

She flushed at the distaste in his voice. 'Then please don't detain me, sire, for fear I should contaminate you in some way.'

Monteagle, looking astonished at the boldness of this reply, took her other wrist and pulled her close. 'How dare you speak to me that way, when I'm a nobleman and you're nothing but a whore. Repeat after me, *I am a whore.*'

Eliza's throat closed up with terror.

'Say it!' he urged drunkenly and, holding both of Eliza's wrists in one hand, he reached to his belt for a small knife. He began cutting off the little glass buttons on her bodice one by one. '*I am a whore.* Say it! And then I'll give you some whore's work to do.'

Eliza struggled, but his grip was strong and his knee was pushing hard against her thigh. She tried to scream, but so terrified was she that the noise came out as little more than a high-pitched sigh.

'Tell me ...' he urged as another button fell to the staircase.

'But I'm not,' she croaked. 'Oh, please don't ... please don't ...'

As the fifth button fell to the floor, Eliza found her voice from somewhere and, gathering her breath, let out a scream. As this echoed around the bare stairwell, Monteagle lifted the knife to her neck.

'Do that again,' he said, 'and I'll cut your whore's throat ...'

There was the clatter of footsteps on the stairs. Eliza heard, 'Monteagle! Hey, Henry!' and Valentine Howard leapt down the last three steps to land beside them. 'What's happening here?'

'What's happening is that I'm teaching this bawd a lesson,' Monteagle said, his voice slurred. He glanced at his friend. 'Have you ever heard of an orange girl who didn't want to do business, Val?'

The other shrugged. 'Maybe she has *other* business.'

Eliza looked from one youth to the other, icy with fear and scared to move in case it provoked Monteagle further.

'Wha' do you mean?' said Monteagle.

'Her other business, to be precise, is an appointment with me,' said Valentine Howard.

'With you? This whore is yours?'

Valentine flicked a glance towards Eliza which told her not to speak. 'She is. We had an arrangement to meet on the stairs but I was on a winning streak and forgot the time.'

Monteagle put his knife back in his belt and stepped back, looking her up and down with such disgust it was as if she'd fallen into a cow turd.

'By all means take her if you must,' he said. 'Although there are fairer whores who are certainly more willing than this one.'

Valentine didn't reply to this, but put his arm under Eliza's elbow and began to guide her down the stairs. Reaching a door at the bottom, he opened this and they went through a small hallway, through an outside door and into a courtyard where there were several sedan chairs and carriages waiting.

Eliza, shaking all over, found she couldn't speak – not even to thank the man who'd saved her.

'I'm sorry I had to refer to you in that manner,' he said, 'but it was all I could think of at the time and it seemed the quickest way.'

'I ... I ...' Eliza began, but could go no further.

'You must take my sedan home.'

Eliza drew in a deep, shaky breath.

'Are you all right?' he asked, and she nodded. 'Then we'll speak of it another time.' He whistled to a sedan, handed her in, and – though afterwards Eliza knew she must have imagined it – seemed to drop the lightest of kisses on to her head. He told the carriers to take Eliza wherever she wanted.

'And now I must get back to my game,' he said, and without another glance turned on his heel and went back in through the same door.

Eliza gave directions to one of the carriers and then sank back on to the cushions, feeling infinitely weary. She wanted to give way to tears, but longed first of all for the privacy of her own room to go over everything that had happened. Mostly she wanted to think about Valentine Howard, muse on what he'd done for her and why. Had that really been a kiss on her forehead? No, surely not ...

The carriers ran the short distance to Pall Mall with Eliza anticipating the sweet safety of her own bed every step of the way. On reaching Nell's house, however, she was appalled to see that there were three people at the front door engaged in a heated conversation. Alighting from the sedan and pulling her cloak tightly around her so that the torn bodice wouldn't show, she saw that these were Mrs Pearce, recently engaged by Nell as cook–housekeeper, Nell's sister Rose, and Old Ma Gwyn.

If she'd seen who was there a moment before, she would have asked the sedan carriers to take her round to the back door of the house, but Ma Gwyn, who was resplendent in the rag-market's finest, had already noticed her and was calling her name.

'It's Little Eliza!' she said, describing her so despite the fact that Eliza was a foot taller than herself. 'Ah, Eliza will take our part and tell Mistress Impudence who we are!'

'Well, thank the Lord,' Rose said to Eliza. 'For since we arrived we've had nothing but gross language and insults from madam here!'

Mrs Pearce, who was built almost as sturdily as Ma Gwyn but was markedly more refined, her stout shape contained in a well-fitting corset and her pale linen dress and apron spotlessly clean, appealed to Eliza.

'These two *ladies*,' she said, indicating she thought them anything but, 'say they are mother and sister to Mistress Gwyn and wish to come into the house.'

Eliza stared at the three of them, bemused. She felt very strange: weary and tearful and all over cold, as if she was suffering from an ague.

'Tell 'er!' Ma Gwyn cried, wiping her nose on her sleeve. 'Tell 'er who we are. An' you can tell her it was me what rescued you with me own money from Clink prison!' She looked Eliza up and down. 'Though to see you now done up like a French dog, a person would never know it.'

'Our Nell said we was to come round any time and

take a jar,' Rose said. 'And that's just what we're doing!'

'Or tryin' ter do!' said Ma Gwyn.

'*Are* these ladies related to Mistress Gwyn?' Mrs Pearce asked Eliza.

'They are,' Eliza replied, nodding. 'But Nell isn't home at the moment,' she said to Ma.

'No matter, my girl,' said Ma. 'I daresay her beer and her whisky is at home!'

There was a tug at Eliza's skirt and she looked down to see Susan. Susan with her carbuncle firmly in place.

'I got four pence on the way over!' she said, slipping it into her mother's hand. 'Four pence and a toffee apple.'

'Good on yer, girl.' Rose pocketed the four pence and looked at her daughter with pride. 'There's not a pissing place about the City that my Susan hasn't begged in.'

'Good heavens,' Mrs Pearce said faintly.

Susan looked up at the house and found she had to step backwards to see it all properly. 'Does our Nell live 'ere on all these floors?' she said, astounded.

'Yers, she does,' Ma Gwyn replied proudly.

'But how did she get such a place?'

No one answered this.

Mrs Pearce coughed delicately. 'So these ladies are related to Mistress Gwyn – but should I really let them in?' she asked Eliza.

Eliza shrugged. She didn't know and much less cared. 'Please could I leave it to you to decide,' she said to Mrs Pearce and, pushing through the little group, she went to her room and climbed on to her bed. Instead of mulling over all that had happened and trying to make sense of things, though, she pulled the blanket over her head and fell into a deep and exhausted sleep.

Late the next morning, Eliza tapped on the door of Nell's drawing room and went in, only to find her sitting before the window in a state of undress.

'I beg your pardon. I didn't realise you were ...' Her voice faded away awkwardly, for she was not quite sure *what* Nell was doing. From the waist up she was naked – or naked apart from a wisp of silk chiffon hanging over one shoulder. She'd not just risen from bed, however, for she was wearing several rows of pearls and some pearl and diamond drop earrings.

'It's all right, Eliza,' Nell smiled. 'Come in.'

Eliza went in and immediately realised they weren't alone, for at the back of the room a brown-smocked artist stood in front of an easel.

'Mr Lely,' Nell said, 'this is Eliza, my maid and companion. Mr Lely is painting my portrait.'

Eliza curtsied. She'd heard of Mr Lely, of course, for he was the most famous artist in England and had painted the royal family, all the leading actresses of the day and a fair number of the royal mistresses too.

'May I move, Mr Lely?' Nell asked. 'I fear that my joints will set as stiff as an old dog's if I don't.'

'You may, madam,' Mr Lely said, and Nell gingerly climbed down from the window seat, stretched out her arms and rubbed at her legs.

'I hear my mother and Rose came a-calling last night,' she said to Eliza.

'They did. Were you in time to see them?'

'No,' Nell said, 'but they left a pile of empty bottles behind so I think they obtained what they came for.' She looked at Eliza's face closely. 'But what is it – did you sleep badly?'

Eliza shot a look at Mr Lely. He was mixing colours on a palette and didn't seem interested in their conversation, however, so she felt able to tell Nell all that had passed at the palace.

'That Monteagle is a lecher and a dog!' Nell said fiercely when she'd heard the tale. 'I pity the person he's been contracted to marry.' She squeezed Eliza's hand. 'But try not to think on it, for he behaves like that with all women. 'Tis his upbringing.' She snorted with laughter. 'To think that Duval is the son of a miller and acts the perfect gentleman, and Monteagle is the son of a wealthy lord and acts like the meanest muckworm.'

'It doesn't make sense,' Eliza agreed.

'Why, Monteagle's father owns half the county of Somersetshire.'

'Really?' Eliza said, disturbed that her home county should be in such hands.

'Or he did. He died recently, so the estates and title now come to Henry. Not that the possession of so much will lighten his disposition, for he's like to remain the perfect beast he's always been.'

Eliza made fists of her hands. 'I hate him!' she said fiercely.

'Of course you do,' Nell soothed, 'but look at it this way: he provided the means for Valentine Howard to come to your aid in the most courteous and genteel manner. So think on *that* instead of allowing yourself to dwell on the miserable wretch who tried to bring you down.'

'I'll try,' sighed Eliza.

The following morning at rehearsal in the theatre, Nell clapped her hands in an effort to draw everyone's attention to her.

'I just want to tell you that a male companion of mine is playing the part of Brown Bear,' she said, 'but as he is fairly well known he wishes not to be seen until the end of the first performance. Until that time, therefore, his part will be taken by George Dunning.'

There was a little stir at this, for most of the theatre people had heard a rumour about who was going to play Brown Bear on opening night, and they fell to speculating excitedly. One did not, however. The wraith-like form of Jemima was seated at the side of the stage holding a script, her job being to prompt the cast when they forgot their lines. Eliza could see that her heart wasn't in it, though, for she was staring unseeingly into the distance and constantly sighing.

At midday Eliza went to speak to her to suggest that they might go together for something to eat.

'I'm not hungry,' Jemima replied dully. Her face was almost grey, and there were dark rings the colour of blackberries under her eyes.

'Have you had breakfast?' Eliza asked, and was answered by a shake of the head. 'You must try and eat something nourishing!'

'Why should I?'

'Well, we have a journey to Barnes on Friday to see little William. You must be strong for that, for I hear the roads are full of ruts and we are like to be jolted to a jelly.'

But Jemima didn't smile at this attempt to cheer her, just sighed again and refused to be tempted outside to buy hot gingerbread or chestnuts or any other sort of delicacy. Eliza went on her own, therefore, and, leaving the theatre and hurrying down Long Acre to the market, was surprised when a smartly painted coach and four stopped just ahead of her and a lady called from its window, 'Maria! Oh, thank goodness!'

Eliza looked behind her, thinking the woman must be calling to someone in a shop, then continued along the cobbles, picking her way carefully across the market rubbish and general filth, for it appeared that the night-soil man's cart had been leaking all along the road.

'Maria!' The lady called again, and then, sounding agitated, flung open the door of the carriage. 'Oh, Maria, do help me!'

Eliza stepped warily across to the carriage. 'I'm sorry,' she said, 'but my name's not Maria.'

The lady, thin and pale, had a handkerchief to her mouth and nose – and indeed London did smell particularly bad that morning. 'Oh!' she said, sounding shocked, and then she looked Eliza up and down. 'No. I can see now that you're not. But you are *very* like a young woman I was recently introduced to.' She stared at Eliza curiously for a moment, and then took a long sniff from the nosegay of flowers she held. 'I'm fair overcome by London, do forgive me.'

'Of course,' Eliza said, then bobbed a curtsy and turned away.

'But tarry a moment – you may be able to help,' the

lady said, 'for my driver's lost and I'm altogether weary. I've been trying to gain entry to the King's Theatre and have been three times up and down the street without discovering the back door.'

'I can help you there,' Eliza nodded. 'Tell your driver to follow me.'

'Oh, thank goodness!' The lady sunk back on the cushions and Eliza, foregoing her shopping for the moment, crossed the road and turned back to the theatre, eventually pausing by one of its back doors.

The carriage stopped and its driver jumped down and lowered the steps. The lady alighted, looking nervously around as she did so.

'Is it all right round here?' she said to Eliza in a whisper. 'I'm dreadfully afeared that some rag-tag beggar will steal my purse.'

'I'll see you safely inside,' Eliza said, and then was suddenly reminded, by the lady's very fair hair and nervous bearing, of Jemima. 'Excuse me for being so bold,' she asked, 'but are you Lady Rotherfield?'

'I am,' said that lady, surprised, putting down her nosegay.

'I'm Eliza Rose. Your daughter's friend,' Eliza said, her excitement gathering. 'It was I who wrote to you; I hope you didn't think me impertinent.'

'I did not!' the lady said, relief and delight spreading across her face. 'For I've been searching for my daughter for many a long month. My dear, you will always have this mother's grateful thanks!'

'Shall I take you to her?'

Lady Rotherfield took one of Eliza's hands in hers. 'Oh, if you would! But how is my daughter?'

'She's very low,' Eliza admitted, 'but I think, with a

mother's care …' She faltered here and could not go on with this sentiment. 'But let me find Jemima and bring her so that you can have a little time together on your own,' she finished.

Eliza asked her to wait in a small sewing room, then, in a flurry of joy, went to find Jemima. She would not, she decided, say who the visitor was, for Jemima might well refuse to see her mother – or even turn tail and run.

'There's someone to see you,' she said on finding her friend. 'Not William!' she added quickly, for Jemima's face had suddenly lifted. She bade Jemima wash her hands and face, made some attempt to arrange her hair and also put a blue shawl around her shoulders in an attempt to add some brightness to her drab appearance.

Jemima submitted to these attentions with no interest nor curiosity, then allowed herself to be led to the sewing room, where Eliza knocked and then pushed her inside.

There was a cry from Jemima – a cry of joy, Eliza decided – followed by a sob, and she heard Lady Rotherfield say, 'Oh, my own darling!' before she went on her way with brimming eyes.

Some half an hour later Jemima, her face stained with tears, came out of the sewing room with her mother's arm about her shoulders.

'I'm going home,' she said to Eliza. She sighed and glanced at her mother. 'Mamma says that Father will forgive me, in time.'

Lady Rotherfield's arm tightened around her daughter. 'You'll return with us to the country and we'll all live there quietly together.' Her daughter smiled tremulously at this. 'We'll invent a story about you being widowed young, and as time passes you'll be accepted back into society.'

Eliza's heart thudded: no one had mentioned the child. 'But there is ...' she began, and both Lady Rotherfield and Jemima looked up at her. 'What about little William?' she asked in a rush. 'Will you take him as well?'

Lady Rotherfield smiled. 'Of course, my dear. Did you think we'd leave without him? No, we'll go to Barnes on our way home and collect him. We'll take his wet nurse too, if she'll come.'

'But surely Father won't allow William in the house!' Jemima said.

'He will,' Lady Rotherfield said firmly. 'Like it or not, you're his child and *your* child is his heir.'

Jemima's grey face had begun to look considerably pinker as she and Eliza hugged each other goodbye. Nell was called for and hugged also, promises were made to keep in touch, then Jemima was taken outside to be taken home in the carriage.

As the coach rolled away, with Eliza waving until she could see no longer Jemima's arm fluttering from the carriage, she felt a mixture of loss and relief wash over her. And a deeper feeling, too: sadness. Everyone, she reflected, had someone to look out for them, be it mother, father, brother, sister or friend.

Everyone had someone except her.

Chapter Twenty-Five

'Are you quite sure you're *rehearsing* when you go to see the king at the palace?' Eliza asked Nell with mock severity a few days later.

'Of course!' Nell said.

'*Really?*'

'A play called *The Prince and the Courtesan*? I'm definitely playing *my* part!' Nell laughed. 'Even though it sometimes ends with us speaking our lines as pillow-talk.'

'And is the king still as keen on play-acting?'

Nell nodded. 'Although he says he will act the role only once, for the great surprise will be when he reveals himself as king, and all that will be lost on subsequent nights.'

With Jemima back at home, Eliza had slipped into the role of prompter, for she was loath to take on the job of orange selling again. It was not, she reasoned, that she felt the work was beneath her, just that people – men – automatically equated the girls who sold oranges with being bawds and whores. Besides, being behind the scenes meant firstly that she wouldn't be so easily noticed by Henry Monteagle, and secondly that she could have a bigger share in the excitement of the king's stage debut.

By early in the afternoon of the first performance of
The Prince and the Courtesan the theatre was
overflowing with people and there were twice as many
as usual crammed into the private boxes. The court
took up the whole of the royal circle, those who were
in on the secret having imparted their excitement to
those who were not. The ordinary, regular theatre-
goers of London had somehow picked up that
something unusual was going to happen, too, but
theories of just what this was varied widely. There
were those who thought that it was merely a new and
controversial play, those who swore that a royal
person was taking part, and those who said that it was
due to the fact that the famous Nell Gwyn would be
retiring shortly to have the king's child, so this might
be the last chance to see her.

The king, escorted by just a valet and without his
spaniels, arrived almost unseen in a hired hackney
carriage with the blinds down, and Nell went out to
greet him. He was then taken to Nell's small dressing
room, which had been hastily improved with a Persian
rug, mirrors and flowers for the occasion. The king's
bear suit was there, Eliza having brushed up the fur
herself – and she had further ensured that there was a
costly embroidered dressing-gown for him to change
into after his peformance.

Eliza stood in the wings as the candle-studded
chandeliers were lit across the stage. She could see,
looking out at the audience, that they were wealthier
than usual by the continuous flashing and sparkling of
the diamonds and precious stones they wore. They
were noisier than usual, too, with shrieking, baying

and whistling coming continually and from all sides. Somewhere out there, she thought, compressing her lips, was the hated Henry Monteagle. And somewhere, too, Valentine Howard.

'Have you ever seen the theatre so full?' Nell said, coming up behind her and breaking into her thoughts.

'Never! Nor with such a quality audience.'

'The street outside is blocked with so many carriage and sixes that many people can't get through. Some have sent their servants to run on ahead and demand that the performance be delayed until they arrive.' Nell nudged Eliza to look at her. 'But what do you think of my costume?'

Eliza turned to admire Nell's outfit which, as she was playing a courtesan, was night attire made of a filmy, gauze-like material, thus ensuring that the men in the audience got a glimpse of her body. It was obvious she was with child, but this plump ripeness suited her. Her hair was loose and flowed in waves down her back, her eyes sparkled, her make-up was vivid.

'You look *very* fine,' Eliza said. 'When you're on stage no one will look at anyone else.'

Nell laughed. 'Brown Bear said he could barely keep his paws off me!'

She looked out to the audience again. 'If Louise is in here with the court tonight, let's hope she's so eaten up with jealousy that she hot-foots it back to France.'

'She can't compare with you,' Eliza said. 'The king will surely never leave you for *her*.'

Nell smiled wryly. 'The king doesn't leave his mistresses, rather he collects them. One wife and one mistress would be enough for most men, but he's a king and so has kingly appetites.'

As Nell spoke the group of musicians on stage struck up and began to play the overture. She put her finger to her lips, then blew Eliza a kiss and went towards the back of the stage, to the doorway from where she was to make her first entrance.

As the overture came to a close the narrator of the play came on to speak the prologue, and then Eliza heard a tremendous cheering, stamping and whooping as Nell entered. This tumult went on for over two minutes until Nell began to speak, and then a hush fell. Eliza relaxed; she knew Nell was word-perfect and wouldn't need any prompting.

The king's entrance would be in about fifteen minutes, Eliza reckoned, and, musing on the secret stage debut of the King of England, felt a shiver of excitement, not least for the fact that there was to be a big party afterwards in one of the Whitehall banqueting rooms, to which she was invited. Monteagle would be there, of course, and she would utterly cut him dead – but she would, perhaps, get the chance to thank Valentine Howard properly for his gallant actions. She'd been in such a state the other evening that she'd acted a perfect goose; she wanted a chance to put this right, to thank him in a gracious and ladylike manner for his rescue of her. She might not be nobility, she thought, but she could act like it when she had to. As soon as that night's performance ended she'd go to the theatre costume department and borrow some finery to wear for the party, and some jewellery, and perhaps she'd put her hair up for the occasion, for it was just long enough now …

Her thoughts were running along happily on these

lines when suddenly she stiffened in fear, sensing that someone had come through the folds of the back curtain and was standing behind her. A hand appeared and touched her shoulder and she all but let out a startled shriek.

'Eliza, don't be afeared,' Claude Duval whispered. 'It is only I.'

She stared at him in shock. 'What are you doing here?' she whispered. She gestured towards the audience. 'The place is full of parliament men and law-makers. If they get a glimpse of you, forty men will storm the stage and take you in.' She gave a sudden little gasp. 'And the king is here, too!'

Claude Duval nodded. 'I thought so.' He took her arm. 'We must be quick, Eliza. I've come to say that under no circumstances must the king be allowed to go on stage tonight.'

'*What?*'

'I was in a coffee house a moment ago and heard three men talking,' Duval said, his voice low and urgent. 'One told the others that he'd heard there was a plan afoot to take the king.'

Eliza swallowed hard, staring at Duval.

'He's going to appear on stage in disguise, yes?'

Eliza nodded dumbly.

'I don't know how, but they're going to take him prisoner. I believe some men are concealed about the theatre and when he's on stage alone they'll capture him.'

Eliza began to tremble. 'Not *really*? Is it true? But what should I do?'

'You must tell him not to go on. You must *insist* that he does not!'

'But I can't! He's already in his bear suit and the queen and all the court are here to see him.'

'If you don't, he'll be captured and they may put someone like Cromwell back in power.' Duval curled his lip. 'Gambling and merrymaking and drinking will be banned and the grand profession of highwayman will be impoverished.'

Eliza stood immobile, fully believing Duval's words but not knowing how to act; longing to ask someone else what to do.

'Could I wait until the interval and ask Nell to tell him?'

Duval gripped her arms. 'That may be too late. You must tell the king now, at once.' He hesitated. 'Say it's information from someone you have great faith in.'

'But who should go on stage in his stead?'

Duval shrugged. 'That doesn't matter. When the plotters find that they've taken the wrong man, they'll let him go.' He pressed Eliza's hands within his own. 'Go now with all haste and God save the king!'

Eliza, fired by his words, hesitated no longer but went straight to the door of the small dressing room and, being admitted by the king's valet, immediately sank into a deep curtsy. She was helped to her feet by a bear and found this so ludicrous that she almost burst out laughing. Then she remembered what she'd come for.

'Sire, I come with a dire warning from someone I trust absolutely,' she said, her words tumbling over themselves, 'and although she does not know this news, Mistress Gwyn trusts this person also.'

'A dire warning *now*?' the king said, muffled from inside his bear's head. 'I'm just about to go on stage!'

'It is about that. Sire, I've been given information that there's a plot against you. That if you go on stage you'll be taken. Kidnapped.'

'Another plot,' the king said. He sighed somewhat wearily. 'So, I'm to be seized from the stage, you say?'

'Yes, sire. The man who told me this overheard it in a coffee house, and was perfectly sure it was true. He's just this moment come to tell me of it.'

'But why didn't he stay to tell me himself?'

'Because ... because he's a wanted man,' Eliza said. She looked up at the king. It was difficult, she thought, from the fixed expression of the bear's face, to know how much he was affected by the news. 'I implore you, sire, don't go on stage tonight!'

There was a moment's pause and then the king sighed resignedly and removed the head.

'I will not, then,' he said. 'But Nelly will be very disappointed – and so am I.'

He returned straight away to Whitehall and George Dunning was called, told there had been a change of plan and that he'd now be playing Brown Bear – although he wasn't told why.

The play proceeded. Brown Bear went on stage and, owing to the fact that George Dunning wasn't as tall as the king, his furry legs bagged somewhat around his ankles. This fact was not lost on Nell, who faltered slightly in the delivery of her lines, while Eliza watched from the wings and waited anxiously for the interval so she could let her know what had happened.

When Nell's scene finished she left the stage to tumultuous applause, making use of some ingenious new moving scenery which simulated a horse-drawn carriage.

The bear was left alone on stage and he approached the front and addressed the audience in rhyming couplets.

'*A man beneath – on top a bear,
I go to seek my mistress fair.*'

The audience laughed heartily, some of them believing that the king was delivering the lines.

'*Is she constant, is she true?
This bear will know, and he'll tell you.*'

Laurence Linkletter, the man playing the bear's rival, entered at the back of the stage laughing a villain's laugh.

'*But this is no bear!*' he said to the audience, getting out a gun. '*I love the courtesan too, and I'll fire a shot to see him off!*'

He took aim and fired, making the ladies in the audience scream, and Brown Bear fell down on cue. Instead of getting up, however, clutching his leg and limping off, he lay writhing on the floor.

Eliza stared at him, puzzled. This wasn't in the script. This wasn't right at all.

Linkletter tucked his gun under his arm and went off stage laughing, and the audience applauded and booed and threw orange peel after him.

Eliza waited for Brown Bear to get up and address the audience, but he didn't. She wondered if he'd forgotten his lines, and hissed from the side of the stage:

'*'Twill take more than a mere shot
To stem the love that this bear's got.*'

But still he didn't stir. The audience began to catcall for him to move himself, to get up and walk. A slow hand-clap started.

As Eliza stared she saw, with horror, that there was a pool of dark liquid spreading from under his body. Others noticed it too and then there was a general outburst of panic and (from those who thought that the king was playing the bear) much terror. As the curtain was brought down and two dozen people ran on to the stage, Eliza, realising that the plan must have been to *kill* the king rather than kidnap him, rushed to tell Nell that he was safe.

'Someone had substituted a real bullet for the dummy one,' Nell said, coming into the tiring room some time later and addressing the members of the company. 'Laurence Linkletter had no idea, of course. He's terrified that he'll be accused of murder.'

Eliza gasped – as did the rest of the company.

'He's dead, then?' she asked. 'George Dunning is dead?'

'He is,' Nell said soberly. 'He bled to death before a physician could be called.'

'And the king?'

'The king has sent a message to say that he's perfectly well but will take no more parts in any plays,' said Nell. 'What's more, the party is off. There'll be no celebrations at Whitehall tonight.' She turned to Eliza and smiled. 'I'm to take you to the palace tomorrow, however, where the king wishes to receive you.'

Eliza stared at Nell. 'Is he … angry at all?' she asked nervously.

'Not a bit! He wants to thank you for saving his life. He'll give you something – a medal of some sort, perhaps. A memento of the occasion.'

Eliza's face broke into a tremulous smile. 'It wasn't really me who saved him, though,' she said to Nell.

'But I don't think that ...' Nell's voice faded and she mouthed the word *Duval*, ' ... will want to go to the palace. And besides, I'm sure he has all the jewels he needs.'

Chapter Twenty-Six

Eliza sat on a window seat in the music room of Whitehall Palace looking outside. She'd never, she thought, seen such a garden before: a formal arrangement of four beds crossed and edged with box hedging and enclosing cobbles, pebbles and stones in decorative patterns. In the middle of each bed stood a pyramid structure covered in ivy, and the whole was surrounded by a succession of lime trees set at the same distance from each other.

A breeze was blowing and the leaves from the lime trees were spinning off and swirling across the garden so that, staring out, Eliza was reminded of autumn days on the Quantock Hills at home. Days when she'd chased her brothers and sisters through knee-high bronze leaves and they'd rolled over and over down the hills and fallen into heaps of damp bracken at the valley floor. But all those days, she thought now, those golden days when she'd considered herself so happy, had been a delusion. She'd merely been tolerated in that family. No one had really loved her. Her every memory of those days was a counterfeit one.

She opened her hand. In her palm was an emerald, a stone as dark and lustrous as the glossy ivy outside. It had been given to her by the king, and after he'd bestowed it he'd taken both her hands in his and told her that he owed his throne to such loyal citizens as herself; that she was truly a child of his kingdom. The whole of this happening, so momentous for Eliza, had taken perhaps forty-five seconds, for there were around eighty other people in the presence chamber, all with seemingly urgent business that His Majesty had to attend to. Whilst she'd been waiting, a furious row had broken out over who was next in line: a group who'd come from the Admiralty to talk about the ordering of some new ships, or a party of architects bearing an exquisite model of what was possibly going to be the new St Paul's Cathedral.

As she'd waited her turn, Eliza had studied everyone surreptitiously. Spies were everywhere; Nell had told her that. And Duval, too, had said that there were always plots against the throne. Which of the men here, then – or the women – were not all that they appeared to be? There were rumours that Monmouth, denied the throne because of his illegitimacy, might seize it by force. Was it he who'd plotted to have the king killed on stage?

Looking now at the glowing emerald she held, she wondered what she should do with it. Have it made into a pendant? Hang it from a silver bracelet? Have it fashioned into a ring? Keep it for ever, that was certain.

'What are *you* doing here?' A child of about eight had come into the music room. She was dressed in a heavy brocade gown and waistcoat embroidered in gold thread; a perfect miniature of the type of dresses worn at court by the fashionable ladies.

'I'm here to have singing instruction,' Eliza said, for

the king, after giving her the emerald, had remembered his promise that she should have lessons with his daughter. 'The king said that I should come,' she added, speaking somewhat shyly, for although the child was perhaps half her own age, it was obvious from her dress and bearing that she was one of the royal children. To show that this was understood, Eliza got down from the window seat and curtsied to her.

The child continued to regard her coldly.

'Are you Anne?' Eliza ventured as she rose.

'No, I'm not!' came the immediate and indignant reply. 'I am Charlotte Fitzroy, Countess of Lichfield.'

Eliza thought swiftly; she was the third child of Barbara Castlemaine, then, so was about seven years old.

'And I don't have my singing lessons with just *anyone*. I won't even have Anne or Mary in with me so I certainly won't have you.'

'Well, I ... His Majesty ... that is –'

'Who are you, anyway?'

'I'm Eliza. Eliza Rose.'

'You have a funny voice. Where do you come from?'

'Originally, I come from Somersetshire.'

'You have a gown which is *very* out of fashion.'

Eliza didn't reply.

'And your hair is not in style,' the child went on. 'Since Louise de Keroualle joined the court we all have our hair done the French way.'

'I'm afraid I'm not conversant with what hairstyles are being worn at court,' Eliza said, trying to sound as polite as possible.

'So if you're not at court where *do* you come from?'

'I'm with the King's Theatre Company,' Eliza replied.

'*Mon Dieu!*' The child took a step backwards. 'You're an actress?'

'Not exactly,' Eliza began. 'Not at all!' she amended, too late, for Charlotte had turned to clip-clop away on her silver leather mules.

Eliza resumed her place on the window seat, wondering what to do next. It appeared that the longed-for singing lessons were still to be denied her – how she hated being so dependent on the whims of others! Now, should she stay and wait for the music master, or make a dignified exit? If so, there was the ever-present problem of just how she was going to locate that exit. So perhaps she'd just sit on the window seat a little longer and enjoy the view.

Nell found her there half an hour later.

'Do you know there are four music rooms in the palace!' she said. 'I've looked into each one of them for you, and this was the last. Have you had your lesson?'

Eliza, laughing a little, told her that she hadn't, and also the reason why.

'I presume that dear little Mistress Charlotte met the singing master on his way in and told him not to attend on me.'

'She's a spoilt miss – she knows full well that she's the king's favourite child.' Nell frowned a little. 'I hope my baby is a girl, for the king greatly favours his daughters. He hands out titles to them like sweetmeats.'

'Does he really?'

'Oh, yes, it's the Countess of this, the Duchess of

that. He's not nearly so generous with his boys.'

'Doctor Deane said you were having a boy,' Eliza reminded her.

Nell frowned. 'But he's not *always* right.'

'No, I'm sure he's not,' Eliza said. He couldn't have been right, for instance, when he'd told her that she was high-born. She knew that. It had just been a play-act on the astrologer's part to cause a stir and a sensation.

The attention of both Eliza and Nell was caught by a pretty scene outside the window, for the queen and several ladies-in-waiting had come into the garden and were playing with a ball, picking up their full skirts and running backwards and forwards to catch it across the cobbles.

'The queen is a goodly sort,' Nell said as they watched, 'for she's heard that I'm with child and sent me a cordial for morning sickness. Not that I've ever been sick,' she added.

Eliza shook her head wonderingly; she'd never understand how the queen dealt so equably with the pregnancies of her husband's mistresses. Staring at them now in the garden, she noticed two ladies-in-waiting she'd never seen before; girls who stood out from the others because they were dark-haired when everyone apart from the queen was a more-fashionable blonde.

'Who are those two girls – the dark-haired beauties?' she asked Nell.

Nell looked. 'Henry Monteagle's sisters,' she said. 'Recently come to court to try and find suitable husbands.'

'Monteagle!' Eliza said, rather shocked, for they

looked much too agreeable to be anything to do with him.

'Coming to live at court is a good road to marriage,' Nell said. 'Girls put themselves on display for a year or two and nearly always find someone to wed.'

Eliza stared down at the two girls. 'But they don't look anything like him,' she said. 'He's broad of hip while they're narrow, and their colouring is very different – they're dark-haired and of a pale complexion, and he's fair-haired and florid.'

'What you mean is, *he* is vile and *they* look perfectly nice!' finished Nell.

'Indeed!' For certainly the girls looked sweet of expression and appeared good-tempered. 'What are their names?'

Nell shrugged. 'I've no idea.'

'And how is it that someone as beastly as he could have such nice sisters?'

'We can't help our relations,' Nell said and, as she raised her eyes to heaven, Eliza knew just who she was thinking of. 'Besides, they may have had a different father.'

'Yes, of course,' Eliza said. She went on looking at the two girls, though she couldn't have said why.

Eliza didn't get a chance to speak to Valentine Howard until a week later when Nell, her dining room now furnished with silver plate and candelabra, her larders filled with game and her cellars replete with fine wines, decided to hold a small house-warming dinner for the king and a few favoured guests. In the normal way Eliza wouldn't have expected to attend such an occasion, but a musician was playing the harpsichord during supper and Nell had asked Eliza to go in and accompany him with a couple of songs after they'd eaten.

In the meantime, Eliza had had some of her money advanced and commissioned a goldsmith to make the king's emerald into a pendant, which had been achieved simply by winding fine gold wire around the stone so that it looked as if it were covered by an elegant golden cage. Hanging from a green velvet ribbon and worn for the dinner party with Nell's moss-green satin gown, it looked very fine.

On entering Nell's dining room after the sweetmeats had been served, Eliza's first fervent hope was that Henry Monteagle was not among the guests. Her second was that Valentine Howard was.

Rising from a deep curtsy towards the king, she was happy to find that both wishes had been fulfilled, for scanning quickly around she saw that Valentine Howard was there, also Monmouth, Rochester and several others of the gang of wits – but of Henry Monteagle there was no sign.

Eliza couldn't follow sheet music nor knew the tunes of any of the newer ballads, so had already arranged with the harpsichord player that she'd sing two traditional airs. These were received with slightly drunken praise by the assembled guests and a request from the king that she should repeat them.

She did so and then curtsied again before making her exit. The men, she noticed, resumed their drinking and carousing before she'd even left the room.

After going downstairs and begging some supper from Mrs Pearce – for she'd been much too nervous about her singing to eat beforehand – Eliza was making her way back to her room with some slices of cold roast goose when she met several of the party moving from the dining to the snooker room. One of these was Valentine Howard.

He stopped on seeing her and gave a short bow.

'Are you well, madam?' he asked.

'I am, thank you, sire.' Eliza bobbed him a curtsy, endeavouring to keep the roast goose on the plate.

'And are you going to join us?'

'*Mais non.*' She coughed nervously. She was anxious to use French expressions, as did the aristocracy, but was not always sure of their correct pronunciation. 'Though I hoped to see you in order to thank you for your kindness to me the other evening.'

'Oh, it was nothing.'

Eliza nibbled at her lip. She thought that he spoke a little too carelessly, almost as if her ordeal had been of no consequence.

'Indeed it was, sire, for I found myself in danger, and who knows what would have happened if you hadn't come along when you had.'

He frowned at her. His brows met in the middle in the most devilishly intriguing way, Eliza thought, and his eyes were the brightest blue she'd ever seen, his eyelashes very long and thick.

'But if you think such situations so dangerous,' he asked, 'why do you persist in getting yourself into them? If you have assignations with fellows like Monteagle, you must perceive, surely, the inherent danger?'

Eliza stared at him, almost too taken-aback to speak. 'I did not ... I *do* not ...'

He nodded to the emerald. 'Oh, and I suppose that

pretty bauble around your neck was obtained by being a mere lady's maid, was it?'

'No, it was not!' Eliza said. 'This pretty bauble, as you call it, was from the king.'

He raised his eyebrows. 'His Majesty seems to be a *very* busy man these days ...'

Eliza was about to protest that she'd been given it for saving his life, but something stopped her. No, if he believed the worst of her, then so be it. She wouldn't be the one to put him right. She was filled with a childish desire to stick out her tongue at him, but managed not to. Instead she pushed her nose into the air, said, 'Your servant, sire!' in as disdainful a manner as possible and, picking up her skirts with her free hand, ran up the stairs and away.

How dare he! What an *infuriating* fellow! What an infuriating, maddening, opinionated ... and devastatingly attractive fellow.

The following evening Eliza was downstairs in the little room which Nell called her closet, sewing new buttons on to the scarlet dress. The bodice being lined with calico, however, it was difficult to insert the needle, and she had also lost her thimble, so more often than not it would stick halfway and then Eliza would have to drive it in with the tip of her finger, sometimes piercing the flesh as she did so. Each time this happened she'd curse Henry Monteagle – and then curse Valentine Howard. How *could* he? How could he think her a common whore? She'd never given him any cause to believe that!

But then, the last of the buttons sewn, she thought about it a little more: Valentine Howard had seen her in Clink, he'd viewed her as a half-naked mermaid at the fair, he'd spoken to her when she'd been an orange girl and now she was Nell's friend and companion. What would *any* man think? Maybe she had been too harsh on him ...

Eliza did not see her friend until near eight o'clock that evening, for Nell had had a day which included shopping, a sitting with Lely, gown fittings, a play reading, a tea party and an appointment with a lace-maker who was to fashion her a sumptuous lying-in gown. When she eventually came in accompanied by a parcel-laden lackey, she was full of news.

'Well, whatever do you think?!' she said as she flung her cloak and feathered hat on to the settle and indicated that the parcels were to be dropped there, too.

Eliza, laughing, said she hadn't the slightest idea.

She dismissed the lackey with a wave. 'Well, why do you think it was that Monteagle wasn't at my soirée last night?'

Eliza shrugged. She knew it wasn't merely that Nell had been solicitous enough of her feelings not to have included him, because if the king had wished to bring Monteagle along then he certainly would have done.

'He's away? He has a new woman – a new *amour*?' Eliza said a little self-consciously.

'No! He's been banned from court!'

Eliza gasped. 'Such good news! But why?'

'Because he's challenged someone to a duel – and you know the king has banned duels.'

'Who is it he's challenged?'

'Someone named Major Whitfield. Monteagle said he was insulted by him and so called him out. The king has told him to withdraw the challenge, or stay away from court – which is exactly what he's doing. They think he means to go through with the duel, though.' Nell flung herself down on the settle. ''Twill be pistols at dawn within the next few days, they say – and Val Howard is to be his second.'

'Oh,' Eliza said anxiously. 'Is there any danger for a second?'

'I think not.' Nell gave Eliza a little sideways look and laughed. 'I'm sure your Valentine will be quite safe.'

Eliza contemplated the happy thought of Monteagle being away from court for ever. 'But what of his sisters?' she asked suddenly. 'How horrid for them to arrive at court just in time to hear that their brother is to fight a duel.'

Nell looked at her. 'Well, why ever should you think of *them*?'

Eliza paused, thought about it again, and shrugged. 'I don't know.' She smiled and pointed to the packages strewn across the floor. 'But what are all those interesting-looking parcels?'

Nell began counting them out, squeezing or sniffing them to try and detect their contents. 'Twelve pairs of scented gloves,' she said, 'two pairs of silver leather slippers, some hair jewellery, two black bodices embroidered in red silk, three painted fans, a nightgown and wrapper of gold-spangled lace and some red and white striped silk undersmocks.' She lifted the last brown-paper package. 'And the most heavenly ribbons in silver-blue to trim the rocking cot

I'm having made.'

'Blue?' Eliza questioned. 'So you *do* think it'll be a boy?'

'I'll send to Doctor Deane to make quite sure. Which reminds me that I've found out Squintabella's date of birth and want the doctor to cast her chart.' Nell went cross-eyed, making Eliza laugh. 'I want to know how long she'll be at court.'

'I'll go tomorrow,' Eliza promised, and she was about to gather her things together and wish Nell goodnight when they heard the bellman outside.

'Eight of the clock!' he called. 'Highwayman taken in Tavern!'

The girls looked at each other.

'I wonder which highwayman?' Nell mused. 'Not my sister's husband, I hope, for I know she'd straight away move in here.'

'And not ...' Eliza's voice faltered and she put down her sewing. 'Shall I run down and ask?' she said. 'I could catch him on the corner and find out more.'

'Do that. Highwaymen are as common as crows and it's probably someone we've never heard of, but 'twould set our minds at rest.'

Eliza flung a shawl around her shoulders, ran downstairs and out of the front door, catching up with the bellman at the top of Thames steps.

'Can you tell me more about the highwayman arrested?' she asked, panting.

'Oh, aye, young missy,' he said. 'They took him in a tavern. They said he was drunk as a lord, for he'd had a mighty good day's thieving and was enjoying a celebration.'

'But who was he?'

'Why, none other than Claude Duval himself.' The bellman winked at Eliza. 'And they say he's to be hanged good and quick before he can get away again!'

Chapter Twenty-Seven

The next morning Eliza, after rising early, went to the stationers at St Paul's to buy a special edition of the *London Newes*. Going upstairs to Nell's room and sitting amid the ruffled silk, lace pillows and be-ribboned hangings of her sumptuous new bed, she read the details of Claude Duval's arrest to her.

'It says they took him at Mother Mabberley's tavern, the Hole in the Wall in Chandos Street. A member of the watch apprehended him when he was talking about a robbery he'd committed earlier on Turnham Green, where he stole a wooden chest containing precious jewels and gold. He was drunk, they say, and off his guard.'

Nell sighed. 'How like a man to be boasting of his success! A chest of jewels, though. No wonder he was full of it.'

'He was taken straight to Newgate and will be tried by Sir William Morton the day after tomorrow.'

'So quickly! That's to make sure he's not sprung.'

Eliza looked further down the paper. 'There follows a list of some of the robberies he's accused of and notable people that he's stolen from over the years.'

Nell waved her hand dismissively. 'But he never used violence,' she said, 'and most of the people he

294

robbed could well afford it.'

'What will happen to him?'

Nell shook her head and shivered, though a large fire had already been lit in the room. 'He'll be sentenced to be hanged for sure.'

Eliza felt her eyes fill with tears.

'Unless,' Nell went on, 'we can appeal to the king to reprieve him.'

'*We* appeal?'

'Well, you and I know that Claude Duval has saved the king's life, so perhaps some sort of bargain can be struck.'

Eliza read further from the *Newes*, and then gave a sudden little cry. 'It says here that they're seeking his accomplices, and that if anyone wants to turn king's evidence, they'll be given a Tyburn ticket.' She looked at Nell. 'What's that?'

''Tis a token against being hanged. If you give evidence against a highwayman, you're allowed to go free even though you may have committed the same crime yourself.'

'They're also giving rewards for the capture of his partners in crime and those who have assisted him over the years.' Eliza suddenly put down the newspaper. 'They are seeking *me*!' she said in a fright.

'But no one saw you that night!'

''Tis possible that Monmouth did,' Eliza said shakily. 'And there are those who saw me with Claude in the coffee house beforehand, too. It could be said that we were in there plotting together.'

'But *who* would have seen you?'

'Anyone! Don't you always say that there are spies everywhere?'

'I do, but ... No, we mustn't think of this! We must seek out His Majesty and beg for Claude to be treated leniently because he's saved the king's life and has never used violence on anyone. And in the meantime I'll send a messenger to Newgate to see if there's anything that Claude needs while he's in there.' Nell shuddered. ''Tis grim there – but at least at this time of the year there's little prison fever about.'

Much to her relief, for she hated going anywhere near prisons, Nell didn't ask Eliza to go to Newgate. Instead she was instructed to go to Doctor Deane's with a slip of paper giving details of Louise de Keroualle.

'And please ask him about my confinement again, and whether he's perfectly sure that I'm having a boy,' Nell had added.

Eliza usually loved walking through the teeming streets of the City, but the news about Duval had unnerved her. Everyone was talking about the arrest; ballad sheets had already been printed with tales of Duval's exploits and posters engraved with wishes for his safe return to the 'fine and ancient business of highway robbery'. Eliza also saw some official bills, however, offering a reward for the handing over of anyone who'd helped him, and after reading these couldn't help but suspect everyone. Was that boy really sweeping the gutters, or was he watching her? Was the street trader selling trinkets from his tray, or had he been placed there to snoop? Why did the green man with his barrow of herbs seem to be following her? She contemplated buying a mask and holding it to her face, but decided that this would make her look more suspicious. Nevertheless, she pulled the hood of her cloak well over her head before going through the City gates.

She passed St Columbus Church, where she'd last seen the man she'd thought was her father, and wondered if he was still working there. The church building seemed to be complete now, so perhaps he'd gone to Somersetshire, back home to her brothers and sisters. Who were, of course, no longer her brothers and sisters. But telling herself not to ponder on that and become downcast, she walked swiftly on towards London Bridge and the consulting rooms of Doctor Deane.

On stating her business, the maid disappeared for a moment and came back with the doctor close behind her. He bowed to Eliza and she returned a curtsy, then handed over the slip of paper.

'This is the date and place of birth of a friend of Mistress Gwyn,' she said. She spoke quickly, for the unpleasant smell in the rooms was making her eyes smart and she wanted to get away as soon as she could. 'She wants you to cast a chart for this lady.'

'And are there any questions in particular that she seeks answers for?' the astrologer asked.

Eliza answered as Nell had instructed. 'She wishes to know how long she'll be at court.'

The astrologer glanced at the paper. 'Ah. Born in Deauville. This is the birth date of Louise de Keroualle, no doubt.'

Eliza marvelled at this rather, but didn't answer.

'Mistress Rose,' Doctor Deane said as she turned to go, 'you may be interested in a strange incident which happened last week.'

Eliza looked at him and shivered. There was something sinister about him, she thought, and something disturbing about the aspect of his rooms: the gloom, the choking smell, the clammy feel of them. What did this man know? Could he tell that she'd assisted Claude Duval? Was this what he was going to say?

'And what was that?' she asked, trying to keep her tone even.

'Last week I was consulted by someone who happened to have exactly the same natal chart as you.'

Eliza blinked at him, not understanding.

'I mean someone who was born in the same place as you, at the same time, and with the same planets in the same houses. That is, with a preponderance of planets in the second and the tenth house.'

'But ... but is this so extraordinary?' Eliza asked. 'One sometimes finds that one shares a birthday with someone.'

'This was not just a birthday. This is someone who in every single aspect is your astrological twin.'

'My astrological twin? Someone at court?' Eliza asked, knowing that was where he obtained most of his clients. 'But who?'

Doctor Deane smiled so that his yellow skin crinkled like paper. 'That, my dear young lady, would be a breach of confidentiality. I didn't disclose your details, and I won't disclose theirs. I won't even say if my client is male or female.'

'Does it mean that there is someone who's very like me in character, then?' Eliza asked, terribly intrigued.

'It does not, for the circumstances of your upbringing have been so very dissimilar that you are different in every possible way.'

'So is there *any* connection between us?'

'The connection is this: with due consideration to your present position in life, I believe that something very interesting and remarkable happened at your birth. That's all I will say.'

And before Eliza could ask anything else he bowed and withdrew.

Eliza walked home, deep in thought. She had no idea what it all could mean. The astrologer had bewildered her so completely, she realised, that she'd completely forgotten to ask him about Nell's forthcoming child.

'The king,' Nell said with some impatience that evening, 'has the Venetian ambassador staying and they've gone hunting wild pig together in Windsor.'

'So you haven't been able to see him?'

'Not even for a moment!' Nell said. 'And tomorrow he is Touching all day – which, before you ask, Eliza, is when those of the population who are afflicted with a disease called the King's Evil come to the palace to be cured by him.'

'I've never heard of such a thing.'

'And pray you never do, for it's a horrid and nasty disease which they believe only the touch of a king can undo.' Nell paused only briefly. 'But how did you fare with Doctor Deane?'

Eliza had already decided not to say anything about the discovery of the person who shared her birth details, for she wanted to ponder on it a while, think what it might possibly mean.

'Well, 'twas very strange,' she said, 'for when I gave

him the paper he knew straight away that it was for Louise de Keroualle.'

Nell smiled. 'As long as he doesn't return the chart to *her*! And what more did he say about the sex of my child?'

Eliza had to admit then that she'd forgotten to ask and Nell, rather cross, said that Eliza should remember that she was her *maid* first and foremost, not merely her friend. Eliza, deeply hurt, turned away with her eyes stinging with tears, and Nell immediately said she was sorry.

'I'm a cross-patch and you must take no notice of me!' she said. She put her arm through Eliza's. 'But when you go back to collect Squintabella's chart you must remember to ask.'

Eliza nodded. 'Of course!' she said, but felt again an anxiety about her situation. Not only might Nell lose her position with the king, but it was possible that she, Eliza, might fall out of favour with Nell. And what would happen then?

The incident now forgotten by her, Nell sighed. 'But did you notice that everywhere on the street the talk is of nothing but Claude? I heard his name dozens of times even from within my carriage.'

'As I walked through the market at Leadenhall I heard a ballad sung about him,' Eliza said. 'And then heard a different one as I was crossing Fleet river!'

'At least our friend wants for nothing. The messenger came back from Newgate to say that he's as well as he can be, has paid for his own cell and is having food sent in from the Fox and Grapes.'

The two girls looked at each other and sighed dismally. Eliza thought that Nell was perhaps a little in love with the so-handsome Claude – and she herself certainly kept a special place in her heart for him.

'We *must* try to save him,' Nell said fervently. 'I'll see the king as soon as I can – I'll send a message to him through Chiffinch.'

The next morning Eliza was leisurely buying ribbons from a peddler outside the front door when the information came down the street from several sources – by whisper, by shouted word, by the forlorn cry of a woman in the street, and lastly from a shout from the bellman – that Claude Duval had been sentenced to hang at Tyburn in two days' time.

Hurriedly taking this news back to Nell, Eliza found that she was receiving Aphra Behn, who'd come to see her with a new play, so had to wait on the landing for that lady to leave. When Nell discovered that sentence on Duval had already been passed, she immediately sent for her carriage so that she and Eliza could go to the palace together.

'I haven't yet heard back from Chiffinch,' she said, 'but we'll go this instant and wait for the king to become free. If necessary, we'll stay there all day.'

Arriving at Whitehall Palace, Eliza was amazed to see a winding snake of people coming out of one of the doors and extending all around the gravelled square where the carriages usually waited.

'So many folk waiting to see him!' she said to Nell.

'The king touched nigh on four thousand last year,' Nell said. She nudged Eliza. 'But don't go too close to any of them, for fear you may become infected.'

'Then doesn't the king catch the disease?'

'Of course not,' Nell said, frowning. 'He *is* the king.'

Eliza was not sure how Nell knew her way, but after entering the palace and travelling some distance through it, they found themselves in a vast presence chamber where scores of afflicted people sat on benches waiting patiently to be seen. Every so often a small line of people would be led off, then the whole audience would shuffle along to sit in these places and more people be let in from outside. It was not just sufferers who were waiting, Eliza saw, for some were accompanied by members of their families and there were also doctors and black-clothed ministers milling about. All of these together contributed to a tremendous bustle and noise.

It was apparent that many of those waiting knew who Nell was – and those who didn't were quickly informed – so that soon Eliza found they were the focus of attention for several hundred pairs of eyes. Nell attempted to get into the next room, into the actual presence of the king, but as those in charge of proceedings all seemed to be churchmen who knew and disapproved of her reputation, she didn't get very far.

She went back to sit with Eliza after another attempt. 'We may have to wait until the whole blooming lot of them have gone in!' she said crossly – and so loudly that a whole bevy of clerics turned and waggled their heads at her disapprovingly. 'And you needn't look so hoity-toity,' she retorted unabashed, 'for I've seen plenty of you at the theatre taking a sneaky look at my privities!'

They waited there for two more hours, until the High Chamberlain, one of the palace officials with whom Nell was friendly, came in and, noticing her, gave leave for them to be taken into the next chamber. Nell was escorted through, smiling triumphantly around the room, and Eliza followed in her wake.

This chamber was about a quarter the size of the other and the king stood within it on a raised dais, a minister to each side of him reading from the Bible in a constant sing-song. Ten patients stood in a line before them.

Nell and Eliza took their places at the back and watched as each of the patients approached in turn. The king laid a hand on their head and the other on the afflicted part and said a few words. A medal of some sort was placed about the patient's neck – which Nell said was of angel-gold and could be sold on afterwards. The ten patients being touched and led off, a basin of water was brought in for the king to wash his hands, then another ten people appeared.

Nell coughed loudly.

'I see you, Mistress Gwyn,' the king said, 'but you'll have to wait your turn to be touched.'

Nell pulled her cloak back to indicate her belly. ''Tis certain, sire, that you have already touched me!'

The ministers looked scandalised and the king hid a smile. 'I'll speak to you very soon, Nelly.'

Another half-hour went by before the king called for a break and, while Eliza sat waiting, he and Nell went off into an inner sanctum.

Nell was away only ten minutes or so, and when she returned her face was grave. She didn't speak until they returned to the carriage.

'The king says he'll try to obtain a reprieve for Claude, but we're not to hope for one,' she said.

'Did you say that it was Claude Duval who –'

'I did,' Nell nodded. 'I told him that he owed his life to Duval.'

'And what did he answer?'

'He said that whatever Duval had done for him didn't excuse the fact that he was a highwayman and villain. He said,' Nell went on sadly, 'that law and order must be maintained.' She put out a hand to take Eliza's. 'I fear that he'll hang, Eliza. There's nothing more we can do to help.'

Chapter Twenty-Eight

'And we're to 'ave seats right in front of the scaffold, you say?' Old Ma Gwyn was very pleased with this news.

Nell nodded. She'd been crying, Eliza could see, and her face was pale under the rouge she'd applied, but her spotted veil hid the slight swelling of her eyes.

Eliza had been crying too, but had not, she thought, managed to hide the results as well as Nell, for her nose was red and her eyes ached. She looked at herself in the Venetian mirror in the hall as they waited for the carriage and adjusted her hat so that its veil fell across her face. She wasn't wearing black, for Nell had insisted that the three of them should wear their best, most beautiful clothes.

'We must look as if we are going to a wedding, not a hanging,' she'd said the night before. 'I'll wear my crimson wool suit, and you, Eliza, must wear your russet dress and embroidered jacket. I want Claude to see that we've dressed in our very best for him.'

Even Ma Gwyn had been prinked up for the occasion, and her unruly shape had been shoe-horned first into a commodious bodice and then a grey linsey-woolsey suit with a frilly white jabot at its neck. Her footwear, unfortunately, let her down, for her packhorse-sized feet were encased in boots which had been tied around with great raggedy squares of sacking to protect them from the mud.

Ma Gwyn and her boots, Eliza thought as they travelled to Newgate prison, seemed to take up most of the carriage, for that lady was sitting four-square in front of the window and blocking out most of the space and all of the light. Nell, in deference to the solemnity of the occasion, had drawn down the blind on her side of the carriage, but Ma Gwyn was waving to people in the street from her window – and had twice spotted someone she knew and insisted that the carriage stop so she could pass the time of day.

'Ma, 'tis not a party we're attending, 'tis a hanging,' Nell said as they travelled down Fleet Street accompanied by a great number of other carriages, sedans and hansom cabs.

''Tis a great and special 'anging and an opportunity for mixing with the 'igh and mighty,' Ma agreed. 'And for making all sorts of deals,' she added in an undertone.

Nell looked at Eliza and sighed.

'I was thinking of a waxworks show,' Ma went on. 'A model of Monsewer Duval and 'is 'orse, and maybe a couple of wax well-ter-dos crying at the wayside. I could 'ave it up and going by next week.' A sly look passed across her face. 'I was wondering, my sweeting, if you could use yer good offices to obtain the great man's clothes for me.'

'No, I couldn't!'

'Pity. Still, I'll try for them meself.' The old lady waved merrily to someone outside and then an indignant look crossed her face. 'I've 'eard that the

Tangier Tavern is trying for 'is body. They wants to embalm it and put it on show there.'

'That would be *very* unseemly!' Eliza protested.

'That's just what I said,' said Ma. 'For they don't know 'ow to do these things with taste and discretion, whereas if *I* 'ad 'im I'd put on a most *hexcellent* show.'

It was not possible, they soon found, to get anywhere near Newgate Prison. The hanging procession was to leave from here, so the road outside was clogged with people who'd either come to catch a last glimpse of the highwayman or to sell refreshments, and carriages jostled for space with pastry-cooks crying gingerbread, fishsellers selling dried hake and milkmaids leading cows.

'Been like this since five o'clock this morning!' a footman on a neighbouring coach informed them.

'Oh-ay,' Ma nodded approvingly. 'There's a mint o' money to be made today.'

'What if there was a last-minute reprieve?' Eliza asked Nell suddenly. 'How would the message get through?'

'A *reprieve*?' Ma echoed, clearly distressed at the idea.

Nell shook her head. 'There won't be,' she said. 'The king tried – he spoke to Sir William Morton himself – but told me that he could do no more.' She sighed. 'And anyway, he's gone to Windsor races today and won't be available for the signing of reprieves.'

As they waited, the tumult about the prison grew greater and Eliza could now hear a faint cry from the prisoners within its walls.

'Claude Du-val!' they chanted as they banged their metal cups on the bars and stamped their feet. 'Claude Du-val! Claude Du-val!'

Nell spoke to her mother. 'I thought Rose and Susan were coming in the carriage with us today?'

'Lawks, no, girl. Susan will be out begging. She always does very well at an 'anging.' She paused and smiled proudly. 'She 'as 'er new carbuncle on today.'

Eliza didn't know whether to laugh or cry at this, so she closed her eyes and waited for the hour of ten to strike. At that time the doors of the prison would open and Claude Duval would begin his journey across London to be hanged at Tyburn.

Her attention, however, was soon drawn back to the moment.

''Ere, I just remembered,' Ma said, nudging Eliza violently, 'I 'ad two people in the tavern last week asking about you.'

'About me?' Eliza asked, startled.

'That's right. Came up to me right boldly and started asking questions. I didn't give 'em no answers, of course.'

'Oh, that's good.'

'Leastways, not until they paid me.'

Eliza looked at her anxiously. 'What did they want to know?'

'Well, they knew I'd rescued you from Clink, and they knew you'd played the mermaid. They wanted to know other stuff – where you come from and who you mix with – that sort of stuff.'

Eliza felt her spine prickle with fear. Someone was spying on her. Someone knew that she'd helped

Claude Duval …

'I hope you didn't give away anything, Ma,' Nell put in sharply.

'Very little,' she said. 'Not for what they paid. For sixpence I gives very little.'

As ten o'clock struck there was an expectant murmur from the crowd and Eliza, peering over Ma's shoulder from the carriage window, could see that the heavy gates of the jail had been pushed open. A moment later a series of carts came into view led by the City marshal on horseback, and he and his sheriffs began to clear a path through the crowd, causing several carriages, including Nell's, to be moved to one side until the procession had passed. A cart pulling a man along backwards on a wooden hurdle came directly after the sheriffs.

''E's committed treason, then,' Ma informed everyone around them. 'And 'e'll be dead afore 'e reaches Tyburn,' she added as the people in the street started pelting him with all manner of rotten vegetables and not a few dead cats and dogs.

A small cart containing four other condemned prisoners came next: three men and a woman carrying a swaddled child in her arms, and then at the last, to a great uproar of laments and shouts from the crowd, came the cart holding Claude Duval.

Eliza let out a long sigh on seeing him.

'Oh, he looks *very* fine,' Nell said, giving a sigh of her own. 'He is a most fiendishly handsome man.'

'What's 'e wearing?' asked Ma Gwyn, trying to peer over their shoulder. 'In case I need to know for the waxworks.'

'A white silk jacket over emerald shirt and waistcoat,' Nell replied, 'and he has high leather boots and his highwayman's hat and mask.'

'Does he look afeared?'

'He does not!' said Eliza. 'There are ladies giving him their *mouchoirs* and throwing flowers into the cart, and he's smiling at them and blowing kisses.'

Nell's carriage not being able to get close to his cart, they followed behind as part of the long procession going slowly down Snow Hill towards Fleet Ditch, with crowds lining the roads all the way. At St Sephulchre's Church the procession stopped and a churchman rang a handbell twelve times and urged all those condemned to die to pray for the salvation of their souls. He handed white flowers and a cup of red wine to each prisoner before the procession went on.

During the last portion of the route along the teeming Oxford Road the crowds were at their most disorderly, and once a surging mob made Nell's coach rock so much that they feared it would be overturned. At some point on this last portion of the journey there was also, they heard later, an armed attempt to free Duval, but owing to the large number of sheriffs present the would-be liberators were thwarted.

Until Eliza saw it, she hadn't been able to imagine the size and scale of the triple tree at Tyburn, the mighty structure, which – as Ma Gwyn cheerfully reminded them – could hang fifteen persons at once. Now as she took her place on the viewing stand erected for the occasion, the three-armed edifice rose before her, large and terrifying. She glanced anxiously back towards the City, praying that she'd see a lone horseman galloping up the road with a document under his arm. Perhaps some high and mighty lawman would step in, perhaps it was not too late for someone to hand over a princely sum which would save Duval ...

The fellow who'd committed treason was, as Ma Gwyn had predicted, dead on arrival at the gallows, but the cart containing the other four prisoners circled the area one last time and then drew up in front of the triple tree amidst mingled shouts of abuse and cries of support. The young woman carrying the child kissed it, again and again, and then, with tears falling down her face, gave it to an older woman standing alongside. As Eliza watched, appalled, the hangman climbed into the cart with the prisoners and fitted the hanging nooses over their heads. He gave the order for the cart to move forward, its driver whipped up the horses and it went off at a smart pace, leaving the four prisoners swaying on the end of their ropes. Eliza screwed her eyes up tightly and turned away.

When Claude Duval's turn came a few moments later, the roar of the crowd rose to a crescendo and, as his cart was manoeuvred into position under the gallows, a woman ran forward and flung herself on to it, sobbing, and was hauled off by the hangman. Another left a nearby carriage and made as if to go towards him, but fell in a graceful faint before she'd taken as many as six steps. Many of the women in the crowd were crying and others were turned away as if they couldn't face the scene.

Eliza stared down the roadway once more, but there was no single traveller on a desperate mission of mercy. Claude spoke to the crowd, but his words were drowned out by sobs and cries. His speech would survive, however, for Eliza could see that what he was saying was being inscribed by two men beside the scaffold.

A church minister spoke a few final words to him; Duval bowed low to the crowd – and, Eliza thought, seemed to see her and Nell in the crowd and wave to them. The hangman fitted the noose around his head. As the order came to move the horses forward a great moan came from the assembled crowd and Eliza gripped Nell's hand and closed her eyes. When, some moments later, she was brave enough to open them again, Claude Duval's body was swinging, lifeless, on the end of a rope.

There had been no reprieve.

Chapter Twenty-Nine

That evening, Eliza stayed within her own room, keeping very quiet. She was immensely sad about Claude Duval, but also concerned about the unknown persons who'd gone to Ma Gwyn's tavern enquiring for her. She'd seen many posters that day asking for information about Claude Duval's collaborators, and feared that at any moment someone might hammer on the front door and march her off to Newgate Prison. Perhaps naturally, then, when Mrs Pearce came to say that there was a gentleman caller waiting in the drawing room, she thought that moment had come.

'He can't want me. Where's Mistress Gwyn?' Eliza asked.

'Gone in the carriage to see Mistress Behn,' said the housekeeper. 'I told him that, and he said he'd like to see you instead.'

'Is he ... does he look like a sheriff or a constable?'

'Not at all,' said Mrs Pearce. 'He looks a fine young gentleman.'

A fine young gentleman, Eliza thought, did not sound like someone who'd come to drag her away, and she went downstairs and, going into the drawing room, found Valentine Howard gazing admiringly at the half-naked Lely portrait of Nell which was now hanging over the fireplace.

Eliza dropped a curtsy, going pink as she remembered their last conversation.

'Forgive my intrusion,' he said, giving a brief bow, 'but I come with some urgency and would ask you to give your mistress a message.'

Eliza nodded and wondered whether to risk a *bien sûr* but decided against it. 'Of course,' she said. She waited for him to say more, but he remained silent. 'Would you like to sit down?' she asked, for he seemed agitated and there were drops of sweat along his upper lip. He didn't seem to hear these words, however, and she had to repeat them before he said abruptly that this wouldn't be necessary.

'Forgive me,' he suddenly burst out, 'I have had a wearying day and I'm trying to get my feelings in order so that I may sound as rational as possible.' He swallowed hard. 'I wished to see Nell to ask her to intercede with the king.'

Eliza did not feel it was her place to enquire what she might be interceding about, so just nodded. After another long silence he went on, 'It concerns my friend Henry Monteagle,' and then turned away – but not before Eliza thought she'd seen tears in his eyes. 'Today,' he continued a moment later, rather hoarsely, 'my friend took advantage of the whole of London being occupied with the hanging of Claude Duval to fight a duel.'

'I knew he was about to,' Eliza admitted.

'I was his second, and saw him hit by the first bullet fired by his opponent.'

A spasm crossed his face and Eliza said, startled, 'Is he dead?'

He gave a slight nod and Eliza drew in her breath, wondering what to say. She couldn't feel any sorrow – or she could, she thought, but only for those he'd left behind.

After a moment she said, 'Then I'm very sorry for his family.'

Valentine went to the window and, pressing his head against the window, looked out on to the darkened street. 'Perhaps ... perhaps you'd be kind enough to ask Nell whether she'd plead with the king. He'd banned Henry from court, you see, but the Monteagle family wish him to have a proper funeral with all due ceremony.' He hesitated. 'The king denies Nell very little, and if she were to appeal to him I'm sure he'd accede to her wishes.'

'I'll speak to her as soon as she returns,' Eliza said, still stunned by the news. She thought hard to recall a redeeming feature of Monteagle's that she might mention. 'You'll miss him very much, I'm sure,' she added after a moment. 'You were good friends.'

'We were,' Valentine said. He swallowed. 'He had a difficult life – a hard childhood.'

'*Hard?*' Eliza couldn't keep the disbelief out of her voice.

'He didn't want for material things,' Valentine went on, 'but his upbringing was brutal. From a very young age he was kept from the arms of his mother and the tenderness of his sisters and given entirely into his father's care, who left no stone unturned to ensure that he grew up a man as arrogant and callous as himself.'

Eliza didn't reply to this. If she had done, she thought, she'd have said that this did not excuse Henry Monteagle his cruelty or his drunkenness or his violent ways. She couldn't say this to Valentine – to his friend – though. Especially not now, when he looked so low. In sympathy she reached out to touch his arm, and somehow his hand grasped hers.

'It must be very hard to lose someone you love,' she said gently.

Valentine managed to smile at her. 'I thank you for your understanding,' he said. They gazed at each other for a long moment – until Eliza, breathless, almost thought that he might kiss her, but when he spoke it was not of kisses. 'There have been some … some misunderstandings between us two,' he said, 'and for my part, I'm sorry for them.'

Eliza stood, spellbound, waiting for whatever was going to come next.

'I would have us friends,' he said, 'but … for someone in my position that could be difficult.'

'For someone in your position?' Eliza asked haltingly, and then realised what he was actually saying. 'Do you mean, rather, for someone in your position … with someone in *my* position?' she asked.

He nodded slightly.

'I am too low for you,' Eliza said, and it was a statement rather than a question.

'It is just that,' he said, and he sounded relieved that the matter was in the open.

Eliza looked at him sadly – although, of course, it was only what she'd known all along. For one moment she found herself tempted to tell him that Doctor Deane had said she was high-born. But why should he believe that when she didn't even believe it herself?

Valentine let her hand fall. 'I'm sorry,' he said, 'but there can be no respectable connection between us.'

And with that he bowed and withdrew.

Eliza spent the next day or so not knowing whether to feel content that there had been some small link between Valentine Howard and herself – that he'd gone some way to admitting that he'd been attracted to her – or frustration at the strictures of society which forbade there should be such a link. She ought to despise him for believing her too low, but knowing this fact to be true, she was unable to. With her background: no family, no name, no dowry, any right-thinking man of high birth would feel the same.

The day of the funeral of Lord Henry Monteagle – titled so for a month following the death of his father – dawned with a fierce and sharp frost, even though it was only the beginning of November. Nell's intercession with the king had worked, and Charles, already regretting that he'd banned Monteagle, had ordered the court into full mourning. This had necessitated Nell's ordering of some gowns and cloaks in black crêpe, together with a quantity of ebony mourning jewellery.

'I hate myself in black,' she'd said that morning, setting off in her carriage for the funeral at St Paul's at Covent Garden. This was the same church, Eliza noted, which was to take the body of Claude Duval when it had finished its lying in state in the popular Tangier Tavern, from where it was drawing people from all parts of the country. Nell had gone to pay her respects there, but Eliza hadn't, for she was convinced that spies would be watching the place and taking note of all those who attended.

'Black makes you look very pallid,' Eliza had agreed

as she'd tied the bows of Nell's wrap. 'Are you sleeping well? Are you sure you don't feel faint?'

'Certainly not,' Nell protested. 'I'm as strong as a horse.'

A little later that morning, however, Eliza received a message from Nell asking that her sable muff and tippet be brought to the church, for she feared that it would be so cold standing at the graveside that she'd take a chill. Eliza hurriedly found these objects and left the house with them, picking up a bag of hot chestnuts from a streetseller in the Strand to warm the inside of the muff.

A great array of black-ribboned carriages filled the square outside the church and, hurrying across to it, Eliza wondered to herself whether anyone else there, like her, was glad to see Henry Monteagle dead – for she realised now that she'd never had a single meeting with him that hadn't been an unpleasant one.

As she wasn't wearing mourning dress she entered the church and hid herself at the back. She'd stand in the shadows and look for Nell, she decided, then try and attract her attention. She might get a glimpse of Valentine, too; although he'd be up at the front with the chief mourners – with Monteagle's mother and sisters.

Eliza craned her neck to see to the front of the church where, on a deep marble pedestal, lay the coffin containing Henry Monteagle covered by a black silk pall on which was embroidered his family's coat of arms: an eagle on a mountain peak. Seeing three figures standing together in the front pew, Eliza imagined the tallest was Valentine, with a Monteagle sister on each side of him. Such pretty sisters, she couldn't help but think again. One, perhaps, was a little too old for Valentine's consideration, but the other was just right. And of the correct social class too, so with due regard for that and for their shared sympathy over the bereavement, it would be entirely natural for them to find comfort in each other's arms ...

Eliza felt sudden tears sting her eyes and quickly blinked them away. She didn't want anyone to think that she was weeping for the man in the coffin.

The service finished and, as the church bells tolled, the congregation started to file out of the church, preceded by the draped coffin carried by several black-robed figures. On seeing that one of these was Monmouth, Eliza pressed herself further back into the shadows, anxious that he shouldn't catch a glimpse of her in case it somehow reminded him of the day he'd been held up by Claude Duval. As Monmouth passed where she was standing, Eliza suddenly saw Nell and, darting forward, pressed the tippet and muff into her hands. Nell, deep in conversation with the Earl of Rochester, broke off to thank her, then Eliza sat down in the nearest pew to wait until everyone else had left the church.

At that point someone approached her. A tall, handsome woman, pale, wearing full mourning dress: black gown with black fur-lined cape and a deep hood. She came over, alone, to where Eliza was sitting and stood before her, and such was her presence and innate nobility that, although she'd no idea who she was, Eliza immediately got to her feet and gave a deep curtsy.

The woman surveyed her kindly. 'Who are you?' she asked.

Eliza gave her name nervously, for to have such a woman notice, let alone speak to her, was quite unexpected and surprising.

'Eliza Rose,' the woman echoed, and her eyes seemed to catch a light from somewhere. 'And do you come here to mourn the passing of my son?'

'Your ... son?' Eliza stammered in surprise, wondering to herself how such a lady, seemingly both gracious and temperate, could have given birth to one like he.

The woman nodded. 'I am Henry Monteagle's mother.'

Eliza hung her head. 'You must excuse my appearance, but I'm not a mourner,' she said when she could trust herself to speak. 'I'm maid to Mistress Gwyn and came here merely to bring her some warm clothes.'

The woman looked away, then touched her eyes with a square of black silk. 'I see,' she said.

Eliza curtsied again. 'I'm immensely sorry for your loss,' she whispered, and found herself, for some unaccountable reason, trembling all over.

The woman nodded. 'It is especially hard to be burying your son on his birthday.' As she spoke these last words, Eliza felt that she looked at her in a strange and penetrating way. So disconcerted did Eliza feel by the woman's presence, however, that she attached no particular significance to this, and it wasn't until she was walking home and happened to look at a bill advertising a play that she realised what the date was that day.

November the third. And her *own* birthday.

Chapter Thirty

Since coming to London, Eliza thought to herself, so many extraordinary things had happened that she no longer tried to make any sense of them. She'd arrived in London as someone's daughter, but was no longer that daughter. Instead she'd been, in turn, a prisoner, a mermaid, an orange seller and a highwayman's moll. And, if she believed the assertions of Doctor Deane the astrologer, then she could add the strangest fact of all to this list: the notion that she was high-born.

November the third. Her birthday; and also Henry Monteagle's birthday.

It had to have been he whose chart Doctor Deane had cast and found to be the same as hers. But how could there be any link or similarity between the two of them? How could she, a humble maid (but perfectly pleasant, she countered), have any similarity to a lord of the realm, and a horrid, callous and drunken one at that? They were astrological twins, the astrologer had said – although he'd allowed that the circumstances of their upbringing would have wrought great changes in their fortunes.

Lying in bed three days after Henry Monteagle's funeral, Eliza tried hard to remember Doctor Deane's exact words to her. He'd said, she thought, that something very interesting and remarkable had happened at her birth. One day, perhaps, she'd go to him again and ask what more he knew, for she yearned to be in possession of any tiny detail about her real family. It was a hard thing, she decided, to have no attachments in life. Some might enjoy this freedom, but she didn't. She longed for connections: a home, a mother, a father, a sister or a brother. And failing any family, then a sweetheart who loved her would suit – and preferably one, she thought now, who was very much like Valentine Howard. In time, someone else might be allowed into her heart, but at that moment it fully belonged to him, be he too high-born or not.

Two more people had been arrested for their connections with Claude Duval: a woman who'd concealed him from the constables and a footpad who'd sometimes worked with him. Eliza had heard this news with fear, especially as the day before the Lord Mayor had bills posted up over the City asking for anyone who'd ever spoken to Duval to come forward so that they might learn more about his habits and his collaborators and thus make the highways safer places to travel. In view of this continued interest, Eliza considered whether she should again change her appearance, but decided that this would be almost impossible whilst living with the famous Nell.

She'd tried to speak to Nell about her worries, but her friend was preoccupied both with the coming child and also with trying to keep the king's attention from straying towards Louise de Keroualle, with whom he seemed somewhat infatuated. Eliza prayed daily that the king would not become jaded with Nell, knowing that her own well-being depended on it. Not that he seemed to love his Nelly any the less, Eliza thought, for she had a new part in a musical play and the king had been in the audience for all three performances. This, however, would probably be the last part Nell played before the birth of her child, for she was becoming rounder and heavier and couldn't dance a jig half as nimbly as she used to.

Later that morning Eliza, visiting the Royal Exchange in order to buy exotic fruit to tempt Nell's appetite, felt a hand on her shoulder and turned to see Valentine Howard, still in the unrelieved black of deep mourning.

He bowed and wished her good day and Eliza said a polite good day also, wondering if he was ashamed to be seen speaking to her.

'I've just been talking about you,' he said. 'In fact, I was making my way to Pall Mall where I hoped to find you at home.'

Eliza's first thought was that the constabulary were after her and that he'd come to warn her of it. 'You hoped … to find me in,' she stammered. 'But why?'

'Nothing untoward, I assure you.' He looked at her closely. 'Mistress Rose, you've gone quite pale.'

'But why were you coming to find me?'

'Because there's someone who wishes to speak with you.'

'Someone connected with the law?' Eliza asked in a flurry. 'For I can assure you that it certainly wasn't me.'

He looked at her curiously. '*What* wasn't you?'

Eliza shook her head, blushing. 'Nothing! I'm sorry. I spoke out of turn.'

He smiled. 'I've no idea why this lady wishes to speak to you, but I'm sure it's nothing untoward. She knows I'm acquainted with Nell and yourself, and asked me to approach you.'

'A woman?' Eliza asked, and her next thought was that it was one of Nell's rivals for the king's affections, somehow trying to obtain information about her.

He nodded.

'Is it Louise de Keroualle?'

He laughed. 'Good lord, no. It is Lady Lucinda Monteagle.'

Eliza's jaw dropped. 'Henry Monteagle's mother? Why should that lady want to see me?'

'I haven't the least idea. Perhaps,' he shrugged, 'perhaps to offer you a job in the household?' He frowned. 'No, it can't be that, for she said that it was on a matter of great delicacy. Have you met her before?'

'Just briefly, in church at the funeral. And I have also seen her two daughters. They are very lovely,' she couldn't resist adding.

Valentine Howard didn't comment on this, but offered her his arm. 'Would you consider coming to Lady Monteagle's residence with me now? I told her that I'd try and bring you to speak with her straight away.'

'Right at this moment?' Eliza looked down at the striped wool jacket she was wearing. 'I'm not dressed to visit a household in mourning. And besides,' she looked at him anxiously, 'how can a mere maid visit a titled lady?'

'I don't think she's even thought of that, for she seemed most anxious to see you. Almost ... agitated.'

Eliza, feeling troubled, began to walk with him out of the Exchange. She knew she didn't have to go, but to refuse to attend on such a lady would be rude in the extreme. Besides, the thought of promenading on Valentine Howard's arm was irresistible.

'Do you think, perhaps, she has heard of Henry Monteagle's reputation – that is,' she corrected herself, 'of his *misunderstandings* with me, and wants to apologise?'

Valentine stiffened slightly and Eliza wondered if she'd offended him. 'I think not,' he said, and then shrugged. 'But I don't know. I'm just to deliver you and leave you to her good offices.'

Lady Monteagle, apparently, had rented a house by the river so that she could be close to her daughters and supervise their welfare while they were at court. It should have been a pleasant walk to her house alongside the Thames, for Eliza was with the man she thought so highly of, it was a brilliant, crisp day and the sun was sparkling on the river's wavelets – but she was much too anxious to enjoy it. Was she to go to the main front door, or round to the servants' quarters? Had she, perhaps, without thinking, said something unkind to Lady Monteagle in the church and was now to be reprimanded? Or had Lady Monteagle heard that Eliza had accused her son of violence and was going to have her arrested for slander? Whatever it was, she would not, she hoped, be called upon to pretend sorrow at Henry Monteagle's untimely death, for this she wouldn't be able to do.

The windows of the large house were draped outside with black, and the Monteagle hatchments hung on a flagpole, signifying the death of the head of the family. The whole house seemed so frighteningly oppressive that, on Valentine leaving her at the front door, Eliza felt almost disposed to run away. He'd knocked at the door before bowing and departing, however, so before Eliza could act upon the urge to bolt, the door was opened by a maid in black cap and uniform.

'Your mistress, please,' Eliza said with as much poise as she could summon. 'Lady Monteagle.'

The maid nodded without speaking and took her into a dimly lit drawing room, its pictures turned to the wall, its mirrors hung about with black crêpe. A great bunch of blue-flowered rosemary stood on a table; its scent the only pleasing feature of the room. Although there was a small fire burning in the grate this did little to heat the place and Eliza stood before it, reflecting and fearing the circumstances that might have caused her to be there.

Lady Monteagle entered the room wearing dull pearls and flowing black garments, her long grey hair plaited down her back. She seemed, as Valentine had said, nervous and troubled.

'You are Eliza Rose,' she said, her voice low, and Eliza curtsied. 'Please sit down, for I scarcely know where to begin and the telling of this will take some long time.'

Eliza, stunned by these words, sat on a stiff chair by the window and began to feel terribly afeared. What *could* she have done to deserve this? Lady Monteagle stood in front of the fire for a moment, and then began to pace the floor. The more she paced, the more anxious Eliza became, for it was clear that something very serious and troubling was about to be imparted and she couldn't begin to think what this might be.

After some moments, Lady Monteagle suddenly looked at her with brimming eyes and cried out in a distracted voice, 'What would you think of a mother who gave away her child?'

Eliza stared at her. Had the poor lady been rendered mad by the death of her son?

'You'd condemn such a woman, would you not? There can be no excuse for such an uncaring and unnatural act!'

Eliza shivered all over. She looked for the bell-pull by the fireplace so that, if necessary, she could summon Lady Monteagle's maid and ask to be shown out again.

'Oh, it is all too horrendous and I cannot begin to explain,' Lady Monteagle went on, wringing her hands. 'And I have no excuses for it – only to say that my children and I would have been turned out on to the streets.'

Eliza didn't speak, startled as she was into complete silence.

'Daughters were not good enough for him!' continued the dowager in a distracted voice. 'We would have been thrown out and starved to death if I hadn't given him an heir!'

At these words, something stirred inside Eliza. Something ... a tiny spark of – not yet an understanding of what was afoot; but something like a mixture of anticipation, expectation and wonder.

Just at this moment, before her feelings and

thoughts had had time to unravel themselves, there came the sound of footsteps outside the door and it burst open to reveal the Monteagle sisters, both dressed in deepest black, their dark wavy hair unbraided.

'Is she come yet?' the younger girl said urgently before she was even halfway through the door, and then they both looked at Eliza and clapped their hands to their mouths in identical manner. The younger girl continued, 'Oh Mamma! We didn't realise.'

'We are so sorry,' said the other, and she took her sister's arm and tugged her out of the room.

'Call us in soon, Mamma!' said the first, as if reluctant to go, and she looked at Eliza and smiled at her with such happiness and joy that the door had no sooner closed than Eliza, for some reason which she was for ever after at a loss to explain, burst into tears. Distressed and confused, she rose from the chair at the same time as Lady Monteagle, who took two steps towards her and clasped her arms about her tightly.

'Oh, my dearest, darling child!' said Lady Monteagle. 'Oh, my own heart, I've found you at last!'

Fully thirty minutes later, Eliza still had not spoken, for at first she'd been crying too hard to speak, then she'd been too stunned and incredulous. Finally, sitting on the window seat with her head on Lady Monteagle's lap, she'd asked her to tell the story over again.

'Of course I will,' said Lady Monteagle. She went on, 'Your father, Lord Monteagle, married me solely so that he could have an heir. I'd gone ten years without conceiving, then had your two sisters a year apart. When I found out that I'd conceived again I knew, because of my age, that this was possibly my last chance to have a child. He said that if I didn't produce a boy to take his title, then he'd divorce me and cast me out on to the streets.' She took a deep breath. 'Sadly, I was bullied throughout my pregnancy upon this matter, so my mother and I contrived a plan. There was a woman in the village –'

'Mrs Rose?'

'Mrs Rose,' the dowager agreed, 'who was expecting a child at exactly the same time. She'd already produced three boys and swore she was having another, and being very poor, was only too pleased to be given the means to improve her situation. My mother, therefore, arranged that if she had a boy, it would be substituted for my child – which I already felt sure would be another girl.

'All happened as predicted, and the changeover of the babies was effected by means of a secret passage which ran from our castle into the local church. I then announced to my happy husband that he had an heir to his fortune and his title. The Rose family moved some distance off and I never heard from them again, although every so often I made discreet enquiries to ascertain that you, Eliza, were alive and well.' Here Lady Monteagle looked down at her child and fondly stroked her cheek.

After a moment she resumed, 'When my husband died my first thought was to find you, and I engaged searchers to monitor your movements, only to find that you'd gone to London.'

'I heard that someone was asking questions about me ...'

Lady Monteagle nodded. 'I persevered with trying to find you, but when I did, I couldn't bring myself to depose Henry. When he died in the duel, however, I was naturally very sad, but knew that nothing could stop me from now claiming you as my own ... '

There followed a long, long silence, with Lady Monteagle stroking Eliza's hair with great tenderness, and Eliza sighing and catching her breath and then sighing again.

'It is the most miraculous fairy tale,' she said at last, 'and one that I can scarce bring myself to believe.'

'I assure you that it's all true,' said Lady Monteagle.

'I am of the nobility, then!' Eliza said, and she began laughing, hardly unable to comprehend such a thing, let alone the implications. What might Valentine have to say to her about it? Indeed, what might she say to him?

'You are of the nobility,' confirmed Lady Monteagle. 'Although you mustn't allow that fact to change you. You have land and property – and a title, too, if you wish to use it.'

'Can I have singing lessons?'

Lady Monteagle smiled, surprised. 'Singing lessons, dancing lessons – and anything else you might care for.'

Eliza thought about this. No more would she be beholden to anyone for her keep and her welfare; she was her own person and would be able to do whatever she wished with her life. And best of all ...

'I have you – and sisters!' Eliza said joyfully.

'You have sisters,' Lady Monteagle confirmed. 'And Kathryn and Maria know the situation and are probably outside the door at this very moment waiting anxiously to be let in.'

'Kathryn and Maria,' Eliza repeated wonderingly, remembering now that Jemima's mother had mistaken her for a Maria.

'Do you want to meet them properly now?'

'Oh, I do,' Eliza said. She looked at her mother shyly. 'Before that, though, will you tell me the story again, for I feel I can't hear it often enough.'

Lady Monteagle smiled. 'Whatever you wish,' she said, 'for we have the rest of our lives together now.' She took a breath and began, 'Once upon a time, there was a beautiful child born in a castle …'

Epilogue

The castle bedroom is large and richly furnished. Paintings and costly tapestries line the walls and in its centre is a vast four-poster bed.

The casements are open wide and the breeze catches the fine silk curtains and billows them across the room. The girl walks about the room slowly, admiring the intricate tapestries and carefully examining each picture in turn. She is looking for family likenesses, for these are her ancestors.

Crossing then to the window, she sees the shimmering water of the castle moat outside, the trees turning golden and, in the distance, the Quantock Hills, purple with heather. She flings her arms out wide as if to embrace them all, and then hugs herself and laughs out loud for no apparent reason.

Her mother comes in and, seeing her daughter laughing, joins in. 'I thought it was right that you should have this room,' she says.

'The room where I was born ...'

Her mother inclines her head. 'Which saw a great deal of unhappiness.'

'But now all departed and disappeared!'

The older woman catches her hand and holds it tightly. 'But I came to tell you that we have a visitor downstairs.'

'Already! How do the neighbours even know we've arrived?'

'Not a neighbour! This is someone from London.'

The girl smiles. 'I wondered how long it would take for the news to spread.'

'He says that your story is being told all across the city from the court to the coffee houses.'

'*He?*' The girl's face suddenly lights up. 'You don't mean *he?* It couldn't possibly be ...'

'It is,' the other woman laughs, for she already knows the state of her daughter's heart. 'He says he came pell-mell along the Bath Road and changed horse three times.'

The girl's cheeks colour pink. 'But what could he possibly – I mean, what shall I say to him?' She indicates their surroundings. 'How can I begin to tell him all that's happened?'

'You must speak the truth. Explain how it occurred, and tell him that you knew nothing about your provenance until I told you of it five days ago.'

The girl suddenly gasps. 'And what if he is here to ask me ...?' And then she stops and thinks a little. 'But in truth he should *not* be here to ask anything, for I wasn't good enough for him before, when I had nothing, was I?'

Her mother smiles ruefully.

'And now that my situation is different, he seems very quick to change his mind!'

'You mustn't blame him for that – 'tis his upbringing,' her mother says. 'But you must now both take some time to get used to your new situation in life.'

The girl nods slowly.

Her mother squeezes her hand. 'Although you are well-born and so is he, so it would be a good match.'

'A good match ...' the girl repeats wonderingly.

'And we mustn't take things too fast. But if he ...'

'*If he*?' the girl prompts.

' ... if he wishes to call on us from time to time, then we will make him most welcome, and we will see what transpires. And when we're back in London and you're living at court ...'

'I'll be at court?'

'Of course. Wherever your sisters are, so will you be.' She smiles. 'When you're at court, there'll be many occasions for you and he to seek out each other's company.'

The girl smiles again, already thinking of how her new life will be in London.

'So, go and see what he has to say,' says the woman, and the girl bites her lips to bring some colour into them, then picks up a silver-backed hairbrush and, pausing just long enough to pass it through her long dark locks, runs out of the room and downstairs to whatever fate holds for her.

Cast of Characters

Eliza is fictional. But she is based, as far as possible, on what it would be like to be a young woman in London in about 1670. The basis of the book came about after I read that midwives in the seventeenth century were required to take an oath that they would not substitute one newborn child for another.

Nell Gwyn The most famous and one of the most enduring of Charles II's many mistresses. She had two sons by him, in 1670 and 1671, and on his death bed Charles asked that whoever came after would 'remember poor Nelly'. High-spirited and mischievous, she really *did* get her rival to take an emetic to prevent her spending the night with the king. She died in 1687.

Old Ma Gwyn Nell's mother, who ran a tavern and a brothel and was said to have 'lain with an army of men'. She died, drunk, in Fleet Ditch, in 1679. Rose, Nell's sister, was married to a highwayman, John Cassells, who was frequently in jail.

Charles II Son of the beheaded Charles I, who came to the throne at the Restoration of the monarchy in 1660. He had numerous mistresses and thirteen acknowledged illegitimate children. He loved the theatre, gambling, horseracing and women. He died in 1685 without a legitimate heir, whereupon his natural son, Monmouth, tried to seize the throne from Charles's brother James.

The merry gang Although the king's gang of wits existed and certainly behaved appallingly, in this book only Charles's son James and the Earl of Rochester are real. The latter's verse is considered good but is mostly unprintable, and one particularly outrageous verse about the king got him temporarily banned from court.

Claude Duval (www.du-vall.net) was a famous, much-admired highway-man who was finally caught and hanged in 1670, aged twenty-six. His body was embalmed and exhibited in the Tangier Tavern, and part of the epitaph on his grave reads:

Here lies Duval
Reader – if male thou art,
Look to thy purse.
If female, to thy heart.

Aphra Behn is usually acknowledged as the first woman to make her living by her writing.

Sir Peter Lely Portrait painter to the aristocracy and the court beauties. He painted Nell several times, once completely nude, as Venus, with her infant son as Cupid.

Places Featured

Stoke Courcey (now called Stogursey) is a small and pretty village in Somerset. All that is left of the castle are some romantic ruins, a moat and a thatched gatehouse.

Southwark(e) The borough extending from the southern end of London Bridge; once the main entry to London from the south. Noted in the seventeenth century for its brothels, inns and taverns (several of which appear in Shakespeare's plays), it was the area of London most generally associated with entertainment and pleasure.

Clink Prison in Clink Street was the most notorious of Southwark's seven prisons and the origin of the expression 'in the clink'. Governors of prisons received money from prisoners for food, lodging and privileges, and this became a source of great abuse.

Fleet Prison Secret, hurried marriages could be performed in the chapel of Fleet Prison without licence, some by clergymen imprisoned in the Fleet for debt, some by tricksters impersonating the clergy. The practice spread to nearby taverns and houses and these would declare their purpose by showing a painted sign depicting a male and female hand clasped together.

Drury Lane A fashionable and wealthy area in the seventeenth century, by the eighteenth it had become a notoriously rowdy place, famous for its brawls and drunkenness. There were several theatres in the locality, and it still remains London's 'Theatreland'.

Whitehall Palace The chief London residence of King Charles and his court, this huge building ran the length of Whitehall and contained, as Nell tells Eliza, some two thousand rooms. Lavish accommodation was provided for two of the king's mistresses here, while his wife had a far simpler apartment overlooking the river.